Dear Target Reader,

I am delighted and honored that [...] *Wedding Date,* for the Target Diver[...] an avid— some might say obsessive—reader since I was a little girl. Reading books about different kinds of people and faraway places taught me so much about the rest of the country and the world. It also helped (and still helps) me to understand and identify with people who have backgrounds and lives very unlike my own. While some of my favorite books feature people like me and my family, many of them have focused on people from different cultures, religions, and nationalities from my own. The thing they all had in common is that the characters were people I related to and cared about, just as I hope you'll care about Alexa and Drew, the main characters of *The Wedding Date.*

I set the beginning of Alexa and Drew's story around a wedding because weddings—and the emotions, anxieties, and desires around them—are universal. No matter if it's a Catholic wedding in Los Angeles, a City Hall wedding in San Francisco, a Jewish wedding in Indianapolis, a Hindu wedding in New Jersey, or a multi-ethnic wedding in North Carolina, there will be excitement, love, passion . . . and a few too many prying questions from friends and family. As someone who has been a flower girl in two weddings, a bridesmaid in eight, and a guest at countless others, I have a healthy fascination with all of the joy, pain, and pure drama that surrounds weddings. From what to wear, to what you'll eat, to what—and how much—to drink, to the seating arrangements, everything about weddings is high stress and seems inordinately important. Tell me another day when people sincerely care about both the color of the tablecloths and Instagram hashtags!

And we all know that emotions are heightened on wedding weekends, especially around relationships . . . and lack thereof. At weddings I've seen people decide to propose, break up, and finally say something to that person they've had a crush on forever. And at weddings, whether because of forced proximity or open bars or all of the feelings in the air, people always ask the questions that shouldn't be asked. There's that aunt who asks, "When is it your turn?" or the well-meaning old friend who says, "Single tonight, huh?" or the frenemy who says, "Where's *your* date this evening?" We can all sympathize with Drew's panic at going to his ex-girlfriend's wedding dateless, and understand why getting stuck in an elevator with Alexa seemed like the answer to a prayer.

When Alexa and Drew get thrown together, they only see how different they are from one another: their race; their jobs; the ways they connect with the world. Haven't we all at first only noticed our differences from one another, especially when the differences can feel overwhelming? But over the course of a wedding weekend, Alexa and Drew learn the many things they have in common. They both care deeply about their jobs, love food, and love and trust their friends. But they also learn that it's even more important to see how their differences complement one another. I've learned that lesson myself, and I bet many of you have too.

Please let me know where you are when you read this book, I would love to see what a diversity of locations there are for readers of *The Wedding Date*! Tag your pictures on Twitter or Instagram with #TheWeddingDate, so I can see them. I hope no matter where you are when you read *The Wedding Date*—in Alexa's Bay Area, in Drew's Los Angeles, on a mountain in Colorado, under a tree in New England, in a cabin by a lake in Minnesota, overlooking the Mississippi River in New Orleans, or somewhere else in the world—that you relate to and care about Alexa and Drew's story.

Thank you for reading, and I hope you love *The Wedding Date*!

Jasmine

The Wedding Date

JASMINE GUILLORY

JOVE
NEW YORK

A JOVE BOOK
Published by Berkley
An imprint of Penguin Random House LLC
375 Hudson Street, New York, New York 10014

ISBN: 9780440000389

First Jove trade paperback edition: January 2018
Jove trade paperback Target Book Club edition: January 2018

Printed in the United States of America
1 3 5 7 9 10 8 6 4 2

Cover design by Vikki Chu
Book design by Kelly Lipovich

To Donna Louise Guillory,
the best mom anyone could ever have.

Acknowledgments

I am so fortunate that I have so many people in my life to thank. I'm more grateful for all of you than I can say.

Holly Root, thank you for everything that you've done for me and my book. I'm happy every day to have you in my corner. To Cindy Hwang, Kristine Swartz, Marianne Grace Aguiar, and the entire Berkley team, you have all been a joy to work with. Thank you for making this dream a reality.

The other writers who helped me along the way are some of the best people in the world. Amy Spalding, I never would have written a single word without your encouragement in the beginning, and I never would have kept writing if you hadn't been there to help me, every step of the way. Thanks for changing my life. Thank you to Akilah Brown, who seemed to know I was a writer before I did. Thank you to Melissa Baumgart, who was the entire reason I started actually writing this book instead of just thinking about it. Thank you to Sara Zarr, who gave me some of my first, and best, writing advice. Thank you to Tayari Jones, Robin Benway, Ruby Lang, Rainbow Rowell, Heather Cocks, and Jessica Morgan, who have all helped me, inspired me, and answered millions of tiny questions. And Mallory

Ortberg and Nicole Cliffe, who have been some of the biggest cheer-leaders in my life, the biggest toast of all to both of you.

Everyone has their talents in life; mine is making really good friends. Simi Patnaik and Nicole Clouse, your love and support (and many, many text messages) keep me going. Janet Goode, you are one of the best friends a woman could ever have. Melissa Sladden and Jina Kim, I love you both so much. Jill Vizas, I'm so glad we became friends so long ago, and Katie Vizas and Sally Vizas, thanks for welcoming me into your family. Thank you to Julian Davis Mortenson, Kyle Wong, Toby Rugger, Leslie Gross, Kate Leos, Lyette Mercier, Joy Alferness, Nanita Cranford, Stephanie Lucianovic, and Laurie Baker. You all have been there for me in countless ways. And Colleen Richards Powell, thank you for the sandwich line that you delivered so memorably that day on the 4th floor of Claflin Hall.

Thank you to every teacher I ever had, but especially Elizabeth Varon, Anita Tien, Pamela Karlan, Bonnie Sussman, and Brad Good-hart. None of you were writing teachers, but you all taught me how to write. Thank you to Wellesley College, who made me who I am.

Michelle Obama, thanks for all of the pep talks, even if they were only in my own head.

And finally, I could have done none of this without my family. Thank you to all of my grandparents, but especially to my grand-mothers, Joyce York-Brown and Lillian Guillory. Thank you to my many cousins, who are always there for me. Thank you to my sister, Sasha Guillory. And most importantly, thank you to my parents, Paul and Donna Guillory, who have always believed fiercely in me. Together and separately they both taught me to dream big and have supported every dream I've ever had. Thanks, Mom and Dad. I love you.

1

Alexa Monroe walked into the Fairmont hotel in San Francisco that Thursday night wearing her favorite red heels, feeling jittery from coffee, and carrying a bottle of Veuve Clicquot champagne in her purse. She took out her phone to text her sister, Olivia, upstairs in one of the guest rooms.

Getting on the elevator!!!

It was always good to give Olivia a little more advance warning than most people. It didn't matter that Olivia had just made partner at her New York law firm; some things didn't change.

Oh no, was just about to get in the shower.

Alexa got Olivia's text just as she stepped into the elevator. She laughed out loud as she pushed the number of her sister's floor, the laughter calming her nerves. Alexa couldn't wait to celebrate with her older sister, despite . . . no, maybe because their relationship was still tricky after all these years.

The elevator glided in the air, in that smooth, noiseless way elevators in expensive hotels do, while Alexa checked her purse for the third time to make sure she'd tossed the fancy crackers and Brie in there. They would need a pre-dinner snack to soak up all of that champagne, after all. She wished she'd found the time to make brownies the night before. Olivia loved her brownies.

She spied the cheese and crackers in the corner of her purse, tucked away from the heavy champagne bottle. Just then, the elevator stopped with a jerk. A second later, the lights went out.

"What's going on?" she said out loud to herself.

A few seconds later, a dim light came on, but the elevator stayed motionless. She looked up and around, and jumped to see a man with a suitcase in the opposite corner of the elevator.

"Were you here this whole time?" she asked.

"What am I, a genie?" He grinned back at her.

"I guess you don't really look like a genie." He was a tall white guy, with tanned skin, rumpled dark brown hair, and about a day's worth of scruff where a beard would be. She had a sudden urge to rub her hand on his cheek to see how prickly it was. How exactly had she missed seeing *this* man get on the elevator with her?

"Thank you, I think. But isn't that what a genie would say?" he asked. "You're not claustrophobic, are you?"

"Um, I don't think so. Why, were you going to bust us out of here with your genie powers if I said I was?"

He laughed.

"I guess you'll never know if I'm a genie now," he said.

"Well, there was that time I got an MRI," she said. "Being inside that tiny machine wasn't much fun. Maybe I am claustrophobic."

"Sorry, you already lost your chance to see my powers." He moved to the front of the elevator and picked up the emergency phone.

"Let's see if they can give us an ETA on getting out of here."

She tried not to stare at him in the dim lighting, but she couldn't miss the opportunity to check out his butt in his perfectly fitted jeans. It was as good as the rest of him. She tried to wipe the grin off her face in case he turned around.

Stuff like this never happened to her. Not the stuck-in-the-elevator thing—her life was full of minor crises like that. No, it was being stuck in an elevator with a hot guy that was the unusual part. She was always the one sitting on an airplane next to a chatty toddler, or a knitting grandma, or a bored college student; never a hot guy to be found.

After about a minute of him saying, "Okay . . . okay," in progressively tenser tones, he hung up the phone.

"Well . . ." He paused and smiled at her. "Wait, I don't even know your name, my new elevator friend."

"Alexa, and you, Genie?"

"Drew. Nice to meet you, Alexa."

"Drew, it's a pleasure, but . . ."

"Right, these circumstances are not ideal. So, the bad news is that there's a power outage in the whole hotel."

Her phone lit up just then with a text from Olivia.

My power went out. Where are you??

"Ahhh, yes, I was just alerted to that." Alexa held her phone up before she texted Olivia back.

Whole hotel, I'm stuck in the elevator.

"At least that means they were telling the truth," Drew said. "The good news, or so they tell me, is that they have generators, so the elevators should start moving shortly."

She slid down to the floor, placing her purse gently beside her. It would be a tragedy to break that champagne bottle.

"We might as well wait in comfort," she said. Her favorite red heels were relatively comfortable for the first five hours, but she'd been wearing them for nine plus.

He shrugged off his leather jacket, gifting her a glimpse of his stomach muscles as his gray T-shirt shifted. Mmmm. Hot, funny guy who occasionally flashed his abs. Was it her birthday?

"So, are you a guest here, Drew? Where are you coming from?" she asked him so she wouldn't stare.

"Just flew in from L.A. And you?" He sat down next to her.

"Oh, I live here. Well, over in Berkeley, anyway. I'm just in the hotel visiting someone."

He glanced at her phone, her shoes, and back up at her.

"A pretty special someone, with those shoes on, and all of that smiling you were doing when you didn't even notice someone else got on the elevator with you."

"A very special someone," she said, and his grin got wider. "Wait, no, not *that* kind of special someone! My older sister! She's in town from New York for work."

Yep, this was how she usually acted around hot guys. Scared to make eye contact, stared at his abs, said something awkward.

"Ahhhh." He laughed. "Okay, yes, I did think it was *that* kind of special someone. Do you two have a hot night in the city planned?"

She crossed her legs and adjusted her black wrap dress so she didn't accidentally flash her underwear at this dude on top of everything else.

"Sort of. We're celebrating. She just made partner at her law firm!" Alexa smiled down at her purse full of treats before looking back up at him. Not even cheese could compete with this dude.

He narrowed his eyes at her. Light brown eyes, with a really dark rim around them. His eyes were so pretty that she looked away again. Thank God her brown skin meant her cheeks couldn't get too pink, otherwise he'd be able to see them glow in the dark.

"Okay, I'm happy for your sister, but what is in that bag? You keep looking at it like it holds the Holy Grail."

She laughed.

"Just champagne and a few snacks. The plan is to drink the champagne here and then go out to dinner . . . Well, that was the plan, but we'll see how long we're stuck in this elevator."

Drew scooted closer to her and looked in her purse. Alexa pushed it toward him, so he could see better in the dim light. She never let people poke around in her purse, but hey, this was a cute guy and a weird situation.

"Okay good, we have sustenance if we're stuck here for hours. Champagne is so convenient because no corkscrew is needed, and then we've got . . . Oh, look at that, cheese and crackers, the perfect stuck-in-an-elevator snack."

She leaned back against the wood-paneled wall.

"Have you been stuck in an elevator before with a variety of snacks and been able to determine which ones are best for this situation?" she asked.

"No, but come on, cheese and crackers are obviously the best possible option here. First of all, you had the foresight to bring a soft cheese, so we won't need a knife to cut it; we can just use the crackers to pull off bits and spread it with our fingers. And second, have you ever not enjoyed cheese and crackers? Ever not thought, 'Oh boy, these cheese and crackers are exactly what I need right now'?"

She considered for a moment.

"Stop, no, stop even thinking about it," he said. "You know the answer is no. Cheese and crackers are objectively the perfect snack."

She laughed and pried his fingers away from the box of crackers.

"Okay, fine, you're right. But you didn't manage to talk me into sharing Olivia's you-made-partner cheese and crackers with you, you know."

He stretched his legs out along the floor and took another glance into her purse.

"I was afraid of that. Well, I can only hope we'll be here so long that you'll take pity on me."

She slipped her shoes halfway off, just enough to relieve the pressure on her toes.

"No offense, Drew, but my goal is not to be stuck in this elevator with you all night." Although those abs . . . No, remember Olivia? Her sister? Right, Olivia, okay, yes, Olivia. Time to ask him another question so she'd stop staring. "Don't *you* have plans tonight? What are you doing here in San Francisco for the weekend anyway?"

He made a face.

"Wedding."

She made a face back at him.

"Don't say it like it's a prison sentence."

He slumped against the wall.

"If prison sentences lasted for a weekend, this one would qualify. Okay, fine, a prison in a cushy hotel, but still."

She looked around at the dim, still elevator.

"Not so cushy right now. What's so terrible about this wedding?"

He threw his hands in the air.

"Let me count the ways." He held up one finger. "One: it's my ex-girlfriend's wedding."

Alexa winced. She'd been there. Exes' weddings were always a trial, even in the best circumstances.

Second finger. "Two: she's marrying one of my best friends from med school."

Alexa covered her eyes. Okay, he maybe had a point.

"Were they . . ."

"No, she wasn't cheating on me with him, but . . . let's just say I wasn't particularly pleased about how it all happened, shall we?"

"Ouch. Well, I understand why you—"

He held up a third finger. "THREE."

She sat up straight.

"There's another one? A third finger?"

"Oh yes." He waved his middle finger in the air. "As a matter of fact, this is the worst of the fingers. Three: I am a groomsman."

She swung around and faced him, mouth wide open.

"Are you kidding me? A groomsman? What? Why? How?"

"Yes, you are asking the important questions. The ones that Josh, Molly, and I all should have asked before this nightmare of a wedding weekend started. What and why indeed. *What* could have possibly inspired him to ask me to be a groomsman? *Why* would he do that? *Why* would she allow it? *WHY* would I say yes? *How* did this happen? All of those questions should have been asked, and yet, here we all are."

"Oh my God, Drew. That's almost enough for me to give you some cheese."

He patted her shoulder. Cheese? Hell, if he'd let his hand linger there for a few more seconds, she would have given him a lot more than cheese.

"Alexa, I'm touched. I truly am. And then"—he waved another finger in the air—"there's four."

"Oh good Lord, what could four possibly be? Are your divorced parents coming to the wedding with their spouses, too, or something?"

He laughed.

"No, but good guess. What a nightmare that would be. No, four is that I am not only a groomsman in the wedding of my ex-girlfriend and former best friend, but I am a dateless groomsman in the wedding of my ex-girlfriend and former best friend. My date bailed on me at the last minute, so I'm going to look pathetic, and I'll probably get drunk and hit on a bridesmaid—the whole thing is going to be a nightmare."

She brushed that off with a wave of her hand.

"Oh please, you'll be fine. Weddings are great places to meet people. It's better that you're without a date. As my friend Colleen always says, 'Don't bring a sandwich to a buffet.'"

He let out a bark of laughter.

"I'm definitely going to steal that saying. And while in most situations I would say that your friend Colleen is totally right, this is that five percent of situations where a sandwich would save me from all of the food poisoning in the buffet. I'm going to get so many pitying looks, you have no idea. And the worst part is that I RSVP'd with a plus-one, so there's going to be an empty seat at the head table. And lots of 'What happened to your girlfriend, Drew, couldn't make it?' And I'm going to have to smile and take it, but there's like a thirty percent possibility I'm going to have one too many glasses of bourbon and go rogue."

She touched his hand and tried not to linger there.

"Okay, yes, sometimes a sandwich is a necessary security blanket. I'm sorry that yours bailed on you."

He looked down into her purse again.

"Alexa, I'm going to need you to stop talking about sandwiches if you don't want me to steal that cheese."

She grabbed her purse and moved it to her other side.

"Now temptation is farther away. Isn't that better?"

He looked at her, at the purse, back at her. She smiled and kept her hand on the strap.

"So, Drew. What happened to your girlfriend?"

He narrowed his eyes at her, and she laughed again.

"Okay, first of all, Emma wasn't my girlfriend. We were just hanging out, that's all."

Alexa frowned at him. This guy had to be in his thirties like her. Hadn't people stopped "just hanging out" with people by their thirties?

"Don't look at me like that! I'm not a girlfriend kind of guy! And when I could tell that she might want something more serious, I ended it. I was nice about it! I don't do girlfriends. I haven't had a girlfriend since . . ." He sighed. "Molly. Anyway. Except I forgot that I needed a date for this damn wedding."

Alexa pointed to the fourth finger that he'd raised in the air.

"Wait," she said. "How, exactly, is that your date 'bailing' on you?"

He shook the finger at her.

"Don't do that! Don't blame this on me. It's not my fault. It's not her fault, either—she was going to come to the wedding with me anyway, but her dad's having surgery tomorrow, so she couldn't come." Those ab muscles moved in a lovely way when he sighed. "And, of course, I'm sorry about her dad. I don't blame her for that at all. I do, however, think this is just more evidence that I've been cursed when it comes to this wedding."

Alexa laughed and relaxed against the wall. If she happened to move closer to Drew while doing so, that was just an extra benefit. Hey, it's not like she was in danger of becoming this guy's not-girlfriend. She could at least get a few accidental touches of his arm in before this elevator started back up again.

"You probably did something to deserve it."

Drew reached around her and grabbed her purse.

"Oh, really? I pour out my heart to you about this nightmare of a wedding and how now I won't have a date and all of the terrible things that will happen to me because of that, and when you hear my tale of woe, you tell me that I did something to deserve it? Just for that, I'm taking some cheese."

He reached into her purse but hesitated for a second and raised his eyebrows at her. She sighed and nodded.

"Okay, fine, you can have a little cheese, but you'd better save some for Olivia. And no tearing it off with your fingers. What kind of a Neanderthal do you think I am? There's a knife in there."

He beamed at her. Good Lord, that was a dangerous smile. She looked away and found the butter knife so she wouldn't throw herself at him.

He'd just bitten into his third cheese-laden cracker when the overhead lights came on and the elevator started with a jerk.

"Wow, are we actually moving?" She sat upright.

"Looks like I won't have to tackle you for the champagne next." Drew got to his feet and reached out a hand to help her up. Was it just her imagination that his hand lingered in hers?

Probably. She had a very active imagination. It helped to make up for her current lack of a romantic life.

In no time at all, they reached the sixteenth floor. Alexa was treated to one more glimpse of those abs as he pulled his jacket on.

"Looks like your sister and I are on the same floor," he said as they got off together.

"Looks like it." She smiled up at him for a second before she had to look away from those eyes again.

"Which way is she?" They both looked up at the arrow signs by the elevator bank.

"This way," she said, pointing to the left.

He consulted his room key.

"Ah, I'm that way." He pointed to the right.

They smiled at each other and didn't say anything for a moment.

"I can honestly say that I've never had a more entertaining time in an elevator. Thanks for that." He reached out a hand.

"Likewise." Alexa shook it. "Good luck at the wedding."

He laughed and grimaced.

"Don't remind me. Congratulations to your sister."

She thanked him and walked down the hall toward Olivia's room. She wished she knew what else she could or should have said to keep talking to him longer. She sighed and kept walking.

♥

"Alexa. Wait." This was crazy. Drew knew, objectively, that what he was about to do was crazy. But as she turned to walk away, he shouted for her to stop a split second later.

"Yeah?" She turned. "You can't have the rest of the cheese, not even as a parting gift."

Okay, here was his opportunity to play it off, pretend that that's what he was asking for, banter with this cute and funny woman with the great cleavage one last time, then turn around and go to his hotel room and get ready for this brutal weekend . . . Well, when you put it like that, maybe this wasn't so crazy.

"You . . . you wouldn't be free this weekend, would you? How long is your sister in town?" No turning back now.

"She leaves tomorrow after her deposition. I'm working on Saturday. I have an event at—"

"Working on Saturday—what about Saturday night? Even . . . Friday night?" Oh please, let her be free, now that he'd gone that far.

"Well, I have to—"

"Be my date this weekend? Please? The wedding isn't until Saturday night, so that would work, right? If you can't do Friday night I understand, but if there's any way you could come to the rehearsal dinner with me, I would . . . I don't know what I would do. Really appreciate it? Buy you all the cheese you wanted?" How did he go from zero to babbling and pleading with this woman in thirty seconds flat?

"Drew, I . . . Are you sure?"

He smiled. With that question, he knew he'd almost got her.

"Positive. Come to the wedding, be my sandwich, protect me from poisoning and disaster. It'll be your good deed for the year. And it's only May—look at you, getting your good deed for the year done before the year is even half over!" He was so close to victory; he could tell by the smile in her eyes as she looked up at him. "Come on, Alexa." He touched her shoulder. "Save me."

She took a deep breath, and he held his as she considered.

"When you put it like that, what else can I say? I'll do it."

He pulled her into a hug. Her champagne bottle–laden purse clanked against his butt, and they both laughed.

"You won't regret this." He pulled back and grabbed his phone out of his pocket. "Wait, give me your number."

He typed in her number as she recited it.

"There, I texted you, so you have mine. I'll send you all of the details later." He turned to leave before she could say anything else.

"Okay, but Drew, are you . . ."

"See you tomorrow, Alexa. Congratulations again to your sister!"

He sped down the hall with his suitcase, not giving her a chance to back out.

2

Alexa stared at Drew's back for a few seconds. Had that really happened? Had that cute stranger just asked her to be his date for a wedding? And had she really said yes?

She turned and raced down the hall to Olivia's room and knocked on the door. Olivia threw open the door and pulled her into a tight hug.

"Get in here!" They grinned at each other and hugged again. It was great to see her sister, it really was.

"Your hair looks amazing," Alexa said. "The pictures on Facebook do not do that 'fro justice."

Olivia looked her over and frowned in that way older sisters can.

"The outfit is great, and I love the shoes, but I thought you were going to get blond highlights? What happened?"

Alexa shrugged. "Sorry, I chickened out. I didn't think I could pull off the blond."

Olivia made a face at her.

"Haven't we been over this? Look at Beyoncé!"

Alexa laughed. "I know I'm the same skin color as Beyoncé, but me in her blond weave wouldn't go over too well during city council meetings. Even though I work in Berkeley, I still work for the mayor, you know."

Olivia plopped down on the bed.

"Oh please, you could get away with some blond highlights, easy. But then, you always were the risk-averse one."

Alexa opened her mouth to argue but thought better of it. She was here to improve her relationship with her sister, remember?

"Look what I brought you!" she said instead.

She pulled the champagne and the cheese and crackers out of her purse. "Not quite sure how cold the champagne is anymore, but we still have to drink it. And I heroically saved most of the cheese and crackers from the guy I was stuck in the elevator with, so we'd better enjoy them."

"Well, of course we still have to drink that champagne! Gimme."

Olivia grabbed the hotel water glasses as Alexa pulled the foil off the champagne bottle.

"I can't believe you were stuck in the elevator all that time. And why weren't you texting me back? Was your battery out?"

"Okay, there's a story there, but let's toast to you before I get into all of that." She twisted the metal tie open and pulled out the cork with a gentle pop. After she poured a healthy amount into each of their glasses, she held hers up.

"To Olivia Monroe, the first black female partner at Palmer, Young and Stewart in over ten years. To a brilliant lawyer, but most importantly the best big sister a girl could have."

"Are you trying to make me cry?" Olivia said. "It's not working. I don't care if you see water in my eyes; it's just because I'm allergic to this carpet."

Alexa smiled and clanked her glass against Olivia's.

"Cheers to you."

They both drank, hugged again, and drank some more.

"What time is our dinner reservation? Are we going to be late?"

Alexa took another sip of champagne and checked the time.

"Reservations are at eight and it's not even seven yet. Have some cheese."

Olivia reached for the champagne bottle and refilled their glasses.

"Oh wait, what was the story from the elevator? Why weren't you texting me back? I was worried that you were, like, eaten by the elevator monster or something."

"'Elevator monster'? Olivia Grace, you couldn't come up with a better fake worry than the 'elevator monster'?"

"The champagne is already going to my head, and I had a six-hour flight today, so give me a break. Tell me this story immediately." Olivia set her glass down on the nightstand and gave her a stern look.

"Damn, do I feel sorry for whoever you're deposing tomorrow. Does everyone you give that look to automatically spill their guts?" Alexa took a fortifying sip of champagne.

The real Olivia slipped out from behind the lawyer face as she grinned.

"Basically, so start spilling."

Alexa took a deep breath. It had just happened a few minutes ago, and this story still didn't seem like it had happened to her.

"So, the other person in the elevator with me was a guy."

Olivia nodded.

"Obviously, otherwise you would have texted me back."

Alexa kept talking so she wouldn't lose her nerve.

"A cute guy."

"Come on, am I an idiot? Of course he was cute. He wouldn't have even known of the existence of the cheese and crackers in your purse if he wasn't. But I feel like that's not the end of this story. Wait." Olivia looked Alexa up and down. "That dress looks like it's easy to get in and out of. I am going to be SO proud of you if you had a quickie in the Fairmont hotel elevator!"

Alexa gasped.

"OLIVIA, eww, no."

Olivia sighed.

"I knew that was too much to hope for. My prude of a little sister strikes again."

Alexa's hand tightened around her glass. Now she was a prude for not throwing her clothes off for a stranger in an elevator?

"I'm not a prude, but thanks for that."

This always had to happen, didn't it? Whenever they got together, her hopes were high, but within the first five minutes either she would manage to say something passive-aggressive to her sister, or Olivia would somehow make her feel inadequate.

Olivia nudged her once and again when Alexa didn't look up the first time.

"It's not an insult, Lexie. You know you've always been the well-behaved one."

Olivia hadn't called her Lexie in a long time. She forced herself to smile.

"Anyway." Alexa stood up and poured the rest of the champagne into their glasses. The bubbles would cheer her up. "You should get ready. Even though you are in San Francisco, I don't think you want to show up to dinner in that robe."

"I bet I could make it the latest style." Olivia grabbed a dress out of her suitcase and pulled it over her head.

"Zip me up." Alexa jumped up behind her. "You distracted me with that whole sex-in-the-elevator thing. What's the rest of the story?"

"Excuse me, *I* distracted *you*?"

"Semantics. Continue." Olivia reached into her purse for a lipstick.

Alexa slid her now-much-emptier purse over her shoulder and her right foot into a shoe.

"To make a long story short: I'm going to be his date to a wedding this weekend."

"WHAT??"

Olivia froze in place with lipstick only on her bottom lip.

"Well." Alexa smiled. "I shocked *you* now. That's a first."

3

Drew tossed his bag on the hotel bed and grinned at the view from his window. He pulled out his phone and texted his buddy in L.A., Carlos, who had heard everything there was to hear about the saga of this wedding.

Found a date for the wedding.

Thirty seconds later, his phone buzzed.

Didn't you swear off women? Like, specifically because of this wedding?

Oh right, he had done that, hadn't he?

Ok yes but this is an exception.

He investigated the sure-to-be-overpriced minibar. What the hell. He opened a beer and sank down on the bed.

Uh-huh. Where'd you find this one, in between SFO and your hotel? Nothing about you should surprise me. And yet.

He knew Carlos would appreciate this.

IN my hotel, if you can believe it. In the elevator.

Drew took a long drink of his beer and pulled off his shirt.

Let me guess, tall, blond, big fake boobs.

Well, this would definitely surprise Carlos.

Short, black, real boobs.

Drew stripped and jumped in the shower, bringing the rest of his beer with him. This morning he had cursed his Friday breakfast meeting in Oakland with his mentor that forced him to get to San Francisco on Thursday night. Now he thanked whichever god had inspired Dr. Davis to schedule that meeting so early in the first place. And also the one that made him follow Alexa onto that elevator.

Even though he was paranoid about running into another member of the Rogers-Allen wedding party, he took a chance and left his room to get a burrito from his favorite San Francisco taqueria. He pulled his hoodie up over his head as he crossed the hotel lobby, though. No need to take too many chances. Luckily, he made it there and back scot-free.

Fate wasn't as kind to Drew the next morning. As he got off the elevator in the lobby, he almost bumped into none other than Josh Rogers, who was holding a cardboard tray with two big Starbucks cups in one hand and a paper bag in the other.

"Drew! Oh man, it's so great to see you!" Josh said, a wide smile on his face.

"Yeah, man, same," Drew lied, happy at least that Josh's hands were full and they couldn't do the full bro hug that he could see Josh wanted.

"You just get here? I just got coffee for me and Molly. Come up to the room and say hi? We're a little crazy with wedding stuff, but I know we'd both love to catch up with you!"

"Oh man, I wish I could." Josh was so nice and cheerful that lying to him was like lying to a puppy. Easy and mean all at the same time. "I have to run. I'm heading out to have breakfast with Dr. Davis. He's at Children's Hospital in Oakland, you know."

"Wow, that's great! I'd love to hear more about what you're—"

"Sorry, Josh, I don't want to be late. I'll catch up with you later?"

"Yeah, yeah, definitely. See you tonight at the rehearsal. Oh, Molly said you RSVP'd with a plus-one? New girlfriend, or . . . ?"

"Yeah, new girlfriend. She'll be there tonight."

"Awesome, man! I can't wait to meet her. Do me a favor and text me how to spell her name? For the place cards, you know." Josh smiled with a dreamy look in his eyes. "Molly's been asking."

"Oh right, of course, of course. I'll let you know. Gotta run. See you tonight!"

Drew was halfway across the Bay Bridge before it hit him. New girlfriend. Shit.

♥

Alexa stumbled into her City Hall office at 7:25 Friday morning, hungover from that bottle of champagne and all the cocktails she and Olivia had had at dinner. As she pushed open her office door, her work phone and cell phone rang simultaneously.

She dropped her bag on the floor, set her full cup of coffee down on her desk, and shook her head. "Not today, Satan. I'm not falling for your tricks today. My coffee hasn't even had time to cool."

"Talking to our coffee again?"

Alexa looked up to see Theo, the mayor's communications director and one of her best friends, standing in her doorway.

"I cannot be expected to talk to anyone except my coffee this early in the morning. I blame you for this." She blew on her coffee in the futile hope that it would cool faster.

"I know you do. Sorry for the early-morning meeting, but the boss gets on a plane to San Diego at eleven, and we've got to . . ."

She waved her hand, stopping him.

"Yeah, yeah, yeah. You did bring me doughnuts, didn't you?"

He grinned.

"I did not bring *you* doughnuts; I brought doughnuts for your boss, the mayor, who should not eat doughnuts but loves them almost as much as you."

She pulled a few files out of her bag and grabbed her laptop and the coffee, and they walked toward the conference room.

"Yes, yes, but did you—"

"Yes, I saved a glazed with rainbow sprinkles for you. What are you, a six-year-old girl? You're the mayor's chief of staff. You should be eating a chocolate croissant or fresh fruit and granola or something."

"Six was a wonderful time in my life. I try to keep it alive at all costs, thank you very much," she said. "Have I ever told you that you look just like a black Clark Kent?"

Theo adjusted his glasses.

"Yes, every time you're trying to sweet-talk me into being your cheerleader. I've got your back during this meeting; no need to butter me up." He frowned at her. "Today, that is."

She grinned at him and snagged her doughnut, just as the mayor and his secretary walked into the room.

"Why, exactly, are we here this early, Theodore?" Mayor Emmitt boomed out, before investigating the pink doughnut box.

"You have a trip to San Diego scheduled for the climate change conference this afternoon, and so—"

"Yes, yes, I know, let's get on with it. Alexa, what's this thing about delinquent teenagers?"

She locked eyes with Theo, took a long sip of her coffee, and flipped open her laptop.

"Well, sir . . ."

An hour later, she finally managed the second bite of her doughnut as the mayor walked out the door on the way to his next meeting.

"Lex, you know how he is. It'll take a little time." Theo handed her the now-lukewarm coffee as they got up to walk to their offices.

She shrugged and tried to smile.

"I know. Thanks for the support in there."

"Anytime. Did you talk to your sister about this last night? You said before that you thought she might have some ideas for you."

Alexa shook her head. She'd almost brought it up a few times, but each time she'd gotten too nervous to say anything.

"It wasn't the right time, Theo. We were celebrating, and . . . anyway, it wasn't the right time." She changed the subject. "How was your hot date last night?"

He rolled his eyes.

"Most boring date I've ever been on. That woman and I had *nothing* to talk about. Buy you more coffee and I'll give you the highlights, such as they were?"

She fought back a yawn.

"Definitely."

Alexa checked her phone when she and Theo got back from their coffee run. A text from Olivia about her hangover; a few from her best friend, Maddie, about the book they'd both been reading; and one from an unfamiliar 310 number.

2 things: 1) we're still on for tonight, yes? 2) what's your last name?

Elevator guy. Tonight. Oh dear God. That hadn't been some sort of alcohol-induced hallucination?

Shit. A rehearsal dinner and a wedding at the last minute? What was she going to wear?

Yes. Monroe. And if I'm coming to this thing, I need some details about when/where/etc.

"Etc." meant "What the hell am I supposed to wear???" but she supposed she couldn't text that to a guy, let alone one she didn't even know.

Rehearsal dinner @7 at Beretta in the Mission. Wedding @6 tomorrow at some church, reception at the hotel. Btw I told Josh you're my new girlfriend, just fyi.

She stared at the phone for two full minutes. His new girlfriend? She had to pretend to be his girlfriend?

I had too much alcohol last night for this.

She had a reply almost immediately.

You and your sister celebrated her partnership in style, I see. Did she enjoy my cheese?

She couldn't help but laugh.

It was HER cheese, and yes, she loved it. Why did you need to know my last name?

She reached for her coffee cup and took a gulp. Thank God she'd gotten the largest size they had.

1) I should probably know my girlfriend's last name, right? 2) Josh asked for it for the place cards.

She looked up at the knock on her door.

"I was going to check to see if you needed coffee, but I see you're all set," her assistant, Sloane, said.

She almost asked Sloane to get her a pastry before she remembered she still had a doughnut sitting on her desk. She took a bite of it. Maybe the sugar would help her figure out exactly why she was going on a fake date with a strange guy tonight.

Oh right, because she'd accidentally said yes, and then Olivia had accused her of being a prude, so now she had to go.

Drew is short for Andrew, I assume? I should know that if I'm your fake girlfriend. I thought you didn't do girlfriends?

She scrolled through her emails and answered the easy ones as she mentally went through her closet to try to figure out what she was going to wear to this wedding. A few minutes later, Sloane poked her head back through the door.

"Oh hey, your lunch meeting just called to cancel. I rescheduled you for Tuesday."

"God bless you." Alexa checked her calendar and saw she was free almost all afternoon.

"She already has," Sloane said on her way out the door.

Short for Andrew yes (don't call me that). And, well, long story. Wait, do you work in SF? What do you do? I should know this about my girlfriend.

She took a sip of coffee and another large bite of her doughnut.

No, I work in Berkeley. For the mayor.

Wait, should she really be eating this doughnut if she was going to have to be in a cocktail dress in a few hours? Shouldn't she be drinking vitamin water or green juice or something?

Eh. She took another bite and went back to her emails.

Are you a lawyer like your sister? I'm a doctor, you should probably know that too.

She laughed. Did this dude think she hadn't listened to every word that had come out of his mouth the night before?

The whole "wedding of my ex-girlfriend and one of my best friends

from med school" thing kind of clued me in there, yeah. I am a lawyer, practiced for a while, am now the mayor's chief of staff.

But seriously, what the hell was she supposed to wear to this wedding? Time and venue were helpful, but that didn't tell her everything.

She hadn't been a bridesmaid a million times for nothing. After a few quick searches of wedding websites for the names Molly and Josh, and Saturday's date, she came up with their wedding website.

Black tie optional?

Alexa groaned and put her head back down on her desk. Her closet definitely was not built for black tie optional. After a few seconds she sat up and scrolled to Maddie's name on her phone— if anyone could save her, her best friend the professional stylist could. Who knew non-celebrities used stylists? Not her, until Maddie had started her business.

Long story but I have a sort of date tonight; wedding rehearsal dinner, going with a guy I hardly know (and that's putting it mildly), and also the wedding tomorrow (I don't even know). I will tell you the whole story you know I will but the important thing is WHAT DO I WEAR HELP ME

Then she shot Drew another text:

Black tie optional wedding with a day of notice. Why am I doing this again?

Because, the voice in her head said, he's hot, and you haven't even had a fake date in over a year.

♥

You're not going to back out on me, are you?

Drew sat in a Berkeley coffee shop, blocks from where he now knew she worked.

Please don't back out on me. Don't make me go to the buffet.

Of course she was going to back out. She was cute and funny and smart, and he oozed desperation. He didn't usually have trouble getting girls to go out with him. But finding a date for this wedding had been such a nightmare, it was like his own personal punishment for everything wrong he'd ever done to or with women: first there'd been everything with Emma, then when he called Julia she had a new boyfriend, and Carlos's sister had laughed in his face when he'd hinted at her coming with him.

He had resigned himself to dealing with what a disaster the wedding and the aftermath would be. Then one power outage and a malfunctioning elevator had saved him, he'd thought. He'd maybe jumped at that solution a little too eagerly, as usual.

Not backing out. Even though . . .

Oh thank God. Sometimes his crazy impulses worked out. He sighed in relief, and his thumbs flew over the keyboard.

No "even though." Don't "even though" me. I will owe you so big for this you'll have no idea. There will be a new Alexa Monroe wing in every hospital in the state. See you tonight then?

I'll be there. Please just text me ahead of time if we become fake engaged in the next few hours, OK? I'll have to borrow a ring.

What, you think I wouldn't buy you a fake engagement ring? You obviously don't know Drew Nichols very well.

Since I didn't know your last name was Nichols . . .

He laughed and downed the rest of his coffee.

Point to you, Monroe.

Another text flashed on his screen as he stood up.

;) Running to a meeting. See you later.

Alexa had looked so flabbergasted when he'd told her the details of the wedding. Everyone else in his life knew most of the Josh-Drew-Molly backstory, so he had kind of forgotten how crazy it was that he was in the wedding. And the worst part was that he hadn't even told her the whole story; he'd actually seemed like a good guy in the story that he had told.

There was no point in telling the woman you were stuck in an elevator with for probably only a few minutes that you'd broken the heart of the nicest person in the world, the snowball that had started this whole avalanche, and you probably deserved all of the looks you'd get all weekend, right? It wasn't like he'd lied to her; everything he said was the truth, just not the whole truth. It wasn't like he'd made Josh or Molly out to be evil, had he?

Well, maybe a little bit, but it was only because this no-date-for-the-wedding thing had driven him out of his mind. He should have just bailed on the wedding and looked like even more of a bad guy.

But now he had Alexa Monroe to come along with him and play the adoring girlfriend. He'd forgotten to tell her that adoring part, but maybe he could help that along some by playing the adoring boyfriend and she would get a clue? Shit, he really was going to have to buy her a hospital wing or something.

♥

"I can't believe you, Alexa. Where are all your cute dresses?"

Alexa's "meeting" was with Maddie—first at Alexa's house so

Maddie could inspect her closet, then at the closest mall when her closet was not miraculously stocked with black-tie-optional dresses. Alexa had opened her mouth to plead that she had too much work to do for a shopping excursion in the middle of the day, she could just wear her one little black dress that was sort of wedding appropriate, but when she saw the look on Maddie's face, she closed it. There was no point in arguing with Maddie when she had that look.

"I have a million cute dresses!" Alexa said as she drove them out to the mall.

"Yes, yes, of course you do," Maddie said. "Cute WORK dresses, but those don't count right now. You need cocktail dresses. Don't you ever go to weddings? I know you do, so where are all of your dresses from those?"

"I've been to ten weddings in the past three years," Alexa said. "I've been a bridesmaid in seven of those. I never get to buy cute dresses for weddings; they are preselected for me. And when do I ever need a cute non-work dress except for weddings?"

"What about the other three weddings?"

"I wore that black halter dress that you vetoed to two of them, and to the third I wore a fantastic gold sequined dress that I rented for the weekend."

Maddie sighed.

"I remember that dress. It looked incredible on you. Well, obviously this mysterious date happened at just the right time. We clearly need to build up your cocktail dress wardrobe. Okay. Now, who the hell is this guy you're going to a wedding with?"

When she told the story without all the adrenaline and champagne, it sounded even more ridiculous. She finished just as she pulled into the packed mall parking lot. What were all of these people doing here in the middle of the afternoon? Shouldn't they all be at work? Shouldn't *she* be at work?

"This is crazy. Why am I doing this? I should not be dragging you all over town in the middle of the workday and spending money on dresses to go to a wedding with some dude I talked to for fifteen minutes in an elevator yesterday. What am I thinking?" She pulled into a parking space and reached for her phone.

Maddie took the phone away from her.

"Nope. You're not allowed to cancel. I'm not letting you talk yourself out of this opportunity for a practice, no-stress date that just landed in your lap."

Alexa sighed and opened her car door.

"The thing is, Mad . . . this guy is out of my league, okay? He's hot, he's funny, he's flirty, and he's a doctor. I'm your standard short black girl with big boobs and hips who can barely look him in the eye without looking away. I don't even have the right clothes to wear on a date like this—this is how far out of my league this is!"

The problem with trying to talk about this with Maddie was that the words "out of my league" had never applied to Maddie. She was at least six inches taller than Alexa, with a body like a Barbie doll, light brown skin that always seemed to glow, and hair that looked perfect no matter if she left it curly or blow-dried it straight. Alexa, on the other hand, was short, what people who liked her called "curvy," and had more than once turned down social invitations because she didn't have the energy to deal with her hair.

Maddie steered her toward the entrance.

"That's exactly why you have to go. Nothing is riding on this! Look: you don't know this guy, he doesn't live around here, none of this matters. Don't overthink everything like you always do.

You'll just dress up, eat free food and drink free drinks, and look fucking hot the whole time if I have anything to do with it."

Alexa rolled her eyes.

Maddie smacked her on her arm.

"Ow! What was that for?"

"I saw that eye roll, and you will look hot, I promise you. And plus, you'll get two great dresses out of the deal."

Alexa opened the Nordstrom door and gestured for Maddie to precede her.

"I have one weekend where I don't have a ton of work to do, and this is how I waste it?"

Maddie threw her arm around Alexa.

"You're not wasting anything. It's practice, remember? Plus, from those text messages you showed me, this dude will freak out if you bail on him now."

When Alexa saw the armfuls of dresses that Maddie brought into the dressing room, she thought about bailing again.

"Maddie, these don't look—"

"Don't argue with me. Try them on."

She was officially an unwilling participant in that *Pretty Woman* shopping scene. Except she was going to have to use her own credit card at the end of it.

She sighed and stripped down to her bra and panties and pulled the first dress on.

"No, next." Maddie barely glanced at her in the dress before she vetoed it and pulled another dress from a hanger. "How's it going with your arts program?"

Maddie knew everything about the program Alexa had proposed to the mayor that morning: a pilot for an arts and writing diversion program for at-risk youth. Alexa had been wanting to start something like this in Berkeley for years, and now she was finally trying to make that dream a reality. It would be a place for teens who had gotten into some trouble to come and find their gifts, to find adults who believed in them, to work hard on something they loved to do, and to get their feet on a different path.

"Well, I proposed it to the mayor this morning, but he didn't say much. I'm not sure what he thinks. I'm worried."

She posed in front of the mirror in dress number two. She sort of liked it, but Maddie shook her head.

"Was Theo there? What did he say?"

"That this is just how he is and I should wait and see, et cetera. And I'm sure he's right. I'm just impatient. You know how important this is to me, Mads."

"I know." Maddie unzipped dress number three without even commenting on it. "I bet Theo is right, though. You know how your boss can be."

When Maddie looked at her in the fourth dress, she smiled and pointed to the shoes that she'd ordered Alexa to bring along with her. Then she spun her finger in a circle, forcing Alexa to twirl. When Alexa caught a glimpse of herself in the mirror, her eyes widened.

"Holy shit, I look hot."

"Mmmhmmm, what did I say?" Maddie had that smug look on her face, but Alexa couldn't even be mad at it.

How did one little dress make her look like a movie star? It was red, with a neckline that showed just enough cleavage, and a full skirt that floated as she twirled and somehow made her waist look tiny.

"Mads, isn't this color too bright for a wedding? Doesn't it make my hips look too wide? Isn't it too . . . boob-y?"

Maddie shook her head.

"Nothing, it's too nothing. It may be too expensive, but we're not going to worry about that right now. This is an emergency. It's the perfect color on you, and your hips are just the right amount of wide. And all that ruching around the waist means you don't have to wear Spanx. I know how much you hate them. Do you or don't you look hot in that dress? Did I not tell you I'd find you one?"

"You don't have to be so smug about it," Alexa said, still staring at herself in the mirror.

"Yes, I do. Okay, well, that's obviously your dress for the wedding, and thank God you have the perfect shoes for it, those gold ones you bought to wear with the gold sequined dress. Now we just need to figure out tonight."

Twenty minutes later, Alexa handed over her credit card for both dresses and tried not to wince at the bill.

"Thanks for this, Mads," she said. "I don't know what I'd do without you."

"I don't know what you'd do without me, either," Maddie replied.

4

Drew went into the bathroom at the church just so he could check his phone for the millionth time without being so obvious about it. His desperation was back in full force—he could tell from his four texts to Alexa over the past hour and a half. Texting a woman this many times was unlike him, but this stupid wedding had him on edge. She'd replied only to the first one where he'd tried to be cool, just confirming she was coming with a *"see you then,"* and the last, where he told her they were about to leave the church for the restaurant (*"on my way"*).

He'd questioned the lack of exclamation points in both texts—women, in his experience, tended to use a lot of exclamation points. Did that mean she was feeling like she should have backed out?

He was certainly feeling like he should have backed out. Not from the date with Alexa—no, that was the only part of the weekend that he was one hundred percent glad was happening. He should have backed out from the rest of it. Josh and Molly were being so welcoming and friendly that he felt like even more of an asshole for hating every second of this. Molly's mother, who had always been so nice to him, was noticeably chilly. Molly's sister, Amy, who had always been kind of a bitch to him, kept looking him up and down and smiling at him in a way that disconcerted him.

When they left the church, he jumped in a cab with Dan, the only other groomsman he knew well, and Dan's girlfriend. He looked down at his phone as the cab pulled up to the restaurant, hoping that maybe he'd missed a vibration and she'd texted to say that she was close, but there was nothing, not even an errant exclamation point.

"Guys, my girlfriend is getting here any second, so I'm going to wait outside for her." He hoped that at least one part of that statement was true. "See you in there, okay?"

His tension rose as other cabs full of the wedding party pulled up and he kept having to explain why he was standing there. He looked down at his phone again and fought the urge to send her a *"you almost here???"* text.

"Drew?" Alexa was standing in front of him. At just the sight of her, his shoulders relaxed. Without even thinking about it, he pulled her into a hug.

"You have no idea how happy I am to see you," he said into her ear.

"That bad already?" Her head rested on his chest for a second until she pulled away.

"Not terrible," he said, looking down at her. "Just not great. You, however, look fantastic." She was wearing a silky pink dress that flattered her golden brown skin . . . and the rest of her body.

"Keep looking at me like that, and we'll have no problem convincing people we're dating." She grinned up at him.

Oh God, he was such an asshole.

"Oh, I . . . I'm sorry." He dropped his hands from where they'd been resting on her shoulders.

She patted him on the arm. "Don't worry about it. Just getting into character, right?"

Not exactly, but if that's how she wanted to play it . . .

"Right." He smiled at her and hoped he hadn't made this girl hate him already. "What can I say? I'm delighted that you're my sandwich tonight."

She smiled. "Well, isn't that one of the loveliest things a man has ever said to me."

He leaned back against the restaurant window.

"I hope *that* isn't true."

She shrugged. A big group of guys pushed past them on the sidewalk, and he pulled her closer to him.

"Hey, Drew?" she said. "We ever going to go inside?"

He stood up straight and slid his hand into hers. Despite the chill of the San Francisco evening, her hand was warm.

"Inside. Right."

She stopped on the stairs on the way down to the private room where the rehearsal dinner was being held.

"Before we walk in there," she said, "is there anything I need to know so we don't look ridiculous?"

He moved closer to her so no one would overhear them. Hopefully, if anyone walked by it would look like they were just having a moment on the stairs.

"I told Josh that we'd been dating a month, so if anyone asks that, that's the story."

"Got it. Wow, only a month and I'm your girlfriend already. Moving fast, aren't you?"

He laughed.

"I'm a smart guy, I make quick decisions, and I know a good thing when I see it," he said.

She smiled up at him for a moment before her smile dimmed. "And now I have a question for you . . ."

Oh God, was she going to ask how long she had to stay? If they could have a fake breakup tonight so she wouldn't have to go to the wedding? He couldn't face this wedding alone. Ugh, maybe she wanted to know the real story behind his breakup with Molly?

"Ask me anything." He didn't really mean it.

"Am I going to be the only black person at this party?" She looked at his chest, his chin, and finally straight into his eyes.

"Oh." He paused. "Huh. I don't know. I didn't think about that."

Her lips curved upward, but she wasn't really smiling.

"Yeah, I figured you didn't. That's why I was asking."

He could hear the murmuring and laughter from the restaurant in the silence between them. He knew she was black, obviously, but he hadn't realized until now that the entire wedding party was white.

Not that he didn't *know* they were all white; he just hadn't thought about it like that.

"Okay." He thought for a second. "I'm pretty sure that this woman Samantha from our med school class will be there, at least for the wedding, and she's black. She and Molly were friends. Oh! And Dan—he's another groomsman—his girlfriend is Asian. Wait, that's not what you asked, is it? Um . . ."

"Don't worry about it," she said. Did she really mean it, though? He couldn't tell. He'd only met her yesterday. He didn't know her "don't worry about it" nuances yet.

"I'm sorry, I didn't think. I should have thought about this and asked Josh, is it going to be . . ."

She held a finger to his lips and smiled.

"Really, don't worry about it, Drew. I didn't get through Berkeley Law School without being the only black person in the room a few hundred times. I just wanted to know what I was in for before I walked in."

"We're okay?" When she nodded, he pulled her in for a hug.

"Oh shit, I think I got lipstick on you." She rubbed her thumb against his chest to try to get it out. After enjoying the sensation for a few seconds, he reached for her wrist to stop her.

"It's okay," he said. "It would look pretty out of character if my new girlfriend and I walked in there after standing around outside for so long and I didn't have her lipstick on me somewhere."

Her smile made him grateful all over again that she was there with him. He wished the two of them could stay here in this stairwell all night. Actually, even better: instead of going to this dinner, they could go back to their elevator and eat cheese and crackers and drink wine and laugh together. And also maybe . . .

She pulled back and took a step down the stairs. There went his fantasy.

"Okay, then, are we ready?" she asked.

He reached for her hand and sighed.

"Ready as I'll ever be."

♥

Boy, was it nice when this guy touched her. The hand-holding was particularly great. She felt like she was back in high school, except instead of the nerdy girl that everyone liked in that generic way, she was the girl holding hands with the hot guy at the party. She'd always wondered how that had felt.

News flash: it felt awesome.

She fought back her smile before she remembered that she was *supposed* to be besotted with Drew, so she let it beam as they walked through the party and up to the bar.

"Full bar, thank God. What's your drink of choice?" He gestured to the bottles of alcohol along the bar with a flourish.

"Tonight? Let's start with a gin martini, please."

Drew handed over her drink and clinked it with his bourbon. They each took long sips of their drinks without breaking eye contact. Alexa glanced at an empty table in the corner and raised her eyebrows to Drew; he nodded and took her arm to steer her over there. As Drew set his glass down, a tall blond guy came over and slapped him on the back before he turned to Alexa.

"So *this* is Alexa? So glad you're here with Drew for the wedding," he said, holding out his hand for her to shake.

Drew put his hand on the small of her back.

"Alexa, I'd like to introduce you to Josh Rogers, the groom. Josh, my girlfriend, Alexa Monroe," Drew said, his hand stroking the small of her back in a way that made her whole body tingle. Or maybe that was the gin hitting her bloodstream. She ignored whatever it was and smiled at Josh as she shook his hand.

"A pleasure to meet you, Josh. Congratulations on the wedding! I'm honored to be here."

A strawberry blonde with soft curls and a knee-length white eyelet dress walked up to them. Alexa had pegged her as the bride as soon as she'd walked into the room—who else would wear white to a rehearsal dinner? At her approach, Alexa moved closer to Drew. He picked up his drink and sipped it, but she knew he noticed, too, because he slid his arm around her waist. Damn, there was that tingle again.

"Drew, is this Alexa? Alexa, I'm Molly. It's so nice to meet you."

Molly gave her a huge smile that felt genuine, and not for the first time, Alexa wondered what the whole story was between the Molly and Drew breakup. Did Josh and Molly feel guilty for what they'd done to Drew? Did they ask him to be in the wedding to assuage their guilt?

She wasn't going to get an answer to that question right now (if ever), so her job was just to stand here next to Drew and turn on the charm. Luckily, she worked in politics; "charm" was her middle name.

Alexa increased the wattage of her smile by at least fifty percent.

"Molly, thank you so much for having me. Everything is lovely. What a wonderful choice for a rehearsal dinner. I can only imagine that the wedding will be just as beautiful."

Drew's thumb traced circles around her hip as she and Molly exchanged bright pleasantries about the wedding, the perfect weather in the Bay Area this time of year, and Josh and Molly's upcoming honeymoon in Hawaii. Between the sensuous feel of his touch and her now-finished martini, she was almost distracted enough not to wonder if he could detect the Spanx underneath her dress. Almost.

After a few minutes, Molly glanced to the corner of the room and sighed.

"My mom is signaling me; I think I have to go talk to one of my aunts. I hope to get to talk to you more later, Alexa. And you, too, Drew. Oh, and don't forget! The hashtag is jollymosh." Molly smiled and glided away.

They only had a few seconds before a tall blond woman in a tight green dress came up to the three of them. She could feel Drew tense up next to her. She reached back to find his hand and interlaced their fingers, and he held on. She didn't have long to wonder who this woman was.

"Josh, there you are. Your mom was looking for you. She had a question about what time we should sit down to eat." As Josh scurried away, her smile at Drew showed all of her blindingly white teeth. "I saw my sister over here. I hope everyone's being nice to her."

Drew squeezed Alexa's hand.

"I hope so, too. Amy, I'd like to introduce you to my girlfriend, Alexa. Alexa, this is Amy, Molly's sister and the maid of honor."

Amy raised her eyebrows at her and immediately turned back to Drew.

"I hope you both have a good time at the wedding this weekend."

Amy's attitude annoyed Alexa just enough that she couldn't resist putting on a show.

"I'm sure we will! It's already been pretty great, hasn't it, Drew?" She winked at Drew and squeezed his hand.

His eyes widened and his smile grew smug. "It sure has, Monroe." He pulled her close. "Amy, great to see you. We were just heading to the bar for another drink. Can we get you anything?"

Her eyes narrowed briefly, then her smile came back.

"No, thanks." She looked at Drew and glanced in Alexa's direction before turning to go. "Nice to meet you," she flung over her shoulder.

♥

As Drew and Alexa walked, still hand in hand, back to the bar, she leaned over and whispered in his ear, "I can't tell whether she hates you or wants to fuck you."

His bark of laughter made a few people look in their direction.

"She definitely hates me," he said against her ear, "but she's also been acting weird all day. You see why I needed you here?"

Her breasts against his chest and her lips against his ear made him want to pull her even closer, but they were in a room full of people.

Oh, and right, she wasn't really his girlfriend.

"I do see," she said. "I think I need another drink after that interaction. I'd better switch to champagne; I can't chug martinis all night or I'll be useless tomorrow."

He wondered if she'd noticed that he was taking every opportunity to touch her all night. Some of it wasn't even conscious; he just liked the feel of her smooth skin, the warmth of her body next to his, the softness of her hand in his.

"I should have said . . . if I do anything that bothers you tonight, you know, with the pretending-you're-my-girlfriend thing, just let me know, okay? Step on my foot or something?"

She turned and grinned at him, her lips so close to his that he could kiss her with just one slight movement. Just as he started to make that move, she stepped back.

"Don't worry, I will," she said. "But you're good so far. Plus, I'd be a pretty shitty fake girlfriend if I didn't let you touch me."

He put his arm back around her waist.

"I would never say such a thing about the best fake girlfriend I've ever had," he said.

As he handed her a glass of champagne, she said, "Oh, and by the way, when did you start calling me 'Monroe'?"

He looked up from his bourbon. "Well, I thought about 'Lexie,' but you don't strike me as much of a Lexie."

She smiled at him over her champagne glass in a way that made him step closer.

"Excellent instincts there. Only my sister can call me that. I'll allow 'Monroe' for the time being."

He stepped closer to her. "I promise I won't do anything you don't like. Cross my heart. Deal?"

She looked at him for a long moment, and he felt the tension between them heat up again. What exactly had he meant by that? Whatever she wanted it to mean, he guessed. Finally, she reached for his hand.

"Deal. Now, let's find some food to soak up all of this alcohol so that you don't have to pour me in a cab at the end of the night."

They followed a waiter to the corner of the room where they loaded up plates of puff pastry pockets and crostini with prosciutto. As soon as their hands were full and they couldn't move, they were surrounded. By bridesmaids.

♥

Though the bridesmaids circling them all had perfect pink lip-glossed smiles, their hostility to Drew and curiosity about Alexa was very clear. She got it, though—if any of her girlfriends' exes had showed up at their weddings, she probably would have smiled big while dropping poison in their drinks. Not enough to kill them, mind you. Just enough to make them humiliate themselves.

At that thought, she glanced down at Drew's drink, but he'd already drained it. Probably for the best.

For the next ten minutes she smiled and chatted and asked questions about their bridesmaid dresses and shared her own bridesmaid-ing stories while Drew never let go of her hand.

Her shoulders relaxed when Josh's dad beckoned everyone to the tables, and Drew's hand moved up and down her bare arm.

"You see why I needed you?" he said in her ear as they sat down. She turned to him and nodded.

"You'd have a peanut butter and egg salad sandwich right about now."

He made a gagging face and she laughed.

Luckily, the rest of the night was less fraught, mostly because they were sitting with two other groomsmen and their dates. As they lingered over dessert, Alexa glanced at the time and sighed at how little sleep she'd be getting that night.

"Something wrong?" Drew asked her, turning from his conversation with one of the other guys about basketball.

"Not exactly," she said in a low voice. "It's just that I have to help my boss build this playground tomorrow, which means my alarm is going off altogether too early for a Saturday, so . . ."

Before she'd even finished talking he had stood up.

"Let's go. You have to get your beauty sleep, though it's clear that you don't need it." She made that gagging face back at him and he laughed. "Too much? Can't you just enjoy the compliment?"

"Thank you, Dr. Drew, you're a sweetheart." She turned to pick up her coat but stopped when she saw him violently shaking his head.

"No Dr. Drew, never Dr. Drew. Dr. Nichols, thank you, though most of my younger patients just call me Dr. Nick."

They walked by Josh and Molly on the way to the door, and Alexa pulled at his hand.

"What?" He turned and saw her head incline toward them. "Oh, right."

"We're taking off," he said to them. "See you tomorrow."

Alexa stopped, which forced him to stop, too.

"Thank you so much, both of you, for your warm welcome. I can't wait to celebrate with you tomorrow."

"Thank you!" Molly beamed and then hugged her. "I'm thrilled that you'll be there!"

After another round of hugs and handshakes, Alexa followed Drew outside.

"Where did you learn to do that?" he said to her, once they were out on the street.

"Do what?" she asked him. He hadn't let go of her hand, and she certainly wasn't going to be the one to let go.

"*Thank you so much, both of you!*" he said in a high-pitched voice. She swatted him with her clutch.

"We have not known each other long enough for you to make fun of my voice!"

"I wasn't making fun of your voice." He squeezed her hand. Okay, so he did realize they were still holding hands. "I was making fun of what you *said*."

"Give me a break." She turned in the direction of the BART station. "Where did I learn basic social graces? Where did I learn how to say please and thank you? I don't know, I think my parents taught me when I was two."

As they moved through a crowd of people, he let go of her hand. But instead, he moved closer and put his hand on the small of her back again. She could feel herself melting inside. Was he just doing this out of habit? Probably.

She tried to remember what Maddie had said. No-stress date, relax and have fun, don't overthink things, just enjoy it. Right, okay.

He cleared his throat. "If I've forgotten to say it, you made this night at least two hundred percent better than it would have been without you. Maybe more."

She smiled at him. "I had a surprising amount of fun myself. Now, what's the plan for tomorrow?"

Classic Alexa. Ignore the compliment; change the topic to logistics. Relaxing was definitely not her strong suit.

"So I was thinking . . ." He dropped his hand from her back and turned to her with a weird look on his face.

Was he bored by her? Was her sarcasm too much? Was he going to say he'd rather have a fake breakup tonight and not have her as his date for the wedding tomorrow so he could enjoy the buffet of bridesmaids, with the maid of honor as the main course? *I had a great time hanging out with you, Alexa,* he'd say, *but I'm going to let you off the hook for tomorrow night. You don't mind, do you?* And of course she would have to say no, she didn't mind.

And she'd have to go return that hot red dress.

"Yeah?" She pulled her coat tighter around her shoulders.

"Maybe you could come get ready for the wedding in my hotel room? You know, so everyone sees you leaving from the hotel, not that I think that people think we're lying, but Amy seemed a little suspicious or something, and then you wouldn't have to . . ."

"That makes sense." She cut him off, trying not to show how relieved she was. "What time?"

His smile widened. He had probably gotten everything he wanted in his life with that smile. Who was she to break the pattern?

"I have to be at the church by five, so just be there before I leave? There's a shuttle from the hotel to the church, and you can take that over so you don't have to sit around during the pictures."

They walked down the street, no longer hand in hand. "That sounds good."

"Great." They were at the entrance to the BART station now. "Okay. See you tomorrow? Text me if you have any questions?"

He leaned in for a hug. Without stopping to think about it, she kissed him on the cheek. He pulled back and looked at her for a long moment.

An ambulance roared by and they jumped apart.

He stroked her cheek with his thumb.

"Good night, Monroe. See you tomorrow."

5

Alexa thanked God the next morning that the real work of building the playground was for people who actually knew what they were doing. She could still keep her boss on message and banter with the press while her mind was constantly wandering to her date that night, but if she'd been operating power tools, it would have been a disaster.

By the time she knocked on the door of room 1624 she was a bundle of nerves. *Maybe he thought better of this? Maybe he already checked out of the hotel and forgot to tell me? Maybe he* . . . She didn't have a chance for another possible worst-case scenario before he opened the door. And then she was speechless for a moment.

She'd thought Drew was hot in his worn gray T-shirt in the elevator, and she'd thought he was hot at the rehearsal dinner, clean-shaven in his pale blue button-down shirt. Now, in a tuxedo, he was so hot she was afraid she wouldn't be able to look him in the eye all night.

He wasn't even fully in the tux—that was the worst part. He had the shirt on and the bow tie untied around his neck, with his hair still damp. He looked like every romantic comedy hero at the end of the night, just before the heroine pulled his shirt out of his pants and started unbuttoning . . .

"Hey!" He interrupted her increasingly lurid train of thought. "You're just in time. I was about to break into the snacks."

"Snacks?" she asked. She followed him into the room, momentarily distracted from her fantasies.

"I got us cheese and crackers . . . and beer. If this is anything like most weddings, we're not going to eat for a while. I don't know about you, but I could use a drink before this night gets under way."

"You read my mind," she said. She dropped her tote bag on his bed and hung her dress up in the closet. "I almost brought a bottle of wine, but I didn't want to start dancing on tables before the wedding even began."

He disappeared into the bathroom and came out a few seconds later with two bottles of beer in his hands.

"Beer's in the bathroom sink. The champagne bucket was too small for a six-pack. Plus, there are two sinks; filling one up with ice was the biggest stroke of genius I've had in a while, if I do say so myself." He cracked open both bottles, handed her one, and then raised his to her. "To my wedding date, and thanks again."

She took a long drink of her beer and looked around the room, trying to find something to distract herself from how much she wanted to lick that drop of condensation off his lower lip. Huge king bed, neatly made up, so housekeeping must have already come and gone. A full-length mirror by the closet—great, she would need that while getting dressed. Floor-to-ceiling windows beyond the bed. She wandered over to the window, beer in hand, and glanced outside.

"Wow." The view stretched out over the sparkling bay. She could see both the gray and white bulk of the Bay Bridge and the gleam of the Golden Gate Bridge, with the bright sun overhead.

"The view is something else, isn't it?" he asked. He came up behind her so close she could feel his body heat. She wanted more than anything to lean back against his warm chest.

"It really is," she said, without turning around. "Olivia was on this side of the hotel, too, but we were so busy talking I didn't even look out the window. Josh and Molly got a perfect day for their wedding." She turned to him, but he'd already stepped back over to the desk.

"I couldn't compete with your fancy cheese and crackers," he said, "but I did what I could."

She walked over to investigate and set her beer down so that she could dig in.

"I love this stuff," she said, dipping a Wheat Thin into the tub of herbed cream cheese.

He followed suit.

"You're not just saying that to be nice? Or because you need to eat something so that you don't jump up on that table and start dancing? Don't hesitate to do that on my account, by the way."

She took another swig of beer and grinned.

"I told you, I love all forms of cheese and crackers, even that gross stuff that I used to get in my lunch as a kid with the little red plastic spreader."

He flopped down on the bed with his beer and grinned at her. She could just push him all the way down and unbutton that shirt of his. Would he have chest hair? If so, not too much—that glimpse of his stomach she'd had in the elevator was branded in her memory, and there hadn't been a ton of hair there.

Oh my God, what was wrong with her? A few sips of beer and her fantasies were trying to take over.

"I love that stuff. I should have bought some of that," he said. Her eyes shot back to his face, and she tried to remember what they'd been talking about. At least if her cheeks were flushed now she could blame the alcohol. Just to make sure that excuse would work, she drained her beer.

"You want another?" he asked. He stood up and moved toward the bathroom.

"Sure." She took out her makeup bag and closed her eyes. This whole thing was such a bad idea—she was getting drunk in the hotel room of a hot guy she barely knew, she was getting drunk enough to fantasize about jumping a guy far out of her league, and her unwelcome fantasies were probably written all over her face because he'd rolled off the bed and moved far away from her.

Oh well, at least she was getting free cheese and crackers out of this. And beer.

He came back from the bathroom with two more beers and stood next to her at the desk as she grabbed more crackers.

"Tell me about your morning," he said. "You built a playground? I'm impressed."

"Oh please, don't be," she said. "The playground building operation was well orchestrated by an actual construction company. My boss and I were just there for show and for the press. I mean, the playground did actually get built—well, started, at least—and I got a few splinters in the process, but everything I did was under the very close supervision of someone who knew what she was doing."

"But tell me." He sat down on the bed. "Where does the construction company come from? How did they figure out where to build the playground?"

"Oh, well, this has been a project that started almost as soon as my boss got into office. Low-income kids are a real priority of his—and mine. We identified a few areas early on that needed safe and attractive playgrounds, and this is the first one that actually got built."

He leaned back on his elbows. Good Lord, was he doing this to torment her?

"Is this your modest way of saying that you found the construction company and you figured out where to build the playground?"

She slipped her sandals off and rubbed her toes into the plush carpet.

"Yes to both of those things, but I'm not that modest; I just hadn't gotten there yet. I can be kind of long-winded."

He laughed and motioned for her to toss him a cracker, which she did.

"Do you have any pictures?"

Alexa beamed at him and reached for her phone. She got so excited when she talked about her work. He liked that about her. He looked over her shoulder as she scrolled through the pictures of what the empty lot had been, the groundbreaking today, and some sketches of what the playground would look like when it was all finished. She was so animated in telling him about it that he couldn't stop himself from moving closer to her on the bed; close enough that their shoulders touched, that her head was almost against his chest.

She turned and looked up at him. They both seemed to realize how close they were at the same time, but neither of them moved away. His hand moved to the small of her back, up her back to the nape of her neck, and back down again. He could smell her perfume. Vanilla, with a hint of spice.

Suddenly there was a loud knock on his door.

"Drew? You ready?"

Dan. Not now. Not yet.

He turned back toward Alexa, but she jumped off the bed and went back to the cheese and cracker table.

"Yeah." He sighed and stood up.

He threw open the door to Dan, who looked altogether too perky for the occasion.

"Hey, man. Oh, hey, Alexa! You almost ready for the wedding? We'll see you over there, huh?"

She looked up and smiled at Dan but didn't look at Drew.

"Yeah, see you there. Is Lauren going to be on the shuttle?" she asked Dan.

"She is! She's still in the room getting dressed, so you guys can ride over together. Here, let me give you her number, so you can be buddies."

"See you at the church," Drew said to Alexa, willing her to look at him. She met his eyes for a second, then looked away.

He was halfway to the elevator before he heard his name from behind him and turned around.

"Drew, aren't you forgetting something?" she said.

He could think of many things he'd forgotten to do in that hotel room, but he could say none of them with Dan standing there.

"Your bow tie?" He glanced down and saw the offending garment dangling from her fingertips.

"Oh. Right." He took the tie from her and smiled. "If you finish the beer, save that table dance for where I can see it, please."

♥

Oh God, she had really been about to kiss him. One and a half beers and a few minutes of him listening to her talk and she was ready to pounce on him. She needed someone to talk some sense into her, and right now the only person to do it was herself.

"Alexa," she said out loud at her reflection in the lighted magnifying mirror. Holy shit, she really needed to pluck her eyebrows. Thank goodness she'd brought her tweezers.

Wait, she needed to focus. She was talking sense to herself, remember?

"Alexa ELIZABETH. This is all fake. This is a fake date; this is a fake boyfriend. You can't just go around kissing hot guys who look like they come straight out of a movie set because they smile at you like that and listen to you prattle on about your job for a few minutes. Just because Maddie told you to practice flirting doesn't mean you get to practice kissing, too."

She cringed to think how humiliating it would have been if she'd actually moved in to kiss him. He would have gently kissed her back for a second. Then he would have pulled back, put his hands on her shoulders, and said that he was very sorry if he'd given her the wrong impression about everything, but she wasn't really his type. All he was looking for from this evening, he would have said, was a buddy to stick by his side and repel other women, and if that was going to be a problem for her it was totally okay for her to go home now instead of to the wedding with him.

And she would have had to suck back her tears like she always did and smile big and say oh no, it was probably just the beer getting to her, it would be no problem. And then things would have been awkward and weird all night.

Well, it was still probably going to be awkward and weird all night, but at least that would be more subtext than text.

Enough pep talk time. All she could do now was look as fabulous as she possibly could. She cued up her girl-power playlist, pulled out her reddest of red lipsticks, and threw herself into getting ready.

♥

"One more with the maid of honor and best man—Amy, you give him your bouquet this time!"

Drew was more than ready for these pictures to stop and the wedding to begin. Especially because that meant Alexa would finally get here. Even though he wouldn't be anywhere near her during the wedding, at least he'd have one person on his side among his sea of blatant or veiled hostility.

She hadn't texted him yet. He should check in and make sure she was on her way.

You on the shuttle over here? Everyone being nice to you?

A few minutes later:

Just getting on now. Dan's girlfriend Lauren is my new date. Glad I met her last night.

He smiled down at his phone. Oh thank God, she was on her way.

Wait, does that make Dan my date? I think I like you better, no offense to Dan.

"Hellooooo, Drew!" He looked up to find the rest of the wedding party, sans bride and groom, staring at him. "Stop texting your girlfriend and pay attention."

"She's—"

Oh shit, close save. He'd been that close to declaring, *She's not my girlfriend*, the way he did every time someone called some woman his girlfriend.

". . . on her way," he trailed off, as everyone stared at him.

"Great, that's great." Amy came up to him and put her arm around his waist. "But can we finish taking these pictures before the wedding starts without us?"

He put a smile on his face and walked over with her to where the rest of the wedding party was waiting for him. He managed to disengage himself from Amy when the photographer ordered the bridesmaids and groomsmen to opposite sides of the church garden.

The groomsmen came back into the church just as the shuttle full of people arrived. Drew searched the crowd for Alexa, and when he finally saw her, laughing at something Dan's girlfriend said, his mouth dropped open. That red dress made him want to grab her hand, pull her out of the church, and bring her back to his hotel room immediately.

Josh's cousin Bill walked up to her before he could get there. What the hell was he doing, looking at her like that?

Apparently, her dress also made Drew want to tell every other man in this room that he wasn't allowed to look at her. Drew walked faster toward her.

"Ladies." He got to them just as Alexa was shaking Bill's hand. "May I escort you to your seats?"

Bill smirked at him.

"Sorry, Drew, I already claimed them. You snooze, you lose."

Drew narrowed his eyes at Bill and slid Alexa's arm into his.

"Oh, Bill, you must have misunderstood. This one is mine."

They walked down the aisle in silence for a few seconds. Once they were out of earshot, she murmured, "I'm sorry, did I interrupt a pissing contest? I can go back to the hotel, I don't want to be in the way."

He laughed and drew her closer to him.

"No, don't worry about it. And I won you anyway."

She raised her eyebrows at him.

"You . . . won me?" she said.

He coughed.

"Wait, that came out wrong. You aren't a thing to win or whatever. Sorry about that. It's just that that dude always rubs me the wrong way."

She smiled and held on to his arm tighter.

"Well, I would much prefer that you win me than him, even though I am indeed not a thing to win, so I guess we agree there."

He stood at the end of the pew with her, not wanting to let go quite yet.

"Excuse us." Dan elbowed him aside to let Lauren into the pew.

"Poor Bill." Alexa laughed up at him. "Cock blocked on both sides."

He didn't remember her looking this hot in the elevator. Good job, Thursday-night-Drew, for somehow knowing that she'd be this hot when she was shoeless sitting on the elevator floor.

Oh wait, at that point he'd been trying not to stare at her cleavage, so maybe he had reason to know.

"Whatever," he said. "He needs to get his own girl and stop trying to grab someone else's."

She went up on her tiptoes and kissed his cheek.

"See you at the reception." She slid past him into the pew and sat down next to Lauren.

"Save me a sandwich," he said, just to make her laugh. It worked.

6

After the ceremony was over, Drew walked back down the aisle after Josh and Molly, with a pink chiffon–clad bridesmaid on his arm. He winked at Alexa as he walked by her, and she winked back. She and Lauren told wedding war stories on the shuttle ride to the hotel and placed bets on who in the wedding party would be wasted first. (Lauren bet on Bill, but Alexa had money on Amy.)

When they got to the hotel, they followed the procession of guests up to the roof for cocktail hour and hung out in a corner with glasses of champagne and plates of something that looked very much like a fancy version of pigs in a blanket.

Thank goodness she'd bonded with Lauren at the rehearsal dinner; otherwise, the ceremony and this part of the reception would have been awkward and lonely. She would have long ago sent dozens of SOS texts to Maddie. It was crucial to have another woman to laugh with, go to the bathroom with, and gossip with during a wedding.

When Lauren was halfway through her "How I met Dan" story, Alexa realized what was coming and set her drink down on a nearby table.

"Hold that thought," she said. "I have to use the ladies' room. Guard my drink."

As soon as she walked into the hall, she pulled her phone out of her clutch.

Hey boyfriend, how did we meet? I can tell Lauren is about to ask me, wanted to make sure our stories were straight.

Just as she got into the bathroom, her clutch vibrated.

The elevator, but a month ago. I was in town for that conference, remember?

Good plan. Keeping to the truth as much as possible was the best way to tell a lie. She'd learned that after working in politics for a while. Not that she made it a habit to tell lies . . . but when she had to, it was best that she knew how to do it believably.

We were so happy that the wedding was back at this same hotel, weren't we?

When she got back out to Lauren, there was another plate sitting next to her drink, along with Bill, the annoying usher.

"Bill grabbed us some crab cakes!" Lauren said. She raised her eyebrows at Alexa where Bill couldn't see her. This was also why it was crucial to have women friends at a wedding: you needed someone to roll your eyes with at all of the creepy dudes.

"Oh, thank goodness, this drink is starting to go to my head already. I don't want to be drunk by the time the bride and groom walk in. Thanks, Bill."

"My pleasure. What's your name again? Alice?" He grinned at her, his eyes dropping to her cleavage. She drained her drink.

"Alexa."

"Alexa, it looks like you need another drink." He brushed some hair from her shoulder. She forced a smile.

"I do, thank you. Champagne, please. Lauren?"

After they sent Bill off to the bar, they both cringed and went back to their conversation.

"Okay, where were we? You reached for the last carton of eggs at the farmers' market and Dan picked them up?"

Alexa had finished two more crab cakes by the time Bill was back from the bar. He handed her the drink with a big smile, his eyes on her cleavage again, and his hand on her elbow. Nothing in the world would compel her to drink *that* glass of champagne.

She moved her clutch from her right hand to her left to shift her body away from him, but he followed. This dude. He had about five seconds to back away before she'd "accidentally" spill the champagne on him.

"What about you and Drew? How did you two meet?" Lauren asked Alexa.

"Well"—an arm went around her waist—"it was actually right here in this hotel." She turned her head, and Drew smiled down at her. "Hey," she said. "You guys are here." She moved closer to Drew and relaxed against him.

"Hey yourself." The rest of the room washed away, and it was just this dream of a guy in a tux, golden brown eyes, his fingers stroking her hip in that way that made her wish there wasn't a layer of clothes in between them and her skin.

Oh God, she was fantasizing about him again.

"Where's Dan?" Lauren asked.

"At the bar. We both need a drink after all of those pictures." Drew leaned down and his lips brushed her ear. "You guys weren't having too much fun without us, were you?"

"Just talking about you guys," Lauren said. "Speaking of, I'll go meet Dan at the bar. I could use another drink, too. Alexa?"

Alexa nodded, only half listening to Lauren. She could stand there all night with Drew's arm around her and his fingers skimming her waist. She felt dizzy from the touch of his hands on her body and his eyes looking down at her. It was almost too much.

Bill's hand tightened on her elbow. She'd forgotten he was even there.

He smirked at Drew.

"I hope you don't mind me stealing your date, but what can I say, I got back to the reception faster."

Drew pulled her closer to him and away from Bill. His fingers kept moving over Alexa's body, drawing circles up and down her waist, moving from there to the small of her back.

"Go away, Billy. The grown-ups are talking." He shooed Bill away with his fingers without taking his eyes off Alexa. After a few seconds, Bill walked away.

Alexa smiled up at Drew and opened her mouth to thank him just as his grip on her waist relaxed. Oh. He'd only been holding on to her like that to protect her from Bill. That was nice of him.

She took a step back, and his arm dropped away from her. She felt colder. And much more sober than a minute before.

"Thank you for that. Did you . . . I mean how was everything with the wedding?" Alexa asked him, crossing her arms in front of her chest and wishing she had that drink.

He shrugged, his hands at his side.

♥

"Mostly fine. Josh was so excited it was almost cute," Drew said, itching to touch her again. He had to keep reminding himself that she wasn't really his girlfriend, or even his real date. She hadn't signed up for him to be all over her tonight, even though he could barely keep his hands off her in that dress. Even though his blood pressure had skyrocketed the second he'd seen Bill with his hand on her. "Want to go find Lauren and Dan now that we got rid of Bill?"

"Now that you got rid of Bill, you mean." She smiled up at him, and it took everything he had not to pull her back against him. But she'd stepped away as soon as he'd relaxed his arm; she probably didn't want that. They walked together toward the bar, close but not touching.

"There you guys are!" Dan said. Lauren and Dan met them halfway, each with two drinks in their hands.

"The bar is swamped, but Dan cut to the front of the line," Lauren said.

"Please, take your drinks. People keep looking at us like we're lushes." Dan handed Alexa her drink. "And I didn't cut! I'm a groomsman. We get front-of-the-line privileges at the bar, didn't you know that?" He laughed. "Plus, I tip well. It's the only way to guarantee a heavy pour at an open bar."

"Oh, you guys were telling me the story of how you met," Lauren said. Oh good, now he had an excuse to touch Alexa.

"Right here in this hotel," he said as he reached for her hand. "We were stuck in the elevator for a while together, and she made me laugh the whole time, even though she openly refused to share the snacks in her purse with me."

She interrupted. "Okay, he says that like I was sitting there eating and ostentatiously not giving him any, which was not the case! He looked in my purse—without my permission, mind you—saw that I had snacks, and tried to sweet-talk me into giving them to him instead of to my sister."

"Probably the first time anyone has ever said no to our Drew. No wonder he was intrigued." Amy. Just who he needed right now.

Alexa gave Amy one of those big, bright smiles like people gave toddlers. "Amy, you certainly won the maid of honor lottery with that dress, didn't you? You all look so *darling* in that pale pink."

Amy's eyes narrowed at the compliment. The night before, one of the bridesmaids had mentioned that Amy had pushed hard for black dresses, but Molly and their mom had insisted on pink, even though Amy claimed the color was juvenile and that it clashed with her hair. Drew squeezed Alexa's fingers since he couldn't laugh out loud. She squeezed back.

Amy's hand was resting on the table right by Drew's. Was that her pinky finger rubbing against his? Yep, yep, it was. He put his arm around Alexa to move closer to her and away from Amy.

"Your dress is great, too," Amy said to Alexa. "I almost bought a dress like that for a wedding I went to last month, but I realized I was just too skinny for it. So glad you can make a dress like that work."

Drew felt Alexa stiffen. He ran his hand up and down her back, not sure if he was trying to calm her or himself down. Probably both, because Amy's words had gotten his blood pressure up again.

"Thanks so much!" Alexa said, lifting up her champagne glass and taking a sip. "I always figure, if you've got them, flaunt them." She gestured to her breasts, causing him—and, he quickly realized, their whole group—to stare at them for a second. Okay, maybe longer than a second. When he eventually raised his eyes to hers, she smirked at him. He grinned back.

"Ladies and gentlemen!" someone said over the microphone. "Please welcome Josh and Molly Rogers!"

They all dutifully turned to the entryway and clapped as the bride and groom entered. Amy disappeared to the other side of the room, but he didn't move his hand from around Alexa, and she didn't move away this time.

♥

Okay, fine. She had to admit to herself that she was smitten with him. It was past time for talking sense into herself. At this point she just had to ride it out for the rest of the night. She knew it was all fake—she knew because she'd been reminding herself of that—but it didn't matter. Not when he was touching her like that.

At first, she'd tried to give him space—after Bill had moved away, Drew obviously hadn't wanted to keep up the pretense, so she'd backed away. But they told their real/fake story to Lauren and Dan, and he introduced her to a million people, and all of those things necessitated them holding hands at a minimum. Or so at least he seemed to think, and it's not like she was going to disagree with him there. So she kept her hand in his and her smile aimed at him, and boy did it feel good, fake or not.

At dinner, they were at one end of the huge wedding party table, along with Amy, a few bridesmaids, and creepy Bill, with Lauren and Dan all the way at the far end. Well, at least she'd had lots of practice eating food with people who were hostile to her. She'd discovered tonight that working in politics had given her a lot of skills useful for being a pretend girlfriend. Drew was talking to Amy, who was on the other side of him, so Alexa chatted away with the bridesmaid sitting next to her.

While they ate their entrées—pork chop encrusted with

chopped almonds for her, chicken cordon bleu for him—he turned back to her while Amy complained to the waiter about something or other.

"How's your food?"

"Good, actually," she said after swallowing. "Better than your typical wedding food. Want some?" She cut a piece and held out her fork to him.

He recoiled. Was this too familiar for someone she'd just met two days before? Did he forget he was supposed to be her boyfriend in this scenario? Or maybe he hated sharing food?

Whatever it was, it didn't make her feel great.

Amy leaned around Drew to laugh at Alexa.

"You trying to kill Drew already? What did he do now?"

Alexa raised her eyebrows at Drew. Now she was pretty sure what the problem was, but she was interested to hear how he was going to play this one off.

♥

"Oh." Drew leaned forward and put his hand on her shoulder. "I guess this hasn't come up yet, but I'm allergic to nuts."

He hated himself for that hurt feeling that had crossed her face before that very bright (and, he suspected, very fake) smile had flashed back on. He rubbed his hand down her arm, trying to apologize with his touch in the way he couldn't with words, not with all of these people listening.

"Weird, because that was one of the first things you told Molly," Amy said. "I remember her telling me that." Was Amy actually suspicious, like he'd wondered last night, or was she just being a bitch?

"Molly and I were in med school at the time. Things like that were more at the front of our minds." He turned halfway to Amy, his hand still on Alexa's arm. "Alexa and I have been busy with other things, but I figured it would come up. And look, it has."

The conversation around them moved on to how good the mashed potatoes were, Josh's stepfather's faux pas at the ceremony, whether people thought the DJ would be good or not. As soon as Amy pontificated loudly about how she'd *told* Molly to get a band instead, he moved his chair closer to Alexa and turned so his lips were almost against her ear.

"That was all my fault. I'm so sorry. Probably should have let you know about my deathly allergy before we ate a meal together."

"It's okay." He could hear the smile in her voice. "Almost killing my date makes a wedding exciting."

He laughed. Okay, good, she wasn't mad at him.

"No chance of that. We're surrounded by doctors, remember? I bet at least ten people have EpiPens on them, just for kicks."

Did she realize her hand was resting on his thigh? It was probably just because of the way he was sitting right against her so he could whisper. Her hand was probably on his thigh by default. He didn't care. He just wished there was a way to keep it there.

"Alexa, I'm heading to the ladies' room. Want to come with?"

He liked Dan's girlfriend, Lauren, but he could cheerfully kill her right now. Hmm, did *she* have any allergies?

He watched Alexa as she crossed the room, laughing about something or other with Lauren. Yep, still hot in that dress from this angle.

For a second, he wondered what the night would have been like if Alexa wasn't there with him. That was easy: miserable. With her here, though, it had been more than okay. Fun, even, which is the last thing he thought this wedding would be.

"Another drink?" Dan plopped down in the seat next to him.

"What? Oh, yeah, sure."

"You've got it bad with that one. Nice going." Dan jerked his head in the direction of where Lauren and Alexa had disappeared. Drew had no idea how to respond to that, so he just shrugged and smiled.

"Yeah," Bill slurred. "I'd hit that one. I've always wanted to bang a black girl. What's it like, Drew?"

Drew didn't realize he'd stood up until he felt Dan pull him in the direction of the bar. He resisted for a second, the rage in his bloodstream pushing him to charge at Bill, but after a second or two he allowed himself to be dragged away. Dan waved at the bartender, who promptly set two neat whiskeys at the end of the bar for them.

"I could throw him off the roof," he said to Dan once he'd calmed down enough to speak.

"You could," Dan said. "And you probably should. But maybe wait until after the wedding? Too many witnesses right now."

Drew picked up his drink and looked around the room for Alexa. At least she hadn't heard Bill.

"All I know is that I'm keeping him the hell away from Alexa for the rest of the night."

♥

Lauren ran up to her room to retrieve her lipstick, so Alexa killed some time texting Maddie an update from inside one of the bathroom stalls. All of a sudden, her ears perked up at a conversation by the sinks.

"I thought Drew was the one to break up with Molly?"

"He was. He totally destroyed her when he did it, too." That was Amy. "But I bet he was pissed when Josh and Molly started dating." She laughed. "When he gets rid of that date of his, I have an idea for a place he can find someone who looks a lot like Molly."

The conversation faded as they left the bathroom. Drew had told her Molly had broken up with him, hadn't he? Had he lied to her, or was she remembering things wrong?

Thirty seconds later while looking in the mirror she got another hit to the psyche. One glance down at her clutch to take out her lipstick, and when she looked back up, she was flanked by thin blond women.

All three of them were in cocktail dresses shorter and tighter than anything she'd dare to wear because of her thighs and hips and butt. Their perky little breasts were obviously unencumbered by bras, and their long, thin legs looked even longer and thinner because of their sky-high heels. And there she was in between them, in the dress that her friends would say made her look "voluptuous," which was just another word for "fat."

She couldn't believe Maddie had convinced her not to wear Spanx. She'd felt great in that dress just a few hours ago when she left Drew's hotel room, but was that just beer and flattering lighting? Maddie had never steered her wrong before, but then Maddie was her friend and loved her. Maddie would give her tough love about many things in life, but she would never say something bad about her body. That was the problem with good friends: they were too damn supportive sometimes.

And she'd spent the night falling deeper and deeper in lust with Drew, with those damn tingles every time he touched her, and the whole time he was probably looking at all of those other women, wishing he was with one of them.

She needed to shake this off to get through the rest of this night. Pep-talk-in-the-hallway time.

Okay, Alexa Elizabeth Monroe, she said in her head, *none of this matters, remember? You're just here because you told Olivia and Maddie about it before you realized you should back out. You're wearing a great dress, you're drinking some free alcohol and eating good food, and you're going to leave in—*

She started when she felt a hand on her shoulder mid–mental pep talk. Not Drew's. How was it that she already knew his touch? She shook off that question and turned to find Lauren behind her.

"There you are! Dan texted me that he and Drew are over at the bar. Let's go find them."

They found them at the bar, all right. Drew, Dan . . . and Amy. Alexa sighed. Maybe she needed another pep talk. Amy's little dig about being too skinny for a dress like Alexa's had already been ringing in her ears, and now she was standing there with her hands all over Drew.

The cotton candy pink did look ridiculous on her, at least.

♥

"Hey!" Drew said as Alexa and Lauren approached. He felt like he'd been scanning the room for her for an hour. "You guys found us." He stepped away from Amy and put his arm around Alexa's waist.

"*Now* are you guys coming?" Amy asked.

Alexa turned and looked up at him with a question in her eyes. Before he could answer it, Amy grabbed his hand.

"They're going to cut the cake, remember?" she said. Yeah, he remembered. Amy had been bugging him about it for the past five minutes. Why he had to stand around and watch two people put a fake cut into a huge cake, he'd never understand.

Plus, he'd rather stand over here in the corner with his arm around Alexa's waist.

"In a second, Amy. We'll meet you over there."

Amy huffed and walked away. He turned his full attention back to Alexa. But instead of looking back up at him like he wanted her to do, she stared after Amy with a weird look on her face.

"Come on," she said. "They're cutting the cake. Let's go watch."

He reached for her hand as they walked across the ballroom and was glad when she took it. Was she upset about the allergy thing? She'd barely even glanced at him when she came back from the bathroom.

As they stood in the crowd surrounding Josh and Molly, she gripped his hand and stared fixedly ahead with that big smile from before planted firmly on her face.

"Are we cool?" he said in her ear. She jumped. Something occurred to him. "Is something wrong? Did Bill say anything to you?"

She turned to him with her eyebrows raised.

"Bill? No, why?"

He looked into her eyes, but she seemed to be genuinely confused. Okay, Bill hadn't gotten to her, and it seemed like no one had told her what Bill had said.

"Nothing, don't worry about it," he said. "It wasn't a big deal."

Her eyes didn't move from his face. Fine, he wouldn't have believed himself, either.

"I'll tell you later," he said, wondering if that would work.

It didn't.

Her laughter had no mirth in it. The crowd around them oohed and aahed at the stupid cake. She put her finger on his chin and tilted his head down to be level with her own.

"It was either something gross about my body or something racist. Which one?" she asked.

Around them, people toasted to Josh and Molly. Alexa let go of him and raised her glass. He lifted his by rote and drank.

"The latter," he said, after a few long moments.

She took another sip of her drink.

"He seemed like that kind of guy," she said.

Molly came up to them before he had a chance to apologize for Bill.

"Drew, Alexa, hi! Alexa, I didn't get a chance to say earlier, you look so beautiful tonight!" Molly was red-cheeked and beaming, not quite drunk but definitely tipsy. Drew knew the signs.

"Oh, Molly, thank you so much, but you look stunning! That dress is incredible and this wedding has been so lovely. Thank you so much for welcoming me," Alexa said, squeezing Molly's hand. No one would have been able to tell from the look on her face that they'd just been having a kind of tense conversation.

"You are so kind. I'm so delighted that Drew has found you!" Molly said.

So was he, he realized.

"So am I," he said, and slid his arm around Alexa's waist. She relaxed against him, and he sighed in relief.

"Oh, you two are so adorable!" Molly said. Okay, maybe she was more on the drunk side of the spectrum. "Anyway, I wanted to let Alexa know that I'm about to throw my bouquet!"

A look of horror flashed over Alexa's face before she covered it with that now-familiar big, bright smile. Big, bright, *fake* smile.

"Oh!" Alexa said to Molly. "Okay, great!"

Molly hugged both of them again and fluttered to the middle of the dance floor, collecting bridesmaids and female wedding guests as she went.

"I guess I should go over there." Alexa drained her champagne glass and handed it to him but made no move toward the dance floor.

"You don't have to sound quite so excited about it." He pushed her in Molly's direction. She rolled her eyes at him but walked over and joined the gaggle of women in cocktail dresses. Lauren caught her arm and said something that caused Alexa to double over in laughter. He wanted to know what had made her laugh like that and how he could duplicate it. Not only to see that glimpse of her boobs in that red bra . . . but partly to see that.

As soon as the bouquet left Molly's hand, Alexa and Lauren took slow, steady steps backward. After a scuffle, one of the brides-maids triumphantly raised the bouquet, but his eyes were on Alexa, by that time at the far end of the dance floor. He saw Alexa and Lauren turn to each other with identical fake pouts on their faces. This time he was the one who doubled over laughing.

Dan nudged him.

"Should we be insulted?" Dan gestured in the direction of Lauren and Alexa, clapping and pouting as the bridesmaid waved the bouquet.

Drew laughed again.

"Nah, I think we should be feeling pretty smug that we're dating the smartest women in the room," Drew told him. Alexa and Lauren had formed a circle with a few other women, all dancing to "Single Ladies" with their hands in the air. "Shall we join them?"

THE WEDDING DATE   71

Alexa danced with Lauren, letting the movement and the laughter shake away her annoying thoughts. When she felt a hand on her waist, she turned to see Drew behind her and laughed again, at how ridiculous the evening had been and how much fun she was suddenly having. He took hold of one of her hands and swung her around to face him and laughed back down at her. Other members of the wedding party joined their group and danced with and around them, but song after song came on, and he never moved from her side.

"Water?" he said in her ear after they'd been on the dance floor for a long time.

"Yes, please." She walked with him over to the bar.

She glanced up at the ornate clock over the bar, surprised at how late it had gotten. And how much she didn't want this night to end. Damn it, it had been fun to be Drew's fake girlfriend, but she knew that once the clock struck midnight, so to speak, the fairy tale would be all over.

He leaned against the bar, his jacket off, his bow tie untied, a little sweaty and disheveled from dancing. Good Lord, this guy was hot.

He rolled up his sleeves, exposing his tan forearms. She wanted to run her fingers up and down them and feel how warm and strong they were.

She needed to stop letting her imagination run away with her.

"Um," she said. "It's getting late, and if I want to make the last BART train back to the East Bay, I should probably leave pretty soon."

Why had she said that? Why, when she was standing next to a

hot guy, basically panting over him? If she was Maddie, hell, if she was *Amy*, she would have grabbed one of those hot forearms and wrapped it around her body, letting him know what she wanted without having to say anything. Sadly, she was Alexa, so she would flee instead.

He put his water bottle down and looked at her.

"Okay."

"Okay," she said. Olivia and Maddie would get mad at her for not throwing herself at him, but they didn't understand that she just didn't know how. Plus, rejection from this guy was the last thing her self-esteem needed. Talk about the opposite of getting back on the horse; that would make her avoid horses, and stables, and all farm animals for another few years. So to speak.

He stepped closer to her and put his hand on her waist. Her hand landed on his arm, and without even meaning to, she ran her fingers up and down. Oh God, touching him like this was as good as she'd thought it would be.

"Or"—he looked straight down into her eyes—"you could stay."

A question was in his eyes, and a smile hovered over his lips. His thumb drew slow circles on her hip and then moved up her side to her ribs. His other hand moved up to her face and traced the outline of her lips with his fingers.

She shivered.

He waited.

"Or," she said, "I could stay."

He pulled her against him and kissed her. Their lips clung together softly at first, then with more urgency. He tasted like bourbon and chocolate cake and everything she'd ever craved. She sighed against his lips and murmured his name, and she could feel his smile. Her hands moved into his hair, that hair that she'd been wanting to touch all night, and he kissed her harder. His hand cupped her cheek, and the gentle touch on her skin as she felt the heat of his mouth had her nerve endings on fire.

It seemed like they were all alone in that crowded ballroom. The people and the noise swirled around them as his lips touched hers, his tongue slid inside her mouth, his body pressed up against hers.

They pulled apart for a moment, and he smiled down at her.

"I've been wanting to do that all night," he said, his golden brown eyes staring straight into hers. He kissed her cheek, her ear, her collarbone. His tongue traced her lips before he claimed her mouth again. She moved her hand in between them so she could touch his chest, wishing there was no fabric under her fingers but just his skin.

Her touch seemed to alight something in Drew. He moved his hands to her back and tugged her against his body. His hands felt like iron against her back, and his rough touch sent a thrill up and down her spine. She bit his lip in retaliation for the bruises she'd have the next day. He laughed and sucked her lip into his mouth.

"Sorry for interrupting," Amy said, sounding not at all sorry.

They pulled away from each other, both breathing hard.

"What is it, Amy?" Drew didn't look away from Alexa. He looked at her like he wanted to throw her over his shoulder, take her into a dark closet, and screw her senseless. Maybe that was just what she wanted him to do.

"Molly and Josh are about to leave. You're needed for the pictures."

He finally looked in Amy's direction. Alexa tried to step out of the way, but he grabbed her hand, not letting her go.

"Great, we'll be there in a second," he said. Amy stood there looking from Drew to Alexa for a few seconds before she sighed and stomped away.

Drew turned back to her.

"How about instead of going to take more pictures, we go upstairs right now?"

Was this really going to happen?

She squeezed his hand and let go.

"Go take the pictures. Patience is a virtue," she said. "Stand still." She reached up and rubbed her thumb against his lips and cheek. "We can't have you in the wedding pictures with my lipstick all over you. Okay, now you're ready."

7

He grabbed his tux jacket from the chair where he'd abandoned it and walked with her, hand in hand, over to the wedding
party. Drew tried to keep Alexa with him, but she pushed him
toward the rest of the groomsmen and faded into the background.

He tried to take this last set of pictures, to look excited and
surprised to see Josh and Molly waving at the crowd, but his eyes
kept straying in Alexa's direction. Her hair was disheveled, her
lipstick had mostly rubbed off, and she looked so incredible that he
wanted to push her against the wall and pull that dress off her
shoulders.

Amy came up behind him.

"Can you just, for the next few minutes, pretend that you ever
cared about my sister and take a few damn pictures without staring
over at what's-her-face over there?"

He sighed. As much as he hated to agree with her, Amy had a
point.

"Yeah, okay, fine." He took a deep breath and turned back to the photographer. Without looking at Amy, he said, "I did care about your sister, you know."

She snorted.

"You had an interesting way of showing it." She moved closer to him and waved as Josh and Molly left the room. He started to walk away, but the photographer spun in their direction and told them to do "something spontaneous." Amy put her arm around his waist and kissed his cheek. He grinned for the camera and hoped it didn't look too much like he was gritting his teeth. He jumped when he felt Amy's hand on his ass.

"I put my room key in your pocket," Amy whispered in his ear. "In case you want to escape that date of yours and compare sisters later. I can promise I'll beat out Molly. I've always been the wild one."

That was a new development. He and Alexa had joked about Amy either wanting to kill him or fuck him, but he hadn't really believed it. Apparently, she wanted to do both?

Now he was even more grateful that Alexa was there. Because he knew himself, and he knew that if he hadn't met Alexa in that elevator, at this point in the wedding he would be just drunk and impulsive enough to make yet another bad decision.

He stepped away from her, and her hand fell.

"No, thanks, Amy. You have a great night." He backed away from her and the rest of the wedding party, and turned to find Alexa.

She was sitting on one of the couches in the corner with Lauren and Dan . . . and Bill. That big, fake smile was back, and her legs were crossed tightly.

"You're in my seat," he said to Bill with a shooing motion.

When Bill didn't get up, he wanted to punch him in the face, but Dan caught his eye. Instead, he reached out a hand for Alexa. She took it and stood up.

"I think it's time for us to call it a night, don't you?" he said. He pulled her close, maybe a little closer than necessary. Dan and Lauren stood up, too, and all four of them walked out of the ballroom without another word to Bill.

"Did he bother you?" he said to Alexa as soon as they were out of earshot.

She shook her head. "He was probably about to, but I had a drink in my hand, and I was not afraid to use it."

They'd been speaking quietly, but Lauren turned around at that.

"That guy is an ASSHOLE."

Dan waited for them to catch up, then whispered to Drew, "Did you tell her what he said?" But his "whisper" was more like a shout. Dan had never been a quiet drunk.

"No, but she figured it out," Alexa said.

"He tried to talk to me in Japanese!" Lauren said. "I'm Korean. Come on."

As they waited for the elevator, Drew stood behind Alexa and wrapped his arms around her. She leaned back against him and set one of her hands against his. Every time she touched him seemed like a secret message reminding him of their kiss and what was to come.

When an elevator finally came, they stood against the back wall, his arms still around her. Her hair tickled his chin when he bent down to whisper in her ear.

"I think this is our elevator."

He kissed her softly when she turned her head toward him.

"I think so, too." She smiled. "I hope we don't get stuck again, no offense to Dan and Lauren."

When the elevator stopped on Drew's floor, Lauren and Alexa hugged.

"I don't know what I would have done without you," Alexa said to Lauren. "Especially during the bouquet toss." The women waved good-bye as he and Alexa got off the elevator. Drew could still hear Dan's laughter echoing in the elevator as they entered his hotel room.

"I really liked Lauren," Alexa said as the room door closed behind them. He didn't give her a chance to say more before his mouth descended on hers. He pushed her up against the door and boxed her in with his arms. Her hands tangled in his hair and pulled him closer. She pushed his jacket off his shoulders, ripped his shirt out of his pants, and slid her hands up and down his chest.

He moved down to her neck, licking and sucking until she wrapped one leg around his waist and pulled him flush against her body. Just kissing this woman was the best thing he'd done all month.

He pushed one strap of her dress off her shoulder and bent down to kiss the curve of her breast.

"I've been wanting to do that all night," he said.

"I've been wanting you to do that all night," she said. Her head was back against the door, and her eyes were closed. She stroked his hair, scraping his scalp with her fingernails in a way that made him shiver. He pushed the other strap down and the dress with it until it hung to her waist.

"Good Lord." He stared at the red lace of her bra, and what was underneath it.

"That's a nice reaction." Her hands drifted to his waist, and her fingers moved against his skin. As he stared, unmoving, she reached up to unbutton his shirt. After she'd unfastened two buttons, he growled and pulled the whole thing off over his head.

She tried to reach for him again, but he pinned her arms against the wall, holding both of her wrists with one hand.

"Tell me," he said to her. "Tell me what you want."

She hesitated, her eyes half lidded and hazy.

"Do you want this, Alexa?" he asked, his free hand moving up and down her torso.

"You know I do," she said, her eyes closed. She pushed her chest against him, but he kept his touch gentle. He could sense her frustration. He loved it.

"Then tell me what you want me to do to you."

Finally, she opened her eyes wide and smiled at him.

"Kiss me."

She didn't specify exactly where she wanted him to kiss her.

"Oh my God, Drew."

But she hadn't seemed to mind the place he chose.

"We've got to get you on that bed." He picked her up by the waist, took three steps across the room, and tossed her on the bed. She laughed as she landed on the pile of pillows. He took a flying leap and landed next to her. He rolled on top of her as they laughed together. He tickled her, and she giggled as she tickled him back.

"This dress has to come off," he said, tugging at the hem.

"These pants first." She reached for his waistband. He sat back and watched her unbutton and unzip him. The sight of her, dress half off, lips swollen and bitten, hands on him, made him grin at his own good fortune.

She grinned back at him, grabbed him by the hair, pulled him down to her, and kissed him. He relished the feel of her body under him, her softness against his hardness, her hands in his hair and rubbing up and down his back. After a long while, he pulled back again and looked down at her half-naked body.

"I really need to get this dress off you," he said.

She pushed the dress off her hips and threw it onto the floor. He saw a flash of red underwear as she lay back against the pillows.

♥

Drew rolled her underneath him and moved his hands to her breasts. Alexa let her eyes flutter closed, enjoying the sensation as his fingers caressed the underside of her breasts and moved upward. But then his hands stopped moving. She opened her eyes, and he looked straight back at her, that small smile on his face.

"Tell me," he said again.

She wiggled underneath him, willing him to start moving again, but it didn't work. He seemed to enjoy frustrating her. Luckily, he was really hot while he was doing it.

"Alexa." He ran his hands through her hair, then down the sides of her face once, twice. "Tell me. You know I want to hear you say it."

She took a deep breath and reminded herself that it was just one night, that she didn't need to be embarrassed. She took his hand in hers and moved it to where she wanted it.

"Kiss me?" It had worked so well the first time.

He smiled and bent down to her.

"That's a start," he said.

Oh wow. Making out with him in bed was even better than it had been against the door. Now he knew what she liked, the moves that made her moan and gasp and sink her fingers into his shoulders.

He sat up and smiled down at her, his eyes on her bright red panties. She mentally thanked Maddie for ordering her to wear a matching bra and panty set. Then all thoughts of Maddie and anyone else left her mind. He moved like a flash down her body, pulling those panties off as he went and throwing them across the room. And then he set about doing things to her with his fingers and his mouth that almost made her black out.

After she collapsed against the pillows, he lifted himself off her, a smug smile on his face. Not that she blamed him. He had every right to be proud of himself after that. He trailed kisses up her body, on her stomach, her breasts, her neck, until he finally dropped a light kiss on her mouth and rolled over next to her.

She turned to face him. She moved her hand to his side and felt the hardness of his chest and the trail of hair that disappeared into his waistband. Holy shit, this guy was something else.

"That was . . ." She tried to think of something to describe what that had been like, and failed. "That made me incoherent."

"I can see that." He leaned forward and kissed her, harder this time. "I liked it."

She tugged at the waistband of his boxer briefs.

"These have got to come off," she said. "And something else has to come on."

"Not going to argue with that." He pushed himself off the bed, pulled his underwear off, and dug into his bag, coming up a few seconds later with a box of condoms.

"This what you were referring to?" he asked. He got back on the bed before she had a chance to admire his naked body. He didn't move from her side and looked over at her.

"Yeah," she said. That seemed to be what he was waiting for. A half second later, she was on her back.

She laughed up at him, and he grinned down at her, and then wiped the smile from his face.

"This is not a laughing matter. We have serious work to do."

Alexa tried to stop smiling, but her lips curved up despite herself.

"Well, never let it be said that Alexa Monroe doesn't believe in the value of hard work."

"Mmmm." He ran his hands up and down her hips, and pushed her knees open. "I would never say that."

Minutes . . . or hours . . . later, he collapsed on top of her.

"Good God," he said. "Why haven't we been doing this since thirty seconds after that elevator got stuck?"

"We are apparently both very stupid people," she said in his ear.

"Very, very stupid," he said.

They stayed like that for a few seconds, both trying to catch their breath. Eventually he reached down, pulled the condom off, and rolled over onto his back, pulling her with him. Her head was on his chest, her legs splayed on either side of his. She could be happy just like this for the next few weeks. Maybe months.

What was it about this guy? Every other first time she'd had sex with someone—and often the second and third and fourth time—she had worried about how he'd felt about her body, or if he was really attracted to her or not, or if he really liked her boobs or would rather they be smaller or perkier, or some other niggling anxiety that had prevented her from really relaxing and enjoying herself.

She'd always enjoyed herself but was still self-conscious, never quite wanting to do certain positions because of how her stomach or her butt would look or what he would see. And she'd certainly never been able to say what she wanted out loud, never at first, sometimes never at all.

But with Drew, she'd been able to throw herself into the whole experience from the first kiss. She'd even thrown her clothes off without worrying about what he would think and how he would react to her body.

Good Lord, was this what one-night stands were like? Maybe it was because she was never going to see this guy again after she left the hotel in the morning. They barely knew each other, they'd met two days before, and he lived in L.A., for Christ's sake. She could be completely honest; she could totally enjoy herself, with no repercussions, no regrets. That must be it.

Whatever the reason, it had been pretty damn great.

"That was . . ." He caressed her back and kissed her shoulder instead of finishing his sentence.

"Mmmmhmmm," she said.

"Sleepy?" He kissed her cheek.

"I can barely move," she said against his chest. "My limbs all feel like they're made out of melted butter."

He chuckled and she felt his chest rumble underneath her face.

"Hold that thought for one minute." He turned her over and got out of the bed. After a trip to the bathroom, he slid back in next to her, tucked the covers over both of them, and pulled her close.

"Good night, Alexa." He wrapped her up in his arms.

She ran her hands up and down his arms and relaxed against his body.

"'Night, Drew."

8

She woke up a few hours later, her back pressed against his chest, his arms circling her. She felt like she was in a snug, warm, masculine cocoon. She had never realized how much that was the ideal place for her until just that moment. There was just one problem.

She had to pee.

Okay, Alexa. Just don't think about it. Just lie here and be content in this cozy sleeping bag of pure male goodness and let that lull you back to sleep.

She listened to his even breathing, felt his chest move against her back and the prickle of the hair on his legs rubbing against hers, and smiled. She could do this.

Her bladder disagreed. It increased the pressure and reminded her of all of that champagne she'd drunk and those bottles of water that had closed out the night. Oh God, she really had to pee.

No, Alexa. Just stay here. Go back to sleep. Don't think about anything liquid. You can do it. Enjoy this perfect moment.

She took a deep breath, clenched everything, and tried to relax against him again, reaching back to that voice in her brain for a pep talk.

I have to pee I have to pee I have to pee!

When even her internal monologue had abandoned the cause, she gave in. She slowly moved out of the circle of his arms in an attempt to not wake him up, pulled back the sheet, and tiptoed into the bathroom.

They hadn't closed the curtains—apparently, they'd been preoccupied—so light shone into the room from the lit-up skyline. That gave her enough light to get from the bathroom to the bed without tripping over the shoes, clothes, and underwear littering the floor.

She got into the warm bed, trying to figure out how she could get back to her perfect cocoon from earlier. He was still on his side, but his arms were folded now; she couldn't very well push herself back against his chest and wrap his arms back around herself, could she?

Well, she could, but not without waking him up, she decided after thinking about it for a few seconds. She lay down on her pillow and admired his naked chest, hoping that maybe he would roll over to her in his sleep and she would get to finish her night off with his arms and legs draped around her again.

"You going to come back over here or are you going to leave me cold and lonely for the rest of the night?" he asked, his eyes still closed.

"I thought you were asleep." She scooted closer, and he wrapped his arms back around her. "I didn't want to wake you up."

He leaned down to kiss her, and their lips clung together. She really liked kissing this guy.

"Even if you had woken me up," he said, "I wouldn't have minded."

Something inside of her melted. At his words, his smile, his touch. She stroked his stubbly cheek and pulled his head back down toward hers.

They kissed again, longer, slower. The urgency of earlier in the night had disappeared. They kissed like they had days, weeks, years to do nothing but lie in this bed and explore each other.

His fingers moved from her back to her neck, then to her hair. His lips touched her cheeks, her eyelids, and the tip of her nose, which surprised a giggle out of her. Not content to be passive, her hands ran down his chest, dancing over his nipples, pressing into his muscles, squeezing his hips.

When her fingers lingered there, he said, "Aren't you going to keep going?"

At this moment, in this hotel room, this night? She would do whatever he wanted her to do. She slid down his body to where she knew he wanted her to go.

"I *really* like the way you do that," he said afterward, once he got his breath back. She crawled up from the bottom of the bed and collapsed on top of him.

After a few minutes, she started to roll off to the side. He stopped her.

"Where exactly do you think you're going?" His hands were on both sides of her waist, holding her in place.

"Oh." She tried to think of a good way to say it and gave up. "I thought I might be too heavy, so I was going to . . ."

His hands gripped her tighter.

"No, you're perfect. Don't go anywhere." He pulled her against him but relaxed his hold almost right away. "Unless you wanted to move? Because if so, I don't want you to—"

"No." She tilted her head back so she could see his face. "I'm happy right here."

He wrapped his arms around her again, and she leaned her head against his chest.

"Good," he said. "So am I."

♥

Drew woke up the next morning with Alexa's body flush against his, his leg draped over her hip, and her hands on his butt. What a fucking fantastic way to wake up. He thought about letting her stay asleep—he really did. But then he remembered that he was leaving in a few hours. He needed to get all of this woman he could.

He ran his fingers up and down her body. My God, her skin was so smooth. He pulled down the covers and looked at those breasts that made him salivate. If he remembered last night correctly, which he thought he did, she really liked it when he played with her breasts.

As soon as he squeezed, she opened her eyes and smiled.

"Mmmm, what a nice way to wake up," she said.

"I thought you might think that."

After round three—or was it two and a half?—they curled up together in bed breathing hard.

"What time is it?" she said into the pillow.

He lifted himself up and looked at the bedside clock.

"Just after nine."

She snuggled against him.

"Hey, Drew?"

He grinned.

"I just met you two days ago, so how do I already know that that's your 'I want something' voice? Haven't I done enough for you this morning?" he asked the top of her head.

He felt her smile against his chest.

"Mmmm, you definitely have done quite a lot. But you know what else you could do?"

He put a hand over hers, trapping it where he loved to feel it.

"Keep doing that and I'll do whatever you want."

She laughed and kissed his shoulder.

"Does that mean you'll call down to room service and order me coffee?"

He flipped her on her back and pressed her against the bed as she smiled up at him. Her hair was wild, she had makeup smudges around her eyes, and he wanted to keep her in this bed all day.

"Coffee?" he said, a fake tone of incredulity in his voice. "I got the 'I need a favor' voice for coffee? Are you that easily pleased or do you love coffee that much?"

Still on top of her, he reached for the bedside phone and dialed room service.

"At this point, I think you know how easily pleased I am," she said as her fingers walked down his body.

He played with her nipple again as he placed a very large room service order. She sighed and moved beneath him while he was on the phone. If they hadn't just had sex, he'd be grabbing a condom just from watching her do that. When he hung up and pulled her back into his arms, he wasn't quite ready for round four, but he was pretty happy to think about getting there soon.

"Hold that thought." He rolled off the bed and into the bathroom. When he came back into the room, he hunted for his wallet so he could tip room service when it arrived. He found it in the back pocket of his pants, along with a stray room key.

"Oh my God, I forgot to tell you: Amy slipped me her room key last night."

"What?" She sat up straight.

He plopped on the bed next to her.

"Yeah, I know, right? She said something shitty about you and then something shitty about Molly and then slid her key into my pocket."

"Wow." Her smile faded for the first time in hours. He wasn't sure why, but he wanted to make her laugh again.

"So I guess you were right, about her either wanting to kill me or fuck me . . . though I'm still not sure which one."

It worked, for a second. But after her laughter subsided, that thoughtful expression came back.

"So, last night at one point I was in the bathroom." She paused.

"Uh-huh?" Was she going to tell him about people having sex in the bathroom? That would start round four off with a bang.

"No one knew I was in there . . ." Oh good, this was getting even better.

"And I heard Amy tell someone about when you broke up with Molly? Am I remembering incorrectly or did you imply that it was the other way around?"

Oh shit. His hand dropped.

After he didn't say anything for a while, Alexa pulled the sheet up to her neck. That did not seem like a good sign for round four.

"So I guess that means I wasn't remembering incorrectly."

He sat up and sighed. Why was it just too much to ask for him to get through this weekend without having to talk about this?

"Yeah, I broke up with Molly. Yeah, I implied that it was the other way around to you. I don't know why."

She sat there for a while looking at him, her knees drawn up and her hands clasped. Guess he could wave good-bye to round four. Oh, the hell with it.

"Fine, I do know why: because I was an asshole to Molly, and I don't like telling people, especially the cute women kinds of people I'm trapped in elevators with, that I was an asshole to a good person."

The tight grip of her hands relaxed, and she touched his arm, just for a second.

"Okay," she said. "Thank you for being honest and not bullshitting me right there."

He shrugged, looking at his knees instead of her. He might as well tell her this whole story now.

"Molly and I dated for about a year and a half. She's a very nice person, as you probably noticed." He could see her nod out of the corner of his eye. "And I really cared about her. I maybe even loved her. I'm not sure if I was in love with her, but I think I loved her. If that makes sense." She nodded again, and her hand went back to his arm, staying there this time.

"Right before her birthday I overheard her on the phone talking to one of her friends. She thought I was planning to propose and was all excited about it." He was still staring at his knees. He had a scar on his right knee from that fall he took while running a few months back. He would be happy to tell her that story instead of this one.

He took a deep breath.

"I pretty much panicked. I wasn't ready for that. I definitely hadn't been planning to propose, and now I didn't want to deal with her disappointment when I didn't. So of course, like an ass-hole, the next day I told her I didn't think it was working out and broke up with her. Right before her birthday. And then I dated three other people in the med school in quick succession. Kind of a jerk move."

Her hand moved up his arm to his. He grabbed it and held on.

Molly had hated him after that. Hell, he'd hated himself. She'd forgiven him eventually, because she was Molly and (he strongly suspected) because Josh had gone to bat for him. Which is why he was at the wedding in the first place.

"And the whole Josh thing?" she asked.

"They didn't start dating right away. In fact, they didn't start dating for well over a year. But I still felt betrayed when they did, even though I had no right to feel that way. And even though Josh asked me if it would be okay. I guess I felt like . . . when I *was* ready to get married, Molly would be around for that."

He sighed and let go of her hand.

"Anyway, we dated, I was an asshole, eventually I apologized for being such an asshole, Josh is a great guy, last night she married him. There, the whole story, more or less."

She tightened the sheet around her body and turned to him.

"So . . . this wedding was kind of your penance, then?" she asked him.

He leaned against one of the pillows they'd pushed out of the way during the night and finally met her eyes.

"I guess so," he said. "Maybe that's one reason why I was dreading it so much. And why I needed a sandwich so badly."

He hoped that she'd laugh at that, but she didn't. She didn't even meet his eyes.

"Hey." He touched her arm. "I'm sorry. I should have been

honest with you before you came here last night and not just because you found out somewhere else."

She met his eyes and nodded.

"Okay," was all she said.

"Are you mad?" he asked. He didn't want to push this. And he
definitely didn't want to keep talking about it. But he didn't want
her to be mad at him. They only had a little while left.

"I'm not mad," she said. She looked at him for a minute, and
her smile became more of a real one. "I did find out last night, you
know. If I was mad, I wouldn't be here right now."

He shouldn't ask. He really shouldn't. She'd think that's why he
apologized, and it wasn't. But he couldn't help himself.

"Does this mean there's a possibility for round four?" he asked,
and he reached for the sheet she'd used to cover herself up.

She looked down at his hand on the sheet and met his eyes.

"Three and a half, you mean."

He pulled the sheet covering her torso down and drew his
thumb over her breasts. Her eyes followed his thumb as it stroked
her body.

"I guess that means that I have some work to do," he said.

He pushed her back down on the bed as she laughed. As they
kissed, his fingers played with her nipples in the way that he now
knew she liked. When his lips trailed down to her breasts, her fingernails dug into his back. Did she know that he liked that? He hoped
so. He'd make sure to tell her in a second. He drew a nipple into
his mouth, and—

"Room service!" came the call from outside.

She groaned and covered her face with her arm.

"Hey," he said as he stood up. "You're the one who insisted on
coffee."

She sighed dramatically and he laughed.

"Don't remind me." She got out of bed, too. "I'm going to the bathroom. The room service guy doesn't need to see me naked, even if it's under a sheet."

Once she was safely in the bathroom, he let the room service guy in and tipped him well. While the guy set up the tray on the bed, Drew double-checked what time his flight was. Noon. Which meant he'd have to leave for the airport in, like, thirty minutes.

Damn it. It wasn't enough time.

But there were a ton of flights from San Francisco to L.A. every day . . .

"Is the coast clear?" she shouted from the bathroom after the door closed behind room service.

He laughed.

"You can come out now." When was the last time he'd laughed this much? He'd been laughing with her ever since that first moment in the elevator.

She padded out of the bathroom, wrapped in a towel this time, and took a big sniff of the air.

"Ahhhh, coffee." She got back in bed and poured herself a cup from the carafe on the tray.

"I'll be right back." He disappeared into the bathroom, his phone still in his hand. In few clicks, he changed his flight to the one at eight that night. Now he could relax.

He came back out of the bathroom—not covered in a towel—and was pleased to see her eyes follow him as he crossed to the bed.

"I thought you were going to start flexing any second," she said as he climbed into bed next to her and reached for his own coffee cup. He pulled his hand back, met her eyes, and slowly made a fist. She laughed at him but bent over and kissed his bicep.

"I poured you coffee," she said, sipping her own. "But I didn't know how you take it."

He poured half the container of cream into his coffee and shook in few sugar packets. She looked from the pale brown liquid in his mug to the unadulterated blackness of her own and laughed.

"I would make a 'I like my coffee the way I like my men' joke, but it would be either inaccurate or just really dirty."

He put his arm up next to her mug, pretending to be injured.

"What, I'm not black enough for you?" he asked.

She put her arm up next to his mug.

"Sweetheart, it seems like I'm too black for you," she said.

His coffee was paler than her skin color; she was right. Oops. Somehow that didn't seem like the right observation to make.

"I didn't mean . . . I wasn't trying to . . ." He looked from his cup, to her, covered up by the white sheets again, and back to his cup. Everything he could think of to say sounded like a terrible idea. "Um."

She turned his face toward hers, forcing him to look her in the eye.

"Stop. It's okay. I was just joking."

He saw the smile on her face and relaxed.

"Now," she said, uncovering the room service plates, "let's eat some bacon so we're all fortified for round three and a half."

Afterward, they lay curved around each other in bed again, his head on her chest, her fingers drifting through his hair.

"Drew?" she said eventually. "When do we have to get out of here? What time is your flight?"

"Not until eight tonight." Hopefully, she wouldn't ask why he was leaving so late. If she did, he could make up something. "I have to check out in"—he glanced at the clock by the bed—"twenty minutes, though. So . . . if you aren't busy for the rest of the day, we could hang out. We'll have to get out of here, but we can go somewhere else. Eat tacos, relax in the park, go for a walk, I don't know." Or go back to her place, maybe? "I mean, unless you're busy. You probably have a work thing to do, or something, so no worries if you do."

He was rambling, but he couldn't help it. Why didn't it occur to him when he changed his flight that she might have something else to do today? Now, not only was he going to have to say good-bye to her very soon, but he would then have to wander around San Francisco alone for the rest of the day. He was so preemptively annoyed that he almost missed her response.

"Sure, why not? Let me jump in the shower."

♥

Alexa grinned at her reflection in the bathroom mirror. How ex-actly was this happening to her? Not only had she had crazy, dirty, great sex all night with a really hot guy, but said hot guy wanted to spend the day with her? For once, she was going to ignore all the work she had to do today.

Thank God she'd gotten ready in his room yesterday, so she had her hair stuff and something to wear other than a cocktail dress.

As they loaded their bags into his rental car, she mused over the past two days, all of which the Alexa of Thursday afternoon would have never believed. Hell, the Alexa of nine a.m. Sunday wouldn't have believed she'd still be with him at noon. The sex had been great—really great—and he'd made it pretty clear that he'd thought so, too. But she had figured he'd want to get out of the hotel as soon as he could on Sunday and leave all of the reminders of the wedding behind. Including her.

She shrugged. He had a late flight back to L.A. and needed something to occupy his time, and she was around and available. It wasn't any more than that. She probably shouldn't have jumped so quickly when he asked her if she could hang out today, but she couldn't fool herself. She didn't want this weekend to end yet. At this point, when he said jump, she'd ask how high.

She could hate herself for that on Monday. Sunday was all his.

"Didn't you just eat a bushel of bacon?" she asked him as he drove toward the Mission. "You're really ready for a burrito already?"

"Number one: I worked off that bacon, as you well know," he said. He grinned at her, and she grinned right back. "Number two: I'm not *quite* ready for a burrito yet, but I know that I will be soon, so we might as well get them and find a good spot in Dolores Park. It's already nice and sunny, and it'll get busy."

She watched his profile as he drove, a little sad he had shaved that day. His smooth skin was nice against her face, but just the thought of the feel of his stubble last night on her cheeks, her lips, and her thighs made her shift in her set.

"You used to live in the Bay Area?" she asked. He'd mentioned something about that to one of the wedding guests the night before. She'd nodded and smiled along like she already knew his whole life story, but now she actually got to ask questions.

"Yeah, had a fellowship for two years at Children's Hospital in Oakland. I loved it. Great hospital."

He glanced to his right as he went to turn and slid his hand onto her leg. She hoped he left it there for a while.

"Why pediatrics?" Apparently, now she couldn't stop asking questions.

He shrugged and laughed.

"Is it corny to say 'because I like kids'? But . . . it's because I like kids. I thought I was going to be a regular surgeon when I started med school, actually. But I did a pediatrics surgery rotation, and it was just so much more fun. The doctors were great, the kids cracked me up, there were always toys around . . ."

She laughed and touched his hand to interrupt him.

"You picked your specialty because of all of the toys? Figures."

He turned his hand over and held on to hers.

"See, I knew you would make fun of me. Tell the truth: if you had to choose between two jobs, one with toys all over the place and one without, which one would *you* pick?" She thought about it for a second, and he squeezed her hand. "*See?*"

He flicked on the blinker, waiting out the people behind him also vying for the parking spot he'd found.

"So, what does a mayor's chief of staff actually do?"

"Everything, really." They got out of the car and into the line outside of La Taqueria. "Manage everything day to day, supervise a lot of different departments, stay on top of major events going on around the city and the Bay Area, crisis management, policy, and on and on."

When they got to the front of the line, they ordered carnitas for him, al pastor for her, and guacamole and salsa and chips for both of them. He won the fight for the bill.

"How did you get a job like that?" They stood in the corner while they waited for their food, his arm around her waist, her body snug against his.

Don't get used to this, Alexa, she reminded herself. She almost pulled away from him but decided to hell with that. She had six hours left with this guy; she might as well enjoy it while it lasted.

"I worked in the city attorney's office one semester in law

school, and I really liked it. You got to do a little bit of everything, but you still felt like you were doing something for the public good. After law school, I managed to get a job there full-time. A few years ago, the old mayor retired, and my boss—then the city attorney—decided to run for the job. When he won, he made me his chief. I'm kind of young for this job. It probably should have gone to someone older and more experienced."

"But you wanted it more," he said.

She smiled at him.

"I did want it more. I worked damn hard for it, too."

She tucked their burritos and chips in her tote bag and they left the taqueria.

"You want to walk or drive to the park?" he asked.

"Walk. We can't count on getting another parking space. This isn't like L.A., you know. There isn't going to be a valet up there for us."

He took her hand as they turned up the street.

"Ooooh, I guess we'll have to see if my slow Los Angeles legs are up to walking up these great big San Francisco hills."

She laughed at him. As they walked the mile to the park, they talked the whole way, about their jobs and what they liked most about them, their daily aggravations, their stress relievers.

The park was crowded, but they found a spot in a sunny corner. He reached inside her tote bag and pulled out a towel for them to lie on.

"Where did that come from?" she asked, looking from her bag to the towel and back at him.

He flopped down onto the towel and gestured for her to sit next to him. She stood there looking down at him, the bag of burritos in her arms, not moving.

"A genie put it there?" he tried.

She raised her eyebrows.

"It was a gift from the hotel? An apology for the stuck elevator?"

She pursed her lips.

"Okay, okay, fine, I took it, but it *should* have been an apology for the stuck elevator. We needed something to sit on. What did you want me to do, take the sheets?"

Alexa gave in and sat down next to him. She handed him the bag of burritos and cracked open her Mexican Coke.

"For the record, just because I sat here doesn't mean I condone this theft. I'm a public servant, after all."

He laughed and reached for his burrito.

They ate their burritos in silence and watched the people go by. Dolores Park on a sunny day in San Francisco was like a public party, everyone coming out to enjoy the brief escape from the fogbank. There were groups of shirtless men drinking beer, women in sundresses eating ice-cream cones, tech bros in dot-com T-shirts and baseball caps checking out the women in sundresses, multiracial families pushing strollers on their way to the playground, teenagers on skateboards, solitary people with books, churro and hot dog and coffee vendors, old men chatting together in Spanish or Russian, the scent of weed wafting in their direction every five minutes.

Alexa wrapped up the second half of her burrito, kicked off her sandals, and lay back. She could feel the grass under her toes and the sun on her face. A few minutes later, she felt Drew lie down next to her. Not quite touching her, but almost.

"I should check my email." She made no move to do so. What she really wanted to do was reach for his hand, but now that they were out of the hotel room—and the hotel room bed—she had lost some of her nerve.

That was a couple-y thing to do, and despite everything that had happened this weekend, the two of them were not a couple. They both knew that they were only together right now because he had time to kill before his flight. And she knew she was there because she didn't want the weekend with him to end yet.

He picked up her purse and moved it to his other side, out of her reach.

"No, no checking email," he said. "You're here with me now—no email, no phones, no checking in with your boss." He put his hands behind his head and gave her that smug—and, okay, fine, sexy—grin. Damn it if she wouldn't do anything to make him keep grinning at her like that.

But . . . she'd felt her phone vibrate a few times through her tote bag as they walked to the park. She really should check.

She looked around, grateful that they were behind a tree for what she was about to do. She rolled on top of him so she could reach into her purse for her phone. Just when she was about to roll back off, his hands came around her waist and held her in place.

His face was so close to hers. This smile was really all for her. Not for show, or for photos, or to convince her to be his date, or to sleep with him. It was just for her, Alexa, right now, in this moment.

"Oh, you think you can distract me with your body so you can get to your phone, do you?" She moved, not really trying to get away, just seeing what he would do. His hands tightened on her hips. "Well, you're right about that. You don't play fair, Monroe."

She grinned and pushed away from him for real. He released her but kept his arm around her as she lay on her side next to him and checked her phone, her head on his chest.

She ignored the texts from Maddie—no way she could answer them with him right there—and went straight to the emails from Theo and a deputy city attorney. She emailed Theo back a quick answer but paused to think for a while about the other email. She finally suggested that they meet on Monday afternoon; some conversations were easier in person than in text.

When she looked up, Drew was looking down at her, no longer smiling.

"Everything okay there? Or do you have to go?" he asked.

She moved away from the curve of his arm and sat up, and he let her go.

"Why do you ask?"

Did he want her to go? Did he want her to say, *Yeah, as a matter of fact, my boss has a public park–related crisis. I need to rush back to Berkeley immediately. It was nice knowing you*? Was he tired of dealing with her and her wide hips and all of her talk about her job and was he ready to go home to L.A. and leave this weekend behind?

He sat up, too.

"You were frowning at your phone. I thought something might be wrong."

Oh, the hell with it. She might as well take one more risk this weekend.

"No, I don't have to go," she said. She paused and looked down. "Unless . . . you're ready to go?"

"No," he answered immediately. She looked up at him, and his smile was tentative now. "I don't want either of us to go anywhere."

♥

When Alexa smiled at him, relief shot through Drew's bloodstream. She lay back down on the towel, and Drew lay down next to her, facing her. They moved the conversation away from the big topics of jobs and weddings and ex-girlfriends. Instead, they made up pretend conversations for the people around them, fed leftover tortilla chips to a friendly puppy who came by with his owner, and tried not to laugh when a teenage skateboarder attempted to fly down the church steps across the way and fell.

"Shhhh," he said when she couldn't hold it in anymore. "You'll hurt his pride."

She giggled, and he giggled with her, and suddenly they were laughing so hard they couldn't breathe. At the delight of watching someone fall down, at the joy that they'd both found it so funny, at the pleasure of being together in the sun, enjoying each other's company so much. He didn't even realize when it happened, but somehow his arms were around her and her head was against his chest as they shook with laughter.

When their laughter finally slowed, and then stopped, he looked down at her. Her cheeks were pink from the laughter and the sun, her hair was tousled, and her eyes glowed. Without even thinking about it, he leaned down and kissed her.

He hadn't kissed her since they'd left the hotel room. He didn't know why—was he nervous to do it in public? Did they have some sort of tacit agreement that all of that had been left behind in room 1624 of the Fairmont? Whatever the reason, it was clearly a stupid one, because as soon as he kissed her, he wondered why he'd spent all of this time with her today without his hands and lips on her.

They lay there in the sun, kissing lazily. He touched her like she was made out of precious china, like he couldn't grab too hard or make any sudden movements. He wanted to throw his leg over her body again, wanted to push her over and roll on top of her, but they were outside in full view of hundreds of people, and she was a public servant, after all. So instead, he kept up the long, slow kisses, the gentle touches on her arm, her neck, her back, and hoped she was as frustrated as he was.

Eventually, she pulled away and rested her head on his chest. He wrote his name on the small of her back with his thumb.

"What time is it?" she asked him.

"After five," he said after checking his phone. Too late.

"You know." He'd just realized something. "My flight is out of the Oakland airport, so I can drop you off at home in Berkeley on the way to the airport. If you want, I mean."

She lifted her head.

"Are you sure?"

"Sure that my flight is from Oakland, or that I can take you home? Either way, the answer is yes."

She pulled his head down to hers and kissed him again.

"That sounds great," she said, and rested her head back on his chest.

"Do you want to get some ice cream on the way back to the car?" she asked him a few minutes later, her voice muffled, her hand on the bare skin of his hip, right above the waistband of his jeans.

"What does 'ice cream' mean exactly in this context?" He pulled back to see her face, to check if he made her smile.

He did.

"I mean ice cream ice cream!" She pinched him, and he laughed. "There's a great place right down the hill."

"Sure." He was willing to go wherever she wanted. "Let's go get ice cream."

She hooked her finger under his chin, pulled him down to her for another kiss, and stood up. After they tucked the towel back into her purse and tossed the remnants of their burritos, they walked back down the hill hand in hand to stand in line for ice cream.

"What's good here?" he asked her. The burrito had been hours ago at this point, and all of the ice cream flavors looked great to him.

"Well, my favorite is the salted caramel, but I also love the coffee toffee. And I always love cookies and cream." She was so animated when she talked about the ice cream that it made him excited about what was coming next. She was like that about everything she cared about, it seemed.

He wondered how she would talk about him.

He moved closer to her and hoped their closeness had the same effect on her as it did on him. She shivered. He smiled.

"All of those sound great," he said. The line ahead of them moved, and they moved up. He stood behind her and massaged her neck. She sighed and leaned back against him.

"Why, exactly, did you wait until now to let me know you could do that? You could have been doing that this whole time?"

"I didn't mean to hold out on you," he said. He ran his thumb down the middle of her neck, and she let out a low moan. "We were a little busy with other things, you know." He kissed her bare shoulder.

"Next customer in line!" the ice-cream lady shouted at them.

"Salted caramel in a cone, please," Alexa said.

"And you?" the woman behind the counter said to him as she packed ice cream into a waffle cone.

"Um . . ." He'd stared at the menu all that time they'd been in line, but he'd been distracted by Alexa's closeness and had barely paid attention. "Cookies and cream?"

They walked slowly back to the car after they got their ice cream, sharing bites with each other.

He drove them across the bridge and followed her directions to a side street off Alcatraz Avenue. The conversation stalled as they got closer and closer to her house. He looked down and saw her hands clasped together, her nails digging into her knuckles.

"So, this is me." She pointed at a little yellow house. He pulled up in a spot in front of it and hesitated for second before he turned off the car and got out. He pulled her bag out of the trunk and walked up to her front door.

She unlocked the door, and he followed her inside. They walked through a long hallway covered in photographs and into a big living room. A plush yellow sofa lined one wall, covered with bright cushions. It was flanked by fat red chairs and faced a big wall-mounted TV. Magazines and nail polish covered the coffee table, and overstuffed bookshelves lined the walls. It suited her. Bright, attractive, warm. He wanted to flop down on that couch and curl up with her.

"Where should I put this?" he asked, gesturing to the bag.

"Oh." She paused. Her eyes darted from her bag to his face, then back to her bag. "My bedroom is easiest, probably."

The afternoon light streamed into her bedroom and lit up the pale yellow walls, the big unmade bed with its green and white striped comforter, the vase full of drooping daffodils on the low bookshelf. He dropped the bag on the floor and turned to her. She had that big smile back on her face. The fake one she'd given Amy and Bill.

"I had a great time this weekend," she said. Even though he knew, *he knew* she'd had a great time, that smile made him unsure.

Screw it.

He cleared the two feet separating them in one step and pinned her against the wall. Her arms went around his neck, pulling him even closer to her.

"I know you did," he said. "And you know I did, too."

He slid one hand up her body and enjoyed her sharp intake of breath when he got to that spot she liked. Her lips parted and her eyes followed his hand. He pulled her dress and bra down. He needed to touch her, without anything in between them. Her fingers tightened on his shoulders. Oh yeah, he knew she'd had a great time this weekend.

"Don't you have to go to the airport?" Her voice was hoarse.

"I'll drive fast," he said. The hand that wasn't on her breast skimmed her knee and slid up her thigh under her dress. He kept going up, and then stopped, surprised.

"Have you been walking around all day with no panties on like this?" Without waiting for an answer, he pressed a finger inside of her and she cried out. She leaned her head back against the wall and closed her eyes.

"Tell me, Alexa," he said. She kept making those noises that he couldn't get enough of. "Have you been like this all day without telling me? When we were in the park, lying in the grass, could I have done this as easily then?"

She opened her eyes a sliver and smiled at him.

"I didn't"—she gasped—"pack extra panties yesterday. I didn't know I was going to sleep over. What was I supposed to do?"

He groaned.

"If I had known that, I would have pulled that dress up long before we left the park. You are evil."

She laughed and gasped all at the same time.

"I'm going to get you back for that sometime," he said. "Just not right now." He fell to his knees. Her fingers slid through his hair. All at once, her fingernails clenched against his scalp, and her whole body relaxed.

"My turn." He stood up, pulled a condom out of his pocket, and pinned her arms against the wall over her head. "Hold on."

He was so turned on from what had just happened, from the thought of her without underwear on all day, from those little noises she made, that he had no finesse. He heard the wall creak and the light fixtures shake, saw her breasts jiggle, felt her writhe beneath him and clench around him.

Her leg slid down his body, her arms fell around his waist, and they stood there, quiet and shuddering for a few minutes until their breathing slowed. God, her body felt good against his.

He kissed her cheek, her lips, and leaned his forehead against hers.

"I hadn't planned that, but I'm not going to pretend I'm sorry."

She laughed. He had maybe gotten addicted to that laugh. There was always so much joy in it. At the wedding, he'd heard her laugh from across the room a few times and each time had wanted to rush to her side to enjoy it. A few times he had.

"I'm not sorry, either. But . . . and I hate to say this . . . shouldn't you head to the airport?"

He moved away from her reluctantly and pulled his pants up. He grabbed his phone out of his pocket to check the time.

"Shit. Yeah, damn it."

She adjusted her dress as he buckled his belt, and they walked to her front door. She reached out to open the door, but he pushed it closed.

"Drew, you have to—"

He reached for her.

"I know. I just have to do this first."

He kissed her, long and slow. He felt her relax against him and wanted to forget about going to the airport. He wanted to pick her up, get in that cozy-looking bed with her, and have a few more rounds, then tuck her against his side all night long. He pulled away from her with a sigh.

She kissed him on the cheek.

"I'm so glad I got stuck in that elevator with you," she said.

"Me, too."

9

After one last hard kiss on her lips, he raced out to the car and peeled away toward the freeway. Alexa collapsed against her front door, almost unable to believe what had just happened. What had happened over the past forty-eight hours.

She stumbled back to her bedroom and flopped on her bed, the stripes of her duvet cover blurring as she stared at it. Thirty minutes later she was in the same spot. She sat up and tried to pull herself together.

She'd known from the beginning that it was just one weekend and she'd never hear from him again. And it was a great weekend, punctuated by some very hot against-the-wall sex at the end there—she would never look at her bedroom wall the same way—so she should be cheerful, not maudlin. *Alexa, snap out of it.*

Her phone buzzed, and she reached for it, expecting it to be another text from Maddie.

Made my flight by the skin of my teeth!

She could feel that dreamy smile back on her face. Oh, the hell with it. She allowed herself that night to swoon and mope about this weekend before falling back to earth.

She texted back before she could overthink her response.

:) Glad you made it!

She should call Maddie and update her. Maddie had forced her to go through with the fake date in the first place, after all. She had to thank her for getting her to break her celibacy streak in an impressive fashion.

But not yet. Right now she needed to hug this whole weekend close to her chest and hold on to it tight before sharing it with anyone.

She puttered around the house, changed out of the dress he'd almost torn off her and into yoga pants and a tank top (and underwear), unloaded her dishwasher, went through the rest of the work emails that had come in this weekend, and made a to-do list for the workweek.

But all the time she thought about Drew. The way he'd laughed whenever she'd laughed; the way he kept touching her, like his hands belonged on her skin; the way he'd smiled at her in the middle of the night like he was so happy to have her there with him in his bed; the way he ate his burrito with tortilla chips as utensils and blushed when she teased him about it.

The whole time she hoped she'd get another text from him after he landed, or after he got home, but her phone stayed silent. She thought about texting him again, but what was she supposed to say? *Had a great time having sex with you this weekend, can't stop thinking about it* was all she could think of, and that was a little too on the nose.

To keep herself occupied, she finally texted Maddie.

Fine you were right. Broke my streak with elevator guy. Sorry I didn't check in before, was occupied with him all weekend ;) Going to bed now & turning off my phone, but I'll give you all the details asap.

Hopefully that was breezy enough that it didn't show she'd been moping over him for the past two hours. Maybe by the time she woke up the next day she would actually feel like that.

She didn't turn off her phone, of course. She left it on all night, hoping he would text again. Which meant she saw Maddie's exclamation-point-filled response, but there was nothing else from Drew.

When she rolled out of bed the next morning, she groaned. She was so sore all over that it felt like she'd gone to the world's hardest yoga class right after running a 10K and right before a weight-lifting competition. Nope, just hours of athletic sex in all sorts of crazy positions.

She grinned in the hot shower; despite the body aches, she felt a lot better this morning than she had last night. She laughed when she saw finger-shaped bruises on her shoulders and hips and hick-eys on her breasts. What was she, twenty-two? Except . . . she'd never had sex that good when she was twenty-two. She whistled as she pulled her robe on and started the coffee maker, and took three Advil along with her first sip of coffee.

She threw on a boatnecked long-sleeved shift dress that covered up all of her sex-related injuries and headed to work. Her boss always got in late on Monday mornings, thank God, so she would have a few hours of relative peace in the office to start the week.

Well, she got an hour of peace, until Maddie called at nine on the dot.

"You were going to call me when, exactly?"

She laughed and closed her office door.

♥

Drew walked into the hospital that Monday morning and jumped into the elevator right before it closed, only to find his friend and fellow doctor Carlos Ibarra part of the crowd inside.

"Just the dude I was looking for," Carlos said. "How was the wedding?"

A hell of a lot better than he'd thought it was going to be, that was for sure. Drew smirked.

Carlos's eyebrows went up and he shook his head.

"Of course. Why would I have thought anything less of you?"

Drew noticed the interested glances sent their way and gave Carlos a warning look. Carlos, of course, exaggeratedly zipped his lips. Always discreet, that one.

They got off on the tenth floor, and Carlos followed him to his office, shutting the door behind them.

"Okay, now you can tell me. Found a woman in the elevator and spent all weekend banging her, huh?"

Drew relaxed into his desk chair and turned on his computer.

"Not quite all weekend." He grinned again.

Carlos sat in the chair on the other side of his desk.

"Oh God, leave it to you. I can't believe you picked up someone in an elevator and made her your plus-one to your ex's wedding."

Drew grimaced.

"Oh, it was even worse. I forgot to tell you: I accidentally told Josh she was my girlfriend, so . . ."

Carlos leaned back in the chair.

"You, a *girlfriend*? So she had to fake it all night? How did you get her to do that?"

Drew grinned.

"Just my natural charm, I guess."

Carlos's phone buzzed and he glanced at it.

"Oh, I bet everyone at the wedding grilled the poor girl. I hope she was up to the pretense."

Was she ever. Man, he really couldn't have picked a better person to be stuck in an elevator with, could he?

"She works in politics, so she's good at stuff like that."

She'd been good at a lot of things. Pretending to be his girlfriend, striking back at Amy, that little thing she did with her hips . . .

"Stop it," Carlos said. "You keep getting this 'thinking about the sex you just had' look on your face, and I'm sick of that look from you."

Drew shook his head to clear it. He had a feeling he'd be thinking about the sex he'd had with Alexa for at least a few days.

"Sorry, but you asked about her. One thought led to another, and . . ." He shrugged. "I'm only human."

Carlos stood up and opened Drew's top desk drawer to grab some of the candy out of it.

"Well, at least you had an ironclad excuse for getting out of there early yesterday. I know how you are with women. Good thing you had to get back here for that golf thing."

Oh shit, the golf tournament.

Carlos laughed at the look on Drew's face.

"What, did you get home and then bail on the golf tournament? Too tired from elevator girl?"

Drew sighed.

"See, what had happened was . . ."

Carlos laughed. "Oh shit, now this is getting good. Go on." Carlos leaned back and propped his feet up on Drew's desk.

He was going to get so much shit for this, but now he'd said too much to not tell the whole story. Carlos would get it out of him eventually anyway.

"I kind of changed my flight to last night. And I forgot all about the golf tournament . . . so, that's what happened. More or less."

Carlos took his feet down and stared at Drew.

"You changed your flight? To hang out with elevator girl?"

Drew shrugged and leaned back in his chair, trying to play it off.

"You know I hate golf. The tournament was just an excuse to get out of there, but once I had Alexa, I didn't need an excuse anymore."

He twitched under Carlos's gaze. His phone buzzed, and he glanced over at it—just an update on a patient. Carlos snatched his phone before he could pull it away.

"Ooh, her name was Alexa, huh? Is that *Alexa* texting you?"

Drew stood up and reached over the desk for his phone.

"Alexa Monroe. And no, as you can see, it wasn't her." Carlos handed him back the phone with a wide grin on his face. "What?"

"Alexa *Monroe*. You like this girl."

Drew shrugged again, pretending that he didn't know what Carlos meant.

"Sure, of course I liked her. We had a great time this weekend."

Carlos shook his head, still grinning.

"No, you *like her* like her. You *wanted* that to be a text from her— you know you did. You should have heard your voice when you said her name and said it wasn't from her. You wanted her to text you!"

Drew shook his head then gave up. Carlos would just keep pushing until he admitted it, anyway.

"I wouldn't be mad or anything if she texted me. But she lives in Berkeley, remember? And I live here? In Santa Monica?"

Carlos reached for Drew's coffee, took a sip, and grimaced.

"So, let me get this straight. You met a great girl this weekend. You had fun with her, you liked her . . . Is she ugly? Was the sex bad?"

Drew smirked again. He didn't mean to. But hell no to both of those things.

"I can see your answer. To recap: you met a great girl, you had fun with her, you liked her, she's cute, the sex was good."

Drew nodded.

"And . . . you're just never going to see her again?"

Hmmm. When you put it that way, it didn't make much sense.

"That was the plan, I guess so, yeah."

Carlos stood up.

"You're such an asshole. I know you're weird about commitment and all, but this is taking it a little far. Text Alexa *Monroe*. Figure out when you're going to see her again. Don't be an idiot. I mean even more of one than you already are." Carlos left his office and then ruined his exit by poking his head back in. "Hoops at six?"

Drew nodded as Carlos walked out, glad he'd remembered to throw his gym bag in the car this morning. Their Monday basketball game would be a good way to get out some of his aggressions from this conversation, where Carlos had somehow gotten the best of him without even trying.

It wasn't like he hadn't thought about texting her again. He had wanted to text her when he'd gotten in bed when he got home, when he stopped on the way to work this morning to pick up coffee and was sure she'd already had some, when he saw a billboard for some new fast-food breakfast sandwich and laughed. But he'd held off, because he figured they'd tacitly agreed that this weekend, as great as it was, was all they'd have. But Carlos had a point.

He reached for his phone. Oh, the hell with it. They could at least have another weekend.

Maybe this is crazy, but I have lots of frequent flier miles. Feel like a trip to LA this weekend?

He didn't let himself think about it and pressed send.

♥

By the time she got off the phone with Maddie, the mayor was in, and she only had time for a brief check-in with Theo before he pulled all of the senior staff into their Monday morning meeting.

After they finished regular business, the mayor looked at her.

"Alexa, you're going to get me a memo on our plan forward with that delinquent teen project. End of the week?"

She locked eyes with Theo across the table from her. He wanted a memo. That was way more than she'd anticipated from his brush-off at their meeting on Friday.

"Absolutely," she said to her boss.

"Great." The mayor stood up, and the rest of the room did, too. "Good work, people. Theo, one more question for you . . ."

He and Theo walked out of the room, deep in conversation about a reporter that the mayor was trying to get on their side, while Alexa stood there stunned.

She was halfway there. Sure, she would have to write the best memo she'd ever written, but she didn't even think he would want that. Granted, just because he was ready to read another memo didn't mean he was ready to throw his weight behind the idea, but it meant he was close.

And she really needed to get him to stop calling it a "delinquent

teen project." She'd thought she'd made it clear when they met that
the correct terminology was "at-risk youth." But in the grand
scheme of things, that was not a big deal.

She walked back to her office, glad she'd made a quick outline
of her arguments on her phone in the middle of the night once
when she couldn't sleep. She reached for her phone to read it over.
And that's when she saw the text from Drew.

She looked over her shoulder. Was she being filmed? Was this
a dream? Was this some kind of "This is Alexa's lucky day!" fake
reality TV show? Her boss was in on her pet project, a hot guy
wanted to fly her to L.A.—was she going to get an email with a
$1,000 gift card to Sephora next?

He'd sent it two hours ago. Right when she was telling Maddie
that she was sure she'd never hear from him again.

Shit, what should she say? *YES, OF COURSE* was what she
wanted to say, but that would be kind of desperate and needy,
right? She checked her boss's calendar: he was at his niece's wedding in Tahoe that weekend. And he'd wanted her memo by Friday
anyway, so work shouldn't be in her way. But still, shouldn't she . . .

She heard Maddie's voice in her head telling her not to overthink it.

She texted him back.

Sure, why not?

She wanted to take it back almost immediately. What the hell
was she doing? Wasting another weekend on this guy? Just because
she'd be done with the—damn it, now she could only think of it as
the "delinquent teens" memo—by Friday didn't mean that she
wouldn't have a ton of other work to do. She'd have to do all the
work that she wouldn't get to bring home every night this week
because she'd be working on the memo.

And when was she going to find time to pack? For a weekend in L.A.? Oh God, she was going to have to go shopping again. She didn't have time to go shopping again! And what if he wanted to go to the beach? Would she have to wear a swimming suit? Didn't he know what she looked like in a swimming suit? Maybe this was all a joke and she'd never hear from him again.

Great, I'll check flights.

"I can't believe you're not spinning around in your office chair," Theo said, standing at her office door.

She jumped.

"How did you know I had something to be spinning about?"

Theo plopped into the chair on the other side of her desk.

"Um, because I was sitting right there when he said he wanted the memo?"

The memo, right. That's what he was talking about.

"Oh. Yeah, right, I was thinking of . . . something else."

Theo paused mid-reach toward her candy jar.

"Wait a minute. What could you possibly be thinking about other than your project?" He looked from Alexa's face to her phone. "Who's the guy?"

She tried to hold back her smile and failed.

"Um. Close the door."

Theo jumped up to close the door and was back at her desk in seconds.

"Talk. We can talk about the memo in a second. I don't have another meeting for"—he looked at his watch—"forty-five minutes. Go."

She rooted through her candy jar to find a Jolly Rancher.

"Soooo, funny story . . ."

10

Some people might say Drew's terrible mood during those two hours after he'd texted Alexa was because he'd convinced himself she wasn't going to write back. After ten minutes of nothing, he'd decided that her gentle way of letting him down would be to never answer, and his desperation would be out there floating in the wind forever.

That wasn't why he'd been in such a bad mood, he insisted to himself, and then to Carlos, when he stopped by on the way to get more coffee. It was just because of those irritating parents he had to deal with this morning. Carlos didn't believe him. He didn't really believe himself either.

It was kind of amazing how little he cared about those irritating parents after Alexa texted back, though.

In the middle of their tame text conversation about flight times, he ventured a suggestion.

You gonna show up to the flight without panties like yesterday?

Her reply came back within seconds.

Maybe.

He grinned down at his phone.

Friday morning, he tried to convince himself the spring in his step was only because his apartment was spotless for the first time in months, thanks to the emergency visit from a house cleaner. Carlos was at the clinic all day, not the main hospital, so there was no one there to argue that point with him.

All he had that day were some appointments in the morning and assisting Dr. Montgomery on a surgery for four-year-old Jack, one of Drew's favorite patients. He'd been hit by a car about a month ago, and one of his bones wasn't healing right. Throughout it all, the kid had been a trooper, and his parents had been attentive and thoughtful.

But Jack's surgery got pushed back. From noon to two. Then at one thirty, word came from Dr. Montgomery's office that it was going to be at least another hour, maybe two. Drew dropped by the waiting room to check on Jack and his parents. Jack was playing happily on the floor with a pile of Legos.

"Dr. Nick! Look what I did!"

"Hey, Jack, good job. Hey, Abby, Fred, how are you guys holding up?"

Jack's mom, Abby, looked up at him and shrugged as she helped Jack pull apart two blue Legos.

"Hanging in there, but we thought we'd be done by now."

Drew sighed.

"Yeah, me, too. Dr. Montgomery had an emergency. I'm so sorry about this."

The frustrating thing was that Drew could have done the surgery alone, but Dr. Montgomery had taken an interest in the case, and it's not like he could tell the parents, *Oh no, don't wait for the expert, he's not worth it.*

"They told us," Abby said. "At least they let us feed him a little once it got pushed back, otherwise this would be even more of a nightmare."

Drew was grateful he'd sent word to the nurses to get Jack some food; sometimes you had to relax the "no eating before surgery" rules with kids.

"Can I get you two anything?" Drew asked them. "Coffee, tea, water?"

Fred smiled at him.

"Thanks, Dr. Nichols. I went on a coffee run, so we're good. Thanks for checking on us. We appreciate it."

When he finally got word that Dr. Montgomery was out of his emergency surgery, he did a quick mental calculation and realized there was no way he was going to be on time to pick up Alexa from the airport. Now he'd be late, she'd be sitting at LAX—possibly without panties on—getting more and more frustrated, and the whole weekend would be fucked up.

Damn it. He called Carlos.

"Hey man, I need a huge favor."

Carlos was clearly in the car; Drew could hear the air whistling through the windows.

"Shouldn't you be getting ready for *Alexa*?" Carlos asked.

Why was he friends with such a jackass?

"Yeah, that's the thing. My surgery got pushed back, so I'm going to be stuck here for a while. Can you pick her up from the airport and bring her to my apartment? You have my keys, right? I'll owe you in beer for the next two months."

He could hear Carlos's car shut off, and he got switched off speakerphone.

"No problem, man. Text me her flight info and how I can find her. Or should I just take all of the short black women with big boobs at LAX to your apartment so you can pick?"

Drew lay his head down on his desk.

"I'm going to regret this, aren't I?"

"Oh, no doubt, you absolutely are. Good luck with the surgery!"

Drew texted Alexa the change of plans. Hopefully, she wouldn't be pissed. She knew he was a doctor, so it would be okay. Right?

♥

Alexa had given her boss two hard copies and an email version of her memo right before he walked out the door on Friday afternoon. She'd barely slept all week, between her regular work, texting Drew, writing and editing the memo every night, thinking about Drew, and, oh yeah, stressing about the upcoming weekend. Thursday night, she'd made her last edits on the memo, after copious notes from Theo, and had packed probably way too many clothes for a weekend trip to L.A.

She slipped into the bathroom at work right before leaving for the airport, stepped out of her underwear, and tucked them into the bottom of her tote bag. When she came out of the stall, she couldn't even look herself in the eye in the mirror.

She sang along to her girl-power playlist in the car on the way to the airport, which helped to psych herself up. But the text from Drew brought her down to earth.

My surgery got pushed back so I'm running late. My buddy Carlos is going to pick you up and bring you to my apartment. He drives a red

**BMW his number is 310-555-4827 if you can't find him, but he's got
your number too.**

Huh. He was a doctor; these things happened. But she felt so
deflated. Now she had no real idea when she was going to get to
see him tonight. How long was this surgery supposed to last? Was
she supposed to just tuck herself in his bed and wait for him?
Thank God she'd thrown her yoga pants in her suitcase. And
brought her laptop.

And the friend picking her up had a red BMW? Oh God, he
was going to be one of those fancy car assholes, wasn't he? Welcome to L.A.

She forced herself to put together a weekend work to-do list
while on the flight. When she read it over, she saw she'd repeated
three different things. Too distracted for more work, she pulled a
fashion magazine out of her bag and updated her Sephora wish
list, just in case that dream gift certificate actually came.

When her flight landed, she had texts from both Maddie and
Theo, wishing her luck (Maddie) and asking a work question
(Theo). And one from a 310 number:

**Hey Alexa, Drew's friend Carlos here. Picking you up bc he can't.
Look for the red car. See you soon.**

She wished tone came through easier on text messages. Was
this guy the asshole that the red sports car would make him seem?
And, oh God, had Drew told him the same girlfriend story he'd
given the people at the wedding, or did he know the real story? She
couldn't even ask Drew because he was in surgery. She'd just have
to play it by ear.

Fifteen minutes later, Alexa stood outside and realized one of
the big differences between Northern and Southern California: a

lot more red sports cars in Southern California. She smiled tentatively at each one, but so far she was 0 for 5 as they sped by. Or
maybe Drew hadn't described her and Carlos was looking for one
of those tall, blond, skinny women like she'd seen in the bathroom
at the wedding?

She looked down at the phone gripped in her hand to see if
maybe Carlos had texted again without her noticing, or maybe
Drew had finished his surgery and sped over from the hospital.

"Alexa?" She looked up, and a red car was parked at the curb
in front of her, a tall Latino guy getting out of the driver's side.

"Carlos? Hi! It's nice to meet you," she said.

"Likewise." He opened the passenger door for her and put her
suitcase in the trunk. She settled into his car, then sat bolt upright.
She really should have stopped in the bathroom and put her underwear back on.

He grinned at her once they were both in the car. Did he know
what she was thinking? Did guys tell one another stories like that?
She had no idea.

"Sorry if you had to wait," he said. "I checked your flight info
online, and you weren't supposed to land until right now."

They were already on their way out of the airport, dodging
cars and rental car shuttles. He definitely drove like a guy driving
a red sports car.

"Oh my goodness, it's no problem," she said. "Thank you so
much for coming to pick me up. I really appreciate it."

He threw a smile in her direction before pulling out of the airport.

"Don't worry. Drew's going to owe me big for this one. By the
way, are you hungry? I have no idea when he's going to be done,
and I don't want you to starve waiting for him. Want to pick something up on the way to his place?"

She set her tote bag down on the floor next to her feet, grateful that he'd asked. Maybe this guy was nicer than she'd assumed. She'd stress-eaten all of her purse snacks over the course of the workweek and hadn't had time to eat anything today except for a salad at noon and a bag of peanuts on the airplane.

"I would love that, thank you. As long as it's not out of your way?" Oh God, she thought, please don't let him say it's out of his way.

He laughed and turned down the radio.

"Tons of stuff in between here and there. Plus I'm hungry, too. Drew didn't give me much warning here."

She pulled off her cardigan and put it in her bag.

"Same here."

He glanced at her as he changed lanes.

"This was a last-minute thing—Drew couldn't have helped it. But he was definitely looking forward to you coming."

She shrugged. That was nice of Carlos to say, but . . . thank goodness he went back to the food topic.

"What are you in the mood for? In-N-Out? Pizza? Tacos? Sush—"

"Tacos, definitely," she said, almost salivating. She relaxed against the leather seat and let her eyes drift shut for a second. She was suddenly exhausted, from the stress of the week, her sleepless nights, the last few hours of uncertainty.

"Awesome." He accelerated and her eyes popped open. She probably should stay alert with him driving like this.

"One question before I decide where to get the tacos: how are you with spicy food?"

She laughed.

"I think my mom used to put Tabasco sauce in my bottles as a kid. I can take anything you're dishing out."

He changed lanes with barely a glance over his shoulder and grinned.

"Excellent."

Thirty minutes later, she carried their food up the stairs to Drew's apartment, while Carlos brought her suitcase. After he opened the door, she walked inside to see big windows, white walls, chrome appliances, and black-and-white prints everywhere. She dropped her tote bag next to the gray couch and looked around for a place to put the tacos.

"Put them on the coffee table," Carlos said. "The game's on. I'll get napkins and beer."

Alexa kicked off her shoes and left them in the corner by her suitcase. She wanted to change into her yoga pants and a T-shirt, instead of the sleek red shift dress she'd worn to work that day. But it felt awkward to wheel her stuff into Drew's bedroom like she belonged there and change into her comfy clothes. She didn't even know where Drew's bedroom *was*.

The spread of tacos Carlos laid out on the table distracted her.

"Oh my God, that looks so good," she said. She'd tried to pay for them, but he'd pushed her wallet aside. To be fair, he'd ordered for her, too.

He turned on the basketball game and plopped in the easy chair. Thank goodness Drew had an ugly throw blanket draped over the back of his couch. She sat in a corner, put the blanket over her lap, and tucked her feet up with a sigh of relief.

"These are so good," she couldn't stop saying as they ate. "Why don't we have potato tacos at every taqueria in the Bay Area? I'm going to be angry about that for months, if not years." She poured more of the habanero salsa over her taco.

Carlos added another taco to his plate and laughed.

"Don't worry," he said. "You can get potato tacos anytime you come down to visit."

How was she supposed to answer that? She doubted if she'd ever be back to visit Drew. Anything she said to his friend about that would either be presumptuous or needy. So instead, she added a dollop of guacamole to her taco and took a bite.

She grabbed a carnitas taco next, and reached for one of the salsas that she hadn't tried yet.

"Oh no." Carlos took it away from her and handed her a container of the tomatillo salsa. "Try this one. That one I got for poor Drew. He can't do too much spice."

She raised her eyebrows at him and opened her mouth, then thought better of what she was about to say.

"I know what you were going to say," Carlos said. "It's a trial having a white dude as a best friend, but I've been working on him."

They both burst out laughing and dug back in to the food.

♥

Drew heard Alexa's laugh from the other side of his apartment door. It made him smile, the way it had ever since her first laugh in the elevator. He opened the door to see her sitting with Carlos, both with plates of tacos from Carlos's favorite taqueria on their laps. Carlos must approve if he'd brought her there. They were laughing so hard they didn't notice him at first.

Hold on. Why was Carlos still here? He hadn't told him to entertain her, just to drop her off at his apartment and let her in.

He wanted to sit next to her on his couch, kiss her, tell her how hot she looked in that dress, see her smile at him, maybe reach up under her dress to check her underwear situation. Instead, she was laughing with his best friend and hadn't even heard him open the door.

"Hey," was all he said.

She looked up and smiled at him, just the way he'd wanted her to. He smiled back, so happy to see her that he had to take a step back.

"You get me any tacos?" he asked Carlos. "I see you're drinking my beer."

Carlos gestured to the table but made no move to leave.

"Tacos for everyone, and I even remembered your favorite salsa. There's more beer in the fridge."

Drew went into the kitchen for a beer. At least there'd been a third plate on the table, so apparently Carlos hadn't completely forgotten that Drew existed.

He sat on the couch next to Alexa and took a swig of his beer. She turned to face him, her smile more tentative now. He reached for her hand, and she gripped his fingers for a second.

"You must be starving," she said. She let go of his hand but moved closer to him on the couch. "Have some tacos. How did the surgery go?"

He loaded up his plate and moved closer to her in the process, so by the time he sat back against the couch cushions they were hip to hip. Carlos was intent on the basketball game, but he had a tiny smirk on his face. He knew Drew was dying to get rid of him, damn him.

He took a bite, realized he hadn't answered her question, tried to talk, then saw the error in that. She laughed at him, and he grinned once he could.

"Surgery went well. This is that kid I was telling you about last weekend, the one who was in the car accident." He took another bite, happy that she was relaxed against him. "Sorry that I couldn't pick you up."

"It's okay," she said. She wiped her hands with a paper towel and set her plate back down on the table. "Will you need to go into the hospital this weekend to check on him?"

He paused, a taco halfway toward his mouth.

"I kind of wanted to. Do you mind? I can go early in the morning so I don't—"

She cut him off with a hand wave.

"No, of course I don't mind. Go whenever it works best for him. We can figure it out."

She sat back against the couch, her leg rubbing against his whenever she changed position. What was her underwear situation? He'd never find out until Carlos left.

He caught Carlos's eye and his "you had better leave my apartment this second or I'll egg your car on a hot day" threat must have been on his face, because Carlos grinned and stood up.

"Alexa, a pleasure meeting you. I hope it's the first of many such meetings. Drew, see you Monday."

Alexa stood up and hugged Carlos.

"Thanks for picking me up, and for the tacos. Great to meet you, too."

Well, wasn't that cozy.

The door closed behind Carlos a few seconds later, and when Alexa sat back down next to Drew on the couch, he put his plate on the coffee table.

"Hi," he said. He'd been dying for Carlos to leave, so why did it feel awkward now? Why did he feel like this? He was never nervous around women.

"Hi." She smiled back at him. But her hands were clasped

together tightly again. It made him feel better that she was nervous, too.

"Sorry I couldn't pick you up," he said again. His hand moved up into her hair, and he rubbed his fingers through the strands.

"It's okay." She turned so her whole body was facing his. Her hands let go of each other, and one of them came to rest on his thigh.

He moved his hand from her hair to her cheek. She closed her eyes and leaned her face into his palm. They sat like that in silence for a minute or so.

Finally, she opened her eyes and looked at him, a dreamy smile on her lips. His hand moved from her cheek to her chin, and he lowered his head to hers.

It had been less than a week, but her lips on his, his arms wrapped around her, her hands in his hair, it all felt like coming home after months away. Like all he needed was this, the gentle pressure of her lips, the soft strokes of her tongue, her touches and sighs, to make him happy.

"I couldn't wait for Carlos to leave," she said against his ear.

He laughed and relaxed back on the couch, pulling her with him. She leaned her head on his chest, and he ran his fingers through her hair.

"He was doing that to fuck with me—I know it—but I was so ready to kill him." He ran his hand down from her hip to her knee over her dress. He paused and slid his hand back up, under her dress this time.

"Did you . . ."

Her wide smile was all the answer he needed. In a flash, he pressed her down on the couch and braced his body over hers.

"Did you plan on telling me this at some point?" He ran his

hand up the outside of her leg again, this time pushing her dress up along with it.

She smiled again from beneath him as she caressed his chest, unbuttoning his shirt as she went.

"You seemed to like the surprise so much last time, I didn't want to spoil it."

"Mmmm. I liked the surprise last time a LOT, that's true." He pushed her legs apart with his knee while she unbuckled his belt.

He kissed her again, harder this time. His thumb ran over her breasts, and she moaned as she kissed him back. She ran her hands up under his shirt. He never wanted her to stop touching him.

Fuck. Condoms were all in his bedroom.

"Hold that thought." He stood up, pushing the coffee table out of the way. One of the containers of salsa spilled everywhere. He couldn't care less. He looked down at Alexa on his couch, dress crumpled around her waist, hair every which way, and grinned. It had been a GREAT idea to have her come down for the weekend.

"Wait right there. Don't move, not one millimeter. I'll be right back." He ran into his bedroom and grabbed a condom out of the box in his nightstand. He ran back into the living room a minute later.

"You moved," he said. She looked up at him, her now-naked body sprawled across his couch.

"You left," she said. "I had to do something to keep myself occupied while I waited for you." Goddamn, this woman.

He threw his clothes across the room and crawled up her body.

"Tell me what you want, Alexa," he said, his naked body suspended over hers.

"I want you to stop asking me stupid questions," she said, and pulled him down so he was flush against her.

He laughed.

"Point taken," he said, and pushed her legs open.

Later, as they lay together on the couch, he looked at the wreckage of his living room—three couch pillows on the floor, clothes in every corner, salsa everywhere.

"Welcome to Los Angeles," he said in her ear. She laughed and turned her face to kiss him.

11

Alexa woke up the next morning, her back tucked against his chest, his arms cocooning her. She couldn't fight the warmth that spread through her chest at the way he held her, the way he touched her. He embraced her like he meant it, like he cared.

He was probably always just like this with women. She knew it wasn't real. But damn, did it feel good.

And then, the times he touched her in other ways . . . holy shit, were those times amazing. What was it about this guy and her reaction to him? She'd never felt so uninhibited around a man before, especially without her clothes on. Her cheeks got hot when she thought about throwing her clothes off on his couch. She hadn't worried about what he would think of her or the cellulite in her thighs or the way her stomach jiggled or how her boobs drooped—she only thought about his pleasure and her own.

Last weekend she'd thought that it was because it was a one-night stand, that it was the craziness of the wedding and the champagne and the knowledge that she'd never see him again that made her so relaxed around him. But now . . . maybe it was just something about him. Whatever it was, she was going to enjoy it all weekend.

She felt him nuzzle the back of her neck and giggled.

"So she is awake," he said, his mouth still on her skin.

"Mmmmhmmm," she responded, not wanting him to move.

But then he started to move, his hands and his lips and his tongue, and it turned out that she didn't mind so much.

Afterward, she snuggled against him, both of them hot and sweaty and breathless.

"Drew?" she whispered in his ear.

She felt him smile against her cheek.

"I'll go turn on the coffee in a second."

They drank coffee in the sun on his balcony, as they looked out at the ocean, him in boxers, her in a flannel robe she'd found in his bathroom. She took her first long sip and sighed. He looked from his own mug to her.

"That was a good sigh, yes?"

She looked at him, then down at her coffee, so she wouldn't smile at him too much.

"Good, yes. You make good coffee."

He leaned back in his chair and laughed.

"A skill I had to learn in med school or get my stomach torn apart by the stuff in the cafeteria."

She laughed and took another sip.

"Hey, Alexa?" Drew said, that little-boy smile back on his face. She would probably do whatever he wanted when he smiled at her like that.

Or any kind of way.

"I'm hungry, too," was all she said.

"The thing is, I don't really have much food in the house. I was planning on going to the grocery store before picking you up at the airport, but . . ."

She stood up.

"I'll jump in the shower."

♥

Drew had noticed Alexa's sweet tooth at the wedding, so he brought her to a brunch place where everyone raved about the waffles. She ordered them with blueberries on top, and he stole a few tastes in between bites of his omelet and bacon. When they walked back to his car, he realized how close to the hospital they were.

"We're only about five minutes from the hospital . . . If you want I can drop you at home first, but I was thinking that I could just run in and say hi to Jack?"

She smiled up at him.

"Sure, of course. You don't have to just run in, you know. I mean, if you have work to do, I get it."

He opened her car door then went around and got in on his side.

"No, really, I only want to say hi. I'm not on call this weekend. I don't want to be that asshole who second-guesses the doctors working that day."

He kept looking over at her as he drove the short distance to the hospital. Her eyes were closed as she leaned back in the seat, her hand in his, her thumb lazily stroking his palm. He liked the way she could give herself up to enjoying things like car rides on a sunny day, her morning coffee, lying in the grass at Dolores Park. Being around her made him enjoy all of those things more, too.

He pulled into the hospital parking lot and squeezed her hand.

"Let's go."

Her eyes widened. She didn't take her seat belt off.

"Shouldn't I just wait here? Confidentiality and all? I don't mind waiting. I have books on my phone."

She was only here for the weekend, and he'd already missed time with her the night before.

"No, come inside. I can show you all the toys. Just step outside the room if I give you the nod."

He didn't reach for her hand on the way into the hospital; there were too many eyes around a hospital. He already knew he'd be getting questions on Monday morning about who the girl he brought in on Saturday was. He didn't need to make the questions even more pointed.

They went straight up to Jack's room on the pediatric floor. Both of Jack's parents were there, looking exhausted. Jack's cheeks were too pale, and he was unusually silent, but he was sitting up in bed.

"Hey, Jack!" Drew said as he walked in. "How are you feeling today?"

Jack swiveled to the door when he heard Drew's voice and giggled.

"Dr. Nick! You aren't wearing your doctor costume."

Drew laughed, moving close enough to the bed for Jack to give him a high five with his good arm.

"I know! I'm off duty for doctoring today. I just wanted to come by and check in on you since I was in the neighborhood." He smiled at Jack's parents. "Abby, Fred, how are you guys?"

"Hanging in there," Abby said to him. He saw her eyes dart to the door, and he realized Alexa was still standing in the doorway. He lowered his voice.

"I was nearby with a friend. Is it okay if she comes in to say hi to Jack? If not, it's no problem; she can wait in my office."

Abby smiled.

"It's fine. Jack's been getting bored with just us for entertainment."

He waved Alexa to his side.

"Hey, Jack, I brought a friend of mine to meet you. Jack, this is my friend Alexa. Can you say hi?"

"Hi!" Jack giggled again. "You're not wearing a doctor costume, either."

Alexa laughed as she offered her fist to Jack.

"No, but that's because I'm not a doctor. Sorry, Jack."

Drew picked up Jack's chart from the end of the bed and checked it, satisfied with Jack's status.

"How's the pain?" he said in a low voice to Fred, as Jack chattered away with Alexa.

"He woke up a few times in the night. Abby was with him, but they seem to be managing it well."

"Dr. Nick, Dr. Nick, Mommy said I couldn't get out of bed yet, but I told her you would say I could, won't you?"

He gave Jack his full attention and let himself get sucked into a conversation about Jack's favorite video game before he realized they'd been there for longer than he'd intended. He looked up, expecting to find Alexa watching him and Jack, but she was over in the corner deep in conversation with Abby.

Huh. It wasn't like he'd brought her here so she could see what a good doctor he was, but she could at least notice.

"Jack, I'm going to have to say good-bye now, but I'll see you in a few days, okay?"

Abby looked in their direction.

"Say thank you to Dr. Nichols for coming by to see you, Jack."

Alexa pulled something out of her purse and handed it to Abby, who hugged her. Alexa waved to Jack as they walked out of his room.

He took her hand as soon as they entered the parking lot.

"How did you get a hug out of Abby? She still calls me Dr. Nichols in that very formal voice," he said.

"Oh, I was just giving her some advice about the kinds of services they could get. She told me about the accident and that it was a drunk driver."

He dug in his pocket for his car key. What did she mean, services?

"They have good health insurance, I think. Fred works for one of the studios."

She checked her phone and frowned at it before looking back up at him.

"I know, she told me, but good insurance only goes so far. I meant all of the crime victims' services that they can get from the state. Counseling, compensation, help at home, stuff like that. She said she vaguely remembered being told about it right after the accident but had no idea how to access that stuff."

No wonder Abby had hugged her.

"So you gave her your card? What's the Berkeley mayor's office going to do about a kid in L.A.?"

She looked back up from her phone and shrugged as they got in the car.

"I have a list at work of all of the right people for her to contact. I told her to email me, and I can send it all her way and introduce her to some victims' rights advocates I know who can help her navigate it all. I can send them quick emails and cc her, just to speed things up a little."

He pulled onto the road for the short drive back to his apartment.

"How did you get all of that out of her in ten minutes? Teach me your secrets, Monroe."

Alexa grinned and put her phone back in her purse, thank God.

"I have a way with people, don't you know? I work in politics."

He put his hand on her thigh. She shifted her body toward him and smiled.

"Mmm, you sure do have a way with people. The way you dealt with the inquisition we got at the wedding was pretty impressive, I have to say."

"Friendly deflection is one of my special talents." She put her hand on top of his. "And Abby looked so worried. It's good to be able to help, if you can."

♥

Oh Lord, he probably thought she was some bleeding-heart interferer now, butting into one of his cases when no one asked her to. But the look on that mom's face had broken her heart. Was she not supposed to try to help?

Fine, she was a bleeding-heart interferer. It was probably in her job description.

When they got to his apartment, he stopped her just inside the door.

"Anyway, thanks for coming along to see Jack. And for being so nice to Abby. They've had a rough time."

Drew pulled her into his arms, enveloping her into a hug that somehow felt more intimate than anything they'd done before. She leaned her head into his chest and relaxed against him. She felt him exhale a deep breath and tightened her grip on his back, the worn cotton of his T-shirt smooth against her fingers. He bent down and kissed her hair, her ear, and when she tilted her head to look at him, her mouth.

"I really appreciated you being there," he said when he pulled away.

She moved her hands up and under his shirt, loving the way he tensed at her touch.

"Show me," she said.

He slung her over his shoulder in one quick motion, making her gasp.

"Drew, no, I'm too heavy!" Ignoring her, he strode with her into the bedroom and tossed her down on his bed. She laughed when she bounced as she hit the mattress, but her laughter faded when he threw his clothes off and stood there naked in front of her.

"Oh my." When he made a move to jump on the bed along with her, she held up a hand to stop him. "Don't move. Just . . . just stand there for a minute."

Despite all of the times they'd had sex so far, she had yet to really see him naked. It had either been too frantic, or too dark, or too early in the morning for her to really pay attention. But now he stood there, the bright afternoon light from his bedroom windows streaming in on his hard body, and she spent a moment in pure awe. She knew just from touching him the contours of his chest, and that light sprinkling of hair, but it was quite another to see it in front of her, golden from the sun, hers to look at as long as she wanted.

She lifted her finger in the air and spun it around to make him twirl like he was a beauty pageant contestant. Glory of glories, he obeyed her. The rush she got out of the pure power of that was only overwhelmed by her sight of his perfect, round, cuppable ass.

"Come here." He didn't have to be told twice. He took a flying leap onto the bed and immediately rolled her underneath him, affording her the perfect opportunity to grab onto that ass and pull him against her.

She ran her hands all over his body, loving the sounds he made as she touched him, loving that he seemed to be enjoying this as much as she was.

"You wore panties today, didn't you?" he said in her ear. Not waiting for an answer, he reached down and grabbed the thong she'd worn, pulled it off her, and threw it across the room. "Your turn," he said, looking down at her.

She didn't pretend to misunderstand him, even though she wanted to. What was that she'd been thinking earlier about how relaxed and confident she was around him? Because that feeling had faded after seeing his perfect body and knowing all of her own imperfections by heart . . . and how bright and sun filled his bedroom was. She suddenly really regretted those waffles at brunch.

He didn't let her hesitate, though. He pulled her dress over her head, reached around her back and unhooked her bra, and then leaned back on his heels to look at her.

She tried to force herself to look at his face, but her cheeks got hot and she had to look away. Her eyes drifted down his body, and that's when she saw clear evidence that he enjoyed looking at her body. She smiled.

"Oh, you like that, don't you?" he said. "But wait. I was supposed to be showing you how much I appreciate you, wasn't I?"

He slid down her body, pressing her legs open with his shoulders. She held her hands against his hair to keep him right where she wanted him. He increased the pace, and she moaned, her head shaking from side to side on the pillow. It felt so good she wanted it to stop and go on forever, all at the same time. Finally, she hit her peak and cried out as the vibrations rumbled through her body.

He crawled up the bed so his head was level with hers and lay on his side next to her, his hand stroking her stomach as her breathing slowed.

"Do you feel appreciated now?" he asked. He kissed her neck and moved down to her breasts, his hand moving up to join his mouth.

"Mmmm," she answered. She leaned forward to kiss his shoulder, then pushed him until he fell on his back. She grinned and climbed on top of him. "I think you've done enough work for this afternoon, don't you?"

She kissed him up and down his body, her fingers stroking his skin. She looked up at him: his arms were crossed behind his head, his whole body looked relaxed, and he was looking straight at her with that look that made her feel like a goddess. She ripped open the condom packet he'd left on the pillow and rolled the condom on.

Usually it made her anxious to be on top. There was so much scrutiny in that position, so many parts of her body that jiggled, so much to make her feel shy. But she couldn't feel anything but pleasure when Drew's eyes worshipped her body like that.

When Alexa came to, she was still on top of him, her head pillowed by his chest. He reached down to pull off the condom, and she tried to roll off him, but he held her in place. She didn't fight it. He massaged her back as she lay there, and she felt like she could easily stay just like that for a few days. Maybe a few weeks.

He leaned forward and kissed her ear.

"Feeling appreciated yet?"

She shrugged as much as she could in her prone position.

"I mean, if that's all you can do, I guess so."

He growled in her ear and rolled her over underneath him as she laughed.

12

Alexa woke up the next morning alone in bed. She assumed that Drew was in the bathroom, but when he didn't get back in bed after a few minutes, she sat up and saw his bathroom door open and the light off. She pulled on his robe and wandered into the kitchen in the hopes that he was making coffee, but he wasn't there, either.

She decided that he'd probably gone for a run on the beach like he said he did some mornings. She sort of wished he'd left her a note but forced herself to shrug it off. She got back in bed with her neglected phone to check her work email. But first things first: she typed out a quick reply to a text from Maddie that just said ????????

Weekend so far: having fun, eating good food, great sex, don't wish you were here.

Just then, she heard Drew's front door quietly open and close.

"Oh, you're awake." He'd tiptoed into the bedroom, holding

two cups of coffee in a tray and a bakery bag. "I thought you'd still be asleep."

She looked at the bag, and then back to him.

"I thought you went for a run, but this is much better. What's in the bag?"

He laughed and handed her one of the coffee cups.

"Don't you want to ask what's in the cup?"

She rolled her eyes.

"I know what's in the cup. I have eyes and a sense of smell. It's coffee! What I want to know is what's in that bag!" She paused. "What I meant to say right there was thank you for the coffee."

He sat down on the bed next to her, still keeping the bag out of her reach.

"Weird, that's not what it sounded like."

She put the cup on the bedside table so she wouldn't spill it and reached for the bag, but he easily dodged her and flipped her over onto her back, the bag still out of reach.

"Drew!"

He kissed her on the tip of her nose.

"Mmm, I like you in this position."

She pulled his face down to kiss him.

"What's in the bag, Drew?"

He laughed and tossed the bag into her lap.

"I thought I'd distracted you there for a minute."

She opened the bag to find a half dozen doughnuts, and her stomach rumbled.

"Oh my goodness! What is all of this? This is amazing!"

He grinned.

"Now I know what you must have been like opening Christmas presents as a kid. A plain glazed, one raspberry jelly filled, one lemon jelly filled, one with rainbow sprinkles, and two with bacon and maple frosting."

"Bacon and maple frosting? What is this place? Is it direct from my wildest dreams?"

Drew laughed as he grabbed one of the bacon doughnuts for himself.

"You have no idea how great this doughnut shop is. I almost woke you up to make you come with me, but you were so sound asleep I didn't want to disturb you. Next time, though, you should come."

Next time? What did "next time" mean in this context? It was Sunday, and she was leaving in less than twelve hours. Did he mean he wanted to go back there today? Or did he mean next time she was in L.A.? If so, what did he mean by *that*?

Don't overthink it, Alexa.

She tried to listen to Maddie's voice in her head and took a bite of the doughnut.

"Oh my God." She swallowed and took a bigger bite. "These are amazing."

He grinned at her and wiped frosting from her cheek with his thumb.

"Did you doubt me?"

After the doughnuts, and her post-doughnut thank-you that went on for quite a while, he jumped in the shower. As soon as he was out of the room, she reached for her phone again. Her boss usually didn't email this early on a Sunday, and he'd had that wedding to go to, but maybe he'd had time to read her memo . . . Nope, he hadn't. To relieve her feelings, she shot off a quick email to Theo in the hopes that he would have some insight on when she might get a reply.

He emailed back a minute later:

> You've been working for him longer than I have and
> you know it. Don't you have better things to do—this
> weekend especially—than sit around on a Sunday
> morning and freak out about this?

She replied:

> Teddy, no matter what other better things I have to
> do, I will always freak out about work, you know that.

"Good news?" She looked up to see Drew standing in the doorway in a towel.

"What?" She was distracted by that rivulet of water running down from his shoulder, down that cleft in his chest, straight down to . . .

"You were smiling at your phone. I was just wondering why." He sat on the bed next to her in his towel.

"Oh." She sighed. For a few seconds there, she actually had stopped freaking out about work. "No, I was just laughing at something Theo said."

He got off the bed and dropped the towel, but too quickly pulled underwear and jeans on. He was still shirtless, though.

"Who's Theo?" he asked.

They'd spent so much time together that it felt jarring that he didn't already know.

"Theo's the mayor's communications director, my work spouse, a good friend, all wrapped into one." She got out of bed and reached for the robe that they'd pushed to the floor.

He pulled on a gray T-shirt, just like the one he'd been wearing when they met in the elevator. Maybe it was that same shirt. She remembered that flash of his chest in the elevator under his shirt, and how much she'd wanted to run her hands up and down his chest. She still couldn't believe it had actually happened.

He looked out the window, not at her.

"Are you guys . . . together or something?"

She tied the robe tightly around her body. Boy, did she not like the implications of that question.

"Me and Theo? First of all, no. But second: do you really think I would be here with you this weekend if we were?"

Weird that he'd think that about her and Theo without knowing anything about him. Even weirder that he'd think she'd cheat on someone.

He looked at her and half smiled. She needed more than his cute little half smile after that. She walked toward the bathroom.

"No, wait, Alexa." He sat down on the bed and patted the spot beside him. She turned but didn't move toward him. "Please?"

Well, she was going to be here for the rest of the day anyway. What else was she going to do? She sat down.

"Sorry, I didn't think . . . That's not what I meant. I asked that wrong. I just wanted to know, for future reference, if there'd been anything between you guys. And plus, you were texting him on a Sunday morning"—his eyes dropped to her cleavage—"naked. I don't usually text my work friends like that."

She thought about asking what "for future reference" meant. But she had no idea how to have that conversation. She was great at difficult political conversations, not so much personal ones.

"I'm just on edge about work and I needed advice. He made

fun of me instead; it made me feel better. It was an email, not a text." She paused. "And I forgot I was naked."

Drew grinned.

"I didn't."

She grinned back.

"Theo and I couldn't possibly have more platonic of a relationship if we tried. He's like the brother I never had."

Drew sat back farther on the bed.

"What were you on edge about? What did you need advice about?" he asked.

"Oh, this arts program for at-risk youth I'm trying to get the mayor to support. I gave him my memo on Friday afternoon, and while I know he probably hasn't even read it yet, let alone made a decision, I still keep checking."

Drew put his arm around her and leaned back against the pillows.

"This program is really important to you, isn't it?"

She nodded, her head against his chest.

"Tell me about it," he said, his fingers moving through her hair.

She hesitated. Was she ready to get into this with him just yet? Or ever, really? Would he understand? Would he even care? He kept waiting, though.

"I've always been interested in how to help teenagers. There are all sorts of programs for little kids, lots of reading groups and playgrounds and stuff like that. But people stop caring about kids once they hit the age of eleven or twelve. And everyone hates teenagers. Which sucks, because that's just the time of life when everything is changing and scary and you need help. And then when teenagers screw up, no one ever wants to give them a chance again. Especially teens of color."

"But an arts program?" She looked up at that tone in his voice and saw his raised eyebrows. "Isn't that just rewarding kids who get into trouble? How's that going to deter them from getting in trouble again?"

She sat all the way up and pulled the robe tighter around herself. She should have known he wouldn't get it. But this kind of attitude from him made her even more disappointed than she thought she could be. Disappointed and angry.

"Sending kids to jail for low-level offenses doesn't deter them from anything; it just makes it worse. People write them off. People like you."

He tried to interrupt, but she talked over him.

"And that just makes them more likely to screw up again, because at that point they know that no one cares about them. A program like this would show them that people care. It's not a reward; they would be required to attend and complete the program, but it would give them different ways of coping with stress, and not push them into a system of punishment that could ruin their lives."

She shook herself and sat up. How was it that she could argue this point totally dispassionately at work, but not with Drew? See, this was why she couldn't be trusted with difficult personal conversations; her temper always got the better of her.

"I'll jump into the shower now, if you're all done with the bathroom."

♥

Well, he'd fucked that up. He'd clearly hit a nerve there, and before he'd had the chance to figure out what to say, she'd fled to the shower.

He wondered if he should say something after she came out of the bathroom, but she gave him that bright smile she'd kept using on Amy at the wedding and said she was hungry, so he didn't bring it up.

Instead, he drove her out to the Valley for dim sum for lunch, to a place Carlos had told him about. After they both had fits of giggles about the embarrassing amount of dumplings on their table, things seemed normal again.

They took a long nap in the afternoon sunlight when they got back to his apartment. He woke up to the breeze blowing her hair into his face and her nose nuzzling his neck. He turned over in bed and pulled her underneath him.

She laughed up at him from the nest of his sheets and pillows and his body, her dark hair fanned around her head like a halo, her brown skin glowing against his white sheets. He laughed, too, just because she was here and he was here with her. He kissed her forehead, her cheeks, her eyelids, and finally her lips. They kissed like that for a while, nothing more, both with their eyes open, looking straight at each other.

After a while, she sighed and put her finger on his lips.

"Drew, as much as I would like to keep doing this . . . what time is it? My flight is at eight thirty, remember."

He took a deep breath and rested his forehead on hers. He wasn't ready for this weekend to be over.

Finally, he looked up at his bedside clock.

"Five."

She sighed and wrapped her arms around him.

"Okay. Did you still want to stop at that burger place on the way to the airport?"

He touched her cheek with his thumb.

"I would rather stay here in bed doing very dirty things with you until we have to go, but if you're hungry . . . ?"

They didn't have time to get burgers.

Right before he got off the freeway to LAX, he cleared his throat.

"I'm not on call next weekend, so I could maybe come up. I mean, if you're free."

She glanced over at him, opened her mouth, and closed it again. Finally, she said, "Yeah, that works for me. You should come. I'll probably have some work to do, but—"

He interrupted her.

"Did you hear from your boss about your memo?"

She shook her head, reached for her phone to double-check, and shook her head again.

"Hopefully tomorrow." She shrugged. "I can't count on it, though."

He cleared his throat.

"Um, I really hope he says yes."

She touched his hand, and he grabbed hers.

"Thanks. Me, too."

Too soon, they pulled into the terminal and he got out of the car to pull her suitcase out of the trunk. Still holding it, he joined her on the sidewalk and kissed her. Her arms went around his waist, and he marveled again at the touch of her hands, how they turned him on and soothed him all at the same time.

She pulled back first.

"I shouldn't miss my flight."

He let go of her but didn't get back in his car yet.

"Right, okay. See you next weekend?"

Her smile almost knocked him down. She nodded.

"Yeah. See you next weekend."

13

Alexa drove herself home from the Oakland airport, still in the combined mood of euphoria and confusion that she'd been in since getting out of Drew's car at LAX. He'd kept making little references to the future all weekend, from saying that they'd go to the doughnut shop "next time," to asking about Theo "for future reference." The whole time, she had been too afraid of destroying the mood to ask him what he meant by all that.

But then when they were almost at LAX, damn it, he'd gone and said that he'd come up to Berkeley next weekend. What was she supposed to have done then? Quiz him on his intentions in the drop-off line at LAX? It's not like she thought this relationship was going anywhere significant. Drew had made it very clear in the elevator that he wasn't that kind of guy.

So instead, she'd just said okay. She wasn't overthinking this, remember?

But she couldn't sleep that night. Her mind cycled around

thoughts of Drew, her boss, her memo and what was probably wrong with it, the weekend and how much fun she'd had, Drew, work the next day, his text asking her to text him when she was home and his increasingly dirty texts after that, the new policy director she was going to have to hire, Drew, the way he'd looked at her when they were in bed. Finally she got up and made a cup of chamomile tea and washed it down with half a Tylenol PM, which gave her about four hours of too-deep sleep.

She woke up groggy but in a much better mood than the night before. She was on her way to the job that she loved, she'd spent all weekend having sex with a hot doctor, and if she was a betting woman, she would bet that Theo would bring doughnuts in that morning.

Sure enough, she ran into him on her way into the building, a pink box in his hand.

"My hero!" she said as she handed him the coffee she'd bought him.

"How did you know I was going to bring doughnuts?" He eyed his coffee and the grin on her face.

"I had a hunch." She popped open the box and took out hers. "Just what I needed."

He tested his coffee for temperature, not taking a sip yet.

"We all know you got lucky this weekend. Do you need to flaunt it?"

She just grinned and took a big bite of her doughnut as he followed her into her office.

"Before I forget, did you hear anything? Normally, I wouldn't have even had to ask, but with you gone this weekend . . ." His voice trailed away as she shook her head. He sat down in one of the chairs in front of her desk.

"Okay, we'll talk about that in a minute. First: the weekend went well, I'm guessing?" He sipped his coffee and reached for his own doughnut.

"It did, thank you." She pushed all of her anxieties from the night before away and grinned at him.

He leaned back in his seat as she sat down and turned on her computer.

"Excellent. Are you going to see him again?"

She shrugged.

"He's going to come up here this weekend."

He toasted her with his coffee cup.

"Good job, Lex. I'm glad one of us is having fun with something that isn't work related."

She laughed.

"Me, too. Now, about my program—when do you think the boss will give me a yea or nay? Or even a maybe or nay?"

Theo took a long sip of his coffee and sat back in the chair.

"Well, either he read it over the weekend and will come in with questions for you today . . . or he didn't even glance at it over the weekend and you'll have to remind him about it today. We'll know that soon, at least."

But she heard nothing from the mayor about her project all morning, even though she sat through two meetings at his side. The third of the day was their biweekly meeting with the city attorney. After the city attorney ran through the list of current lawsuits against the city (protestors, slip-and-fall cases, employment matters, something about a clown) and pending settlement offers, the mayor looked up from the doodles on his notepad.

"Great. Now that we're done with all of that, Alexa has an idea to run by you. It's not a legal problem, but I want to make crystal clear that there are no liability issues before we bring this to the council, got it?"

Thanks, boss, for springing this on me. She didn't even have her notes with her. Luckily, she could recite this from memory.

"Yes, sir. Susan, here's my proposal."

She floated back into her office. She hadn't won yet, and there was a long fight ahead, but at least the mayor was with her now. She walked into Theo's office to shout the news at him. But it was empty.

"He's having coffee with a reporter," Theo's assistant called out to her.

Damn it.

She needed to share this joy with someone. When she pulled her phone out to text Maddie, she saw a text from Drew.

How's your Monday? Any word from your boss about your idea?

Huh. After their not-quite-fight about it on Sunday, she was surprised he'd brought it up again. She was so excited that she wanted to text him with about forty exclamation points, but she tempered her impulse.

Just talked to him. He's in! Good start to the week.

Fine, one exclamation point, so sue her.

Great news! What did he say?

She made a mental note to reward him for giving her an exclamation point back.

Hardly said anything, sprung it on me during a meeting with the city atty.

She plopped down at her desk, slid off her shoes, and twirled around in her office chair. By the time her rotation slowed, she had another text.

Great work, I'm happy for you.

She spun her chair again and beamed down at her phone.

I'm happy for me too!!

She couldn't hold back on the exclamation points that time, because it was true. She was happy about her project, happy that she had Drew to tell about this battle she'd fought, happy that he was happy for her. She was so busy smiling and spinning and looking at her phone that she didn't even notice Theo come into her office.

"You were looking for me?"

She jumped up, almost knocking over her chair in the process.

"Theo! Listen to what just happened."

Just as she finished telling him the whole story, her phone buzzed again.

We'll have something good to celebrate this weekend.

She beamed at her phone again. Theo's eyebrows shot up.

"You told him?"

She shook her head. "What do you . . . I didn't . . . How did you . . ." She sighed and gave up.

"I knew because I know you. Okay, we have to plan this out. Coffee in an hour?"

She nodded and waved him out the door. Maybe all of her middle-of-the-night anxieties—about everything—had been for nothing.

♥

Carlos had been so busy on Monday he'd barely nodded at Drew, and he'd gotten to their basketball league at the last minute. Drew hoped that meant he'd managed to escape the Carlos brand of humor about Alexa.

But he heard a shout after the game when he was almost at his car.

"I liked her, you know."

Drew turned around to find Carlos jogging toward him, a broad grin on his face.

"I noticed. You sure seemed to want to spend extra time with her."

Carlos caught up with him.

"How long did it take for you to jump her after I walked out the door?"

Drew flashed back to Friday night. They'd barely stopped to take off their clothes. He shook his head.

"None of your business."

Carlos laughed.

"That fast, huh? I thought you'd throw me out the window if I was there for another minute."

Drew unlocked his car and tossed his bag in the trunk.

"If you had stayed another minute, we might have tested that theory."

Carlos wiggled his eyebrows.

"Soooo, when are you going to see her again? You *are* going to see her again, right?"

Yeah, he was going to see her again.

"This weekend." He tried and failed to hold back a grin. "Flying up there for the long weekend."

Carlos patted him on the shoulder.

"Finally. Good job, dude. Proud of you."

Drew shook Carlos's hand off his shoulder and opened his car door. Oh great, now Carlos was smug because he got him to text

Alexa in the first place. He never would have done it if he'd known he was in for this.

Okay, never mind that, yes, he would have.

"Proud of me for what, asshole?"

Carlos grinned.

"Oh, you'll see. Tell Alexa I say hi."

♥

"Is he sleeping with anyone else?" Maddie asked as she sipped her second margarita.

Alexa paused, her own drink halfway to her mouth. That hadn't occurred to her. Why hadn't it occurred to her?

"I don't know." Because she hadn't wanted to think about him with anyone else, that was why. "Why do you ask?"

"You said he isn't really one for commitment, so I wondered," Maddie said. "Are you going to ask him?"

Alexa took a sip of her drink. This wasn't what she'd expected from margarita night with Maddie. Taco Tuesday was not supposed to be stressful. She didn't want the third degree about Drew; she just wanted some uncomplicated applause.

At least she'd gotten that from Theo.

"I hadn't thought about it."

"Okay. So I guess asking if you guys are dating now is going to get the same non-answer, isn't it?"

Alexa set her drink down.

"What happened to 'Don't overthink everything, Alexa'?"

Maddie laughed.

"I guess sometimes you do listen to me. But that was different! And even now, I'm not saying you need to *overthink* things . . . just don't under-think them."

"Great, perfect thinking balance, that doesn't sound hard at all. Why didn't I think of that? Now can we talk about you instead? Who was the client who pissed you off this week?"

Maddie's styling business was thriving, which meant she always had great stories. Alexa laughed throughout the tale of graduation dress shopping for a whole family, ages seventy, fifty-five, eighteen, and nine.

Unfortunately, now that she'd been given permission to start thinking more about the Drew situation, it was all she could think about.

"Should I ask him?" Alexa asked, midway through her second drink.

"I guess that depends on how much you want to know the answer," Maddie said.

♥

Wednesday afternoon, Drew's phone buzzed in his pocket while he was in the middle of an appointment with Jack and Abby. He grinned, almost certain of who had just texted him. He and Alexa had been texting each other all week, both in innocent and creative ways, though she'd been strangely silent today. He fought the urge to pull his phone out of his pocket and concentrated on Jack.

When Abby and Jack were walking out the door, she stopped and turned around.

"Your friend Alexa's been so helpful. She's gotten me in touch with help that I didn't even know existed. Please thank her for me."

Alexa hadn't even told him she'd been in touch with Abby.

"I'm sure she'll be happy to hear that," he said. Jack high-fived him with his good arm as they left.

He ducked into his office in between patients to text her. But then he saw the text that had come in during his appointment.

Are you sleeping with anyone else?

Whoa, wait, what had prompted that? He responded before he stopped to think.

Not at the moment, I'm at work.

Why did he never stop to think?

I see. What about after work, will I get a different answer?

Maybe another joke would help.

No, tonight is basketball night.

There was a knock on his office door, and he looked up.

"Dr. Nichols? Your one thirty is in the exam room."

"I'll be right there!" he said, and looked back down at his phone.

How about this: now you have the weekend free so neither work nor basketball nor I will get in the way.

What the fuck? How did that escalate so quickly? And why the fuck had she brought this up right now in the middle of the day? In a text message?

Come on, can you just calm down about this? I was just joking.

He sat down on the edge of his desk, ignoring the files that fell onto the floor.

Hahahahaha so funny.

Somehow, he didn't think those were genuine hahahahas. While he was still thinking about what to say to her, his phone buzzed again.

Look, Drew, I'm too busy to deal with this. I don't think this is a good idea.

Drew barely caught himself from cursing out loud, and luckily remembered that there were small children and their parents just outside the door.

"Dr. Nichols?" The knock on his door was louder. Shit, he was running even later than usual.

"Coming!"

Come on, Alexa. What the hell?

He slammed his phone down onto his desk and opened his office door hard enough for it to bang into the wall. Why the fuck did women have to do things like this?

"Everything okay there, Dr. Nichols?" the nurse asked.

"Fine. Who's next?"

He raged through his next four patients. He forced himself to smile at the kids, but he was particularly curt to one of the moms, and he knew he'd hear about that later.

Carlos came into his office at the end of the day when he was getting ready to go.

"Why are you still in those clothes?" Carlos dribbled an imaginary basketball on his office floor. "Basketball tonight!"

He flashed back to the text he'd sent Alexa that day and cringed.

"Gotta bail, sorry." His general plan was to go home and drink all of the beer in his fridge.

"Why, gotta call your girl?" Carlos asked. "You really going to ditch us for her? Though, I have to say, she is really . . ."

He didn't want to hear the end of that sentence.

"She's not my girl." He threw his bag over his shoulder and walked out the door. Carlos, of course, followed him. Still talking.

"Yeah, yeah, of course you'll say that. I know how you are. But anyone who sees you together knows the truth."

"She's. Not. My. Girl." Drew got in the elevator, not looking at Carlos, but he could feel his scrutiny.

"Okay. What happened?" Carlos pressed the button for the lobby, still staring at him. Of all people, he did not want to talk to

Carlos about this. He'd make it a whole big thing, and it wasn't a big thing. It had just been two fucking weekends, it was over, and he didn't want to deal with it or think about it anymore.

"Nothing." They rode down the whole way in silence. Carlos followed him across the street to the parking garage and got in the elevator with him there.

"Are you going to tell me now?" Carlos got off the elevator with him and walked with him toward his car.

"Don't you have somewhere to be? Why are you following me? Go play basketball."

Carlos gestured to the left, and Drew saw his gleaming red BMW. "I parked two cars away from you this morning, jackass. I'm not following you." He leaned against Drew's much more battered car and studied him. "Though, that is a good idea. You realize that I do have a key to your house, right? If you don't tell me what got you in this mood, you know I'm just going to follow you home until you do. And I know it's about Alexa, so don't try to bullshit me."

Drew sighed. As much as he'd fought it, he'd known it was inevitable.

"Fine, follow me home, but you'd better stop to get us food on the way. And you're paying."

Twenty minutes later, Carlos walked into his apartment carrying two In-N-Out bags. Drew ripped them open, bit into a Double-Double, and washed that down with his second beer. Then he flipped to Alexa's text messages and tossed his phone to Carlos.

"You might as well just read what happened today, so I don't have to tell you. Scroll down."

Drew watched Carlos's face as he read. In seconds it went from puzzlement to amusement, to outrage, and finally landed on exasperation. He set the phone down in the center of the table, popped open a beer, took a long sip, and sat back against the couch cushions. Finally, he looked at Drew.

"'Not at the moment'? Really?"

Drew thumped his empty beer bottle down on the table.

"It was a joke!"

Carlos unwrapped a burger for himself.

"Oh yeah? Did you think she would think that was funny? Did you think that *any woman* would think that was funny?"

Drew got up and went into the kitchen for another beer.

"I wasn't thinking! I wasn't prepared for that question! Why did she text me that? In the middle of the day? On a WEDNESDAY?"

Carlos squeezed out three ketchup packets onto his hamburger wrapper and grabbed a handful of fries. Ugh, he always took all of the ketchup. Drew should have just gotten his own damn hamburgers and gotten drunk at home alone in peace.

"So, what, a Thursday would have been better?"

He wanted to throw his beer bottle at Carlos's head. Instead, he drank from it and sat back down in his corner of the couch.

"What?" Carlos asked. "Just making a joke."

Okay, that was it. He didn't have to take this shit in his own house.

"Fuck you! Go home."

Carlos had the audacity to laugh at him.

"No, I mean it, fuck you."

Carlos stopped laughing at him, but he settled himself and his burger and beer more comfortably on the couch.

"So you're going to call her, though, right?

Drew slammed his beer bottle on the table. The beer fizzed up and overflowed everywhere.

"No, why would I? I can find another girl. I have before; I will again."

Carlos didn't say anything as Drew went back to the kitchen for another beer. Drew sat back on the couch and took a gulp.

"It was going to have to end at some time anyway. Better it end now before she *really* hates me."

He looked up and saw Carlos looking at him.

"What do you mean?"

Drew shrugged off the question and reached for the food. When he looked up, Carlos was still staring at him.

"What? What's wrong with you?" he asked.

Carlos shook his head.

"Nothing, dude. Finish your burger."

♥

Alexa spent the rest of the afternoon first furious at Drew, then at herself. Why had she decided to text him in the middle of the day on a Wednesday, for God's sake? Did she have to do this right when she was about to go into three back-to-back meetings where she had to concentrate and be diplomatic and pay attention? Shouldn't she have waited to talk about this in person?

After the last of her meetings, not only did she have to drive her boss home, but he made her sit in the driveway with him and talk about their transportation plan for fifteen minutes.

She felt like she was going to crawl out of her skin. She was angry that she had gotten so invested in a relationship that had lasted all of thirteen days, angry she'd done all of that for something that wasn't even a relationship in the first place, angry at Drew for being such a jackass, angry at Drew for being such a great guy for ninety-eight percent of those thirteen days, angry at herself for being on the point of tears for six straight hours when she prided herself on never crying, angry at her boss for still talking about fucking bicycles when she just wanted to go home.

Finally, the mayor's wife called him from inside the house and told him that unless he came inside in two minutes she was going to eat their dinner without him.

All Alexa wanted to do was go home and wallow, but even that made her angry—how dare she need to wallow after such a short time? She barely even knew him! Why couldn't she be like one of those women who could sleep with a guy for a few weeks, never see him again, no big deal? She envied those women.

She put on her most comfortable yoga pants when she got home and texted Maddie.

The Drew thing is over, I don't want to talk about it.

Her phone buzzed a second later.

You OK?

She dropped her favorite bra on her bedroom floor and shook her head.

I don't want to talk about it.

Maddie knocked on her door thirty minutes later with two bottles of wine poking out of her purse and a large pepperoni pizza in her hands.

"We don't have to talk," she said. "But I'm hungry, and I thought you might be hungry, too. And there's a marathon of *Say Yes to the Dress* on right now, so . . ."

Alexa took the pizza out of her hands and turned toward the couch.

"I'll get the wineglasses."

14

Alexa sat in her office the following Tuesday with the door closed. She'd closed it for a conference call, but the call was long over. She needed some time when no one would walk by and pop their head in, time when she wouldn't have to smile and act professional and interested. Time to studiously not think about what her long weekend would have been like if she hadn't sent those texts. She put her head down on her desk and closed her eyes.

She wished she could throw herself into work, but the whole day had been super slow because of Memorial Day the day before. Even though she was furiously making lists of who to talk to next and doing more research for her program, it felt like busywork more than anything else. Normally, she enjoyed quiet weeks at work where she could put her head down and clear things off her plate. But this week she needed all of the chaos that she wasn't getting.

Her phone buzzed, but she ignored it. It was probably Theo,

asking if she was free, or Maddie, checking up on her, or her cousin, needing a favor, and she just couldn't deal with anyone right now.

But even so, she pushed her phone under the curve of her arms and opened one eye to see who it was. Just in case.

Theo. The wave of disappointment hit all over again. It wasn't like she expected Drew to text her. There had been no word from him for a week, and she hadn't reached out to him, either. So why was she still hopeful?

She left her office without responding to Theo's text and walked up two flights of stairs to go to the bathroom. Less of a chance she'd see people that she'd have to talk to on another floor. She splashed cold water on her face, repaired her makeup, and installed a smile on her mouth before she went back down and knocked on Theo's door.

"You needed me?" She leaned against the doorframe and hoped this was short.

Theo looked up from his computer.

"Yeah, but this isn't about work. You're still coming to my birthday thing this weekend, right?"

Shit, she'd totally forgotten about Theo's birthday. On top of everything else, she was a terrible friend.

"Of course! Wouldn't miss it!"

Theo narrowed his eyes and beckoned her into his office.

"You forgot, didn't you?"

She gave up and slumped into a seat in front of his desk.

"Okay, yeah, but I'm sure it's on my calendar. It's not like I wasn't going to come. What's the plan, again?" She knew she'd talked to Theo about this at some point, but it was all mixed in with her cousin's engagement party and the grand opening next week of that new bar on Telegraph that the mayor had decided to attend.

"Now I know something is wrong with you. We're meeting at the Royal Arms in the Mission for drinks."

She made a face. "I hate that place."

"Yes, I know, that's what you said the last time we talked about it. But my buddy Nate is a part owner and is giving us a fat discount."

"I hate your buddy Nate," she said without any heat. She'd said that the last time, too; it was all coming back to her.

"I know. Dave will be there. He's always had a thing for you. Maybe he can pull you out of this funk."

She thought about denying that she was in a funk, but what was the point?

"I'll snap out of it at some point. Just stressed about everything with my program, that's all." She stood up to go back to her office and stopped in the doorway. "Who all else is coming? Can I bring Maddie?"

"People you like, I swear. I invited the whole crew from the campaign. But yeah, bring Maddie if you want."

♥

Drew went for two long runs on the beach over Memorial Day weekend. He repeatedly reminded himself that if he'd been up in Berkeley with Alexa, he wouldn't have been able to do that. He walked back home along the beach, checked out all of the women in bikinis, and tried and failed to make himself hit on one of them.

He went to a birthday party, one that he would have happily bailed on to be in Berkeley. He left before the blonde in the strapless dress who reminded him of Amy could put her hand on his ass again. Sunday afternoon, he almost texted Vivian, a girl he'd been sleeping with for a while in the fall, but he watched golf on the couch all afternoon instead. He was relieved to fill in for someone and be on call on Monday.

Carlos burst into Drew's office on Wednesday afternoon.

"Hey man, my trip to Hawaii was great, thanks for asking."

Drew looked up from his stack of files.

"You were in Hawaii?"

Carlos rolled his eyes and dropped into a chair.

"You're such an asshole. My cousin's wedding? I was a grooms-man? I left Friday morning, which is why you had to cover for me on Friday?"

He shrugged.

"Right, sorry that your travel schedule isn't on the top of my mind at every moment of the day. You have my apologies." He went back to puzzling out his own handwriting in his files.

"Wow, someone is still in a shitty mood, huh?" Carlos settled into the chair. Damn it, he should have just smiled and asked him about his trip and he would have been gone after a few minutes. Now he was going to have to deal with this bullshit.

"Just busy, that's all."

Carlos looked at the pile of files on his desk and raised his eyebrows. Drew only did this work when he was forced into it or had nothing else to do to keep him occupied, and Carlos knew it.

"So I'm guessing from the look on your face that you didn't go to Berkeley last weekend? Did you even try to fix it?"

Drew kept his eyes on his computer and attempted to keep his voice level.

"Leave it alone, Carlos."

Of course he'd thought about trying to fix it. But what was the point?

Carlos stood up, thank God.

"Fine, keep brooding. But you'd better have pulled yourself together by the time we go to San Francisco this weekend."

Drew's head shot up. What the hell was he talking about? Why the hell would he be going to San Francisco?

Carlos laughed. At, not with him, he was pretty sure.

"The American Association of Pediatric Hospital Medicine Conference? We planned it, like, two months ago? We're the only two junior peds from this hospital who get to go? We leave tomorrow?"

Drew laid his head down on his desk, lifted it, and banged it back down. Luckily, the files on his desk cushioned him.

"You remember now, I see." Carlos walked to the door. "Have fun packing."

Drew let out a sigh when he was finally alone again in his office. Great, just the place he didn't want to go. He jumped when Carlos poked his head back in the door.

"You should call her and tell her you'll be in town."

Drew got up and slammed the door in Carlos's face.

♥

Maddie was all in for Theo's party, especially since her on-again, off-again relationship with Chris was off, this time (she said) for good. Thank God; Alexa had never liked that guy. Maddie volunteered to be the designated driver for the night on the condition that Alexa wear whatever she ordered.

This meant that Alexa sat in Maddie's car Saturday night in a leather jacket and a strapless black dress, wearing altogether too much eye makeup and heels at least an inch too high. Sometimes giving the reins over to Maddie wasn't the best idea.

"Are you sure about this outfit?" she asked Maddie again, even though it was too late to change. "I have way too much cleavage with this dress, and this makeup isn't me. Plus, this is San Francisco. All of the dudes there will be in jeans and hoodies."

"Just because their standards are low does not mean that we should lower ours." Maddie backed into the parking spot on a side street that they'd found after ten minutes of circling. "And why do you care about your cleavage? What happened to 'If you've got them, flaunt them'?"

Alexa checked her reflection in the car mirror one last time.

"There are going to be a ton of douchebags here tonight, that's what happened. All of those tech bros that Theo's friend Nate knows. And the rest of the people there will be people I've worked with. I don't want them to think . . ."

Maddie jumped out of the car and shut the door. Alexa knew a hint to stop talking when she heard one.

She grinned when she looked at Maddie, wearing a hot pink minidress and tall black boots. Hopefully, at least Maddie would get some action tonight. She needed to find someone good to her after that asshole Chris.

"All right, fine," Alexa said. "Let's do this."

15

"I can't handle this for one more minute," Drew whispered to Carlos.

It was the awards dinner at the conference. The ballroom of the Palace Hotel was filled to the brim with self-congratulatory doctors. Drew wanted to stab himself in the head with a fork.

"On it," Carlos said. "I'm going to the bathroom in two minutes. Three minutes later, you go up to the bar for another drink. We'll meet up by the taxi stand outside and get the hell out of here."

In ten minutes, the two of them were in a cab, laughing at how well they'd executed their plan. It was the first moment of fun Drew had had in two days. The conference had been educational, sure, and he'd gotten to spend more time with Dr. Davis, his mentor from med school, but it had been two full days of networking and listening and smiling and taking notes, even in the hotel bar at night. And the whole time he kept trying to not remember that

Alexa was just a bridge away. Thank God Carlos was there, too. He would have died from either boredom or frustration otherwise.

"Where are we going?" He hadn't paid attention when Carlos had yelled out an address to the cabbie.

"I just told him 24th and Valencia. I figured we could find somewhere good to go around there, and no one from the conference is going to get that far from here." He thought for a minute. "And if they do, we want to know who they are so we can find them at next year's conference."

They walked into the first bar they found and were soon drinking bourbon and watching basketball with everyone else sitting at the bar. Halfway through the first bourbon their jackets were off and their ties were loosened. By the time they'd finished their drinks, they'd made friends with the bearded dudes on either side of them and their tattooed bartender, so much so that they ordered a large pizza for delivery to the bar, with the bartender's blessing.

After his third drink, Drew got up to find the bathroom. His new friends pointed him to the back of the bar, so he weaved through a crowd of people to get there. On his way back to his barstool he heard the laughter. He turned his head and saw her.

She was over in the corner, and a black dude in glasses had his arm around her. Without thinking about it, he walked toward them and stopped just outside their circle.

"Alexa."

She turned, and when her eyes met his, her smile blew him away all over again. It was hesitant at first, and then grew in strength, like a light with a dimming switch being turned up. He smiled back at her, trying to think of what to say, but between the bourbon and the hunger and her smile, his mind was blank.

"Drew. What . . . what are you doing here?"

She didn't sound upset to see him, and she was still smiling at him. Those were good signs. But that guy's arm was still around her.

Suddenly, instead of being on the other side of the circle of people from her, he was right in front of her.

"What am I doing at this bar, or in San Francisco?" he asked. He wanted to reach out for her but stopped himself.

"Either." She raised her eyebrows and her smile dimmed a little. "Both."

He touched her hand but didn't take it. Had he forgotten how good it felt to be around her, or had he forced himself to block that out?

"Conference. Carlos and I are both here." He inclined his head in the direction of the bar. "We had to bail on the awards dinner tonight, and somehow we ended up here." He moved closer to her, so their bodies were almost touching. He could feel her body heat through that tight dress she was wearing. She didn't move away. "And you?"

She looked away from him and at the pack of people surrounding them. Most of the people who'd been in the circle around her had melted away. Except for the dude in glasses and the woman in pink; they were both staring at him.

He stood close to her, hoping that the dude in glasses would get the hint. He didn't. Wait, was Alexa with this guy?

"It's Theo's birthday party, and—" The woman in pink elbowed her, not at all subtly, and she laughed again. "Sorry, sorry. Drew, this is Theo, the birthday boy, and this is my friend Maddie. Maddie, Theo: Drew."

Of course it was fucking Theo. Maddie shifted her drink to her other hand so they could shake hands.

"Maddie, nice to meet you. I've heard a lot about you." He turned. "You, too, Theo."

At least Theo'd had to move his arm away from Alexa's shoulder to shake Drew's hand.

Maddie grinned at him, her eyebrows dancing.

"Likewise, Drew. Now, if you'll excuse me, I've got to freshen up this drink. And I think the birthday boy needs another, don't you, Theo?" She disappeared in the direction of the bar with her almost-full drink and with an iron grip on Theo's arm. Drew was pretty sure he was going to like Maddie.

"Hi," he said, once they were alone. He touched her bare arm and this time didn't let go. "Can I, um—can we talk for a minute?" Now that he'd seen her, he couldn't just walk back to his barstool.

She looked in the direction that Theo and Maddie had disappeared in, and then back at him. Shit, was she going to tell him to go away?

"Sure," she finally said. He grabbed her hand and pulled her deeper into the corner.

"Look, I'm sorry about what I said. In the texts, I mean. I wasn't thinking," he said, once the din around them was a little quieter. He wanted to step closer but didn't want her to back away.

She squeezed his hand.

"No, Drew, I'm sorry. I shouldn't have started all of that. It wasn't . . . I didn't want . . ."

He looked down at her. That strapless dress she was wearing . . . he wanted to pull down the neckline and kiss her in that hollow between her breasts.

"I wasn't," he blurted out. "I mean, I'm not. I mean . . ." She looked up at him with a question in her eyes, and he realized how incoherent he was being. "What you asked me in that text. I'm not sleeping with anyone else."

When she met his eyes and smiled, he stepped closer to her. She didn't move away.

"You look great tonight," he said. She released his hand, and his heart fell for a second. When he felt her fingers stroke his waistline and pull him against her, he sighed in relief.

"I'm glad you're here," she said.

His hand moved from her arm to her waist. He bent down to kiss her just as she reached up to him.

The kiss was familiar and a surprise all at the same time. It was like coming home to kiss her, like sliding naked into a freshly made bed with sheets just from the dryer, warm and sexy and everything he wanted. He cupped her face and kissed her harder.

She bit his lip and he jumped.

"Were you getting me back for something there?" He licked her lip.

She laughed against his mouth, and he laughed with her. How had he even thought about giving her up?

"Just checking to make sure it's really you. That you're really here."

He felt a hand on his back and flinched. He turned his head and shielded Alexa with his body. If this was that Theo . . .

He relaxed when he saw Carlos behind him.

"When you're done here, there's pizza up at the bar, and . . . Alexa!" Carlos's voice lost the stiffness, and he backed away. "I'm sorry. I didn't realize it was you. Don't mind me. Good to see you, Alexa."

"Carlos!" She wiggled out from behind Drew to hug him.

"Good to see you, too. It's my friend Theo's birthday party. Let me introduce you guys to some people."

Alexa brought them both to the group around Theo and Maddie and did introductions all around. Theo didn't quite look thrilled to see him, but at least he didn't throw him out of the bar, not even when Alexa went off to the bathroom.

♥

Alexa was not at all surprised to find Maddie lying in wait for her outside the bathroom door.

"So that's Drew, huh?" Maddie said with a wide grin.

Alexa grinned back at her. Damn, had it felt good to flaunt him around the bar. And while he'd looked good every time she'd seen him, he looked especially good tonight, wearing a white button-down shirt with his tie loosened in that way that made her want to pull it all the way off and throw it on her bedroom floor. Or any bedroom floor.

"That's Drew."

Maddie grabbed her arm as she tried to walk back toward Drew and dragged her over to the bar.

"Is everything okay? Between you two, I mean."

Alexa smiled and shrugged.

"I think so."

Maddie raised one eyebrow. Damn, did she hate that Maddie could do that. She'd spent hours in front of the bathroom mirror as a teenager trying to figure out how to do it, with no luck.

The biggest problem with it was whenever Maddie did it to her, it worked.

"Last week . . . we had a fight. I started it—well, we both

said stupid things, but I started it. He definitely made it *worse,* though. Anyway, we made up. And no, he's not sleeping with anyone else."

Maddie grinned and took a sip of her weak gin and tonic.

"Excellent. So . . . back together, then?"

Alexa laughed.

"I don't know if 'together' is the right word. How about, I'm back to trying to not overthink things. I'm just . . . happy he's here right now, Mads. And that he seems happy to be here. With me. I'm going to enjoy being happy for now, okay?"

Maddie handed her a drink and clinked their glasses together.

"I am one hundred percent in favor of you being happy."

She walked back over to Drew to find him deep in conversation with Nate. She turned to go ask Theo if he needed another drink, but before she could move away, Drew's arm slid around her waist and secured her to his side. It turned out she didn't even mind douchey Nate so much when she had Drew's arm around her and his warm body against hers.

After a few minutes, she saw Maddie whisper something in Theo's ear. Weird to see Theo and Maddie being friendly; they'd only ever barely tolerated each other before.

"Hey, Nate, what was that bourbon you wanted me to try?" Theo asked a few seconds later.

"Oh, it's behind the bar. Let me go with you to show you. I brought it back from my trip to Kentucky. There are only a hundred cases of it produced a year. You're lucky that I . . ." As they walked away, Theo turned back to her and winked.

She turned to Drew to make fun of Nate, but his mind was elsewhere.

"As much as I like your friends," he said, his fingers stroking her waist, "I haven't seen you in two weeks, and I've missed you. You think we can take off anytime soon?"

She should probably play it cool, right? Not show how much she couldn't wait to be alone with him, how delighted she was that he'd told her he missed her; not admit how much she'd missed him, too, and that she desperately wanted to be naked in a bed—or out of a bed—with him. Not jump when he said how high. Yes, she absolutely should play it cool.

"Give me thirty seconds to get my jacket and tell Maddie I'm leaving."

"I like that jacket," Drew said as they stood outside, after summoning a ride by pressing a button on his phone.

She zipped it up against the frigid San Francisco summer night.

"Thanks, Maddie made me wear it tonight." The way he was looking at her, she owed Maddie a bottle of wine for forcing her into this outfit. She remembered the bottles Maddie had brought over to her house after she'd sent those ill-fated text messages. Okay, maybe she owed Maddie a few bottles of wine.

"I'd like it even more if you were naked underneath it." He played with the zipper, running it up and down while his eyes followed his fingers. She shivered.

"How much would you like it?" She stared at his fingers moving along her chest. She wanted him to stop and linger, but he just kept up that slow movement. Had she thought it was cold tonight? If she stood there with him any longer, she'd get so hot she would combust.

"Mmmm." He took her hand and let her feel how much this was getting to him, too. "This much, I think. What do you think about that?"

She moved her fingers up and down over him like he was doing to her. She was gratified to hear his intake of breath.

"I think we'd better get to your hotel as soon as possible."

♥

All Drew wanted was to make out with Alexa in the back seat like teenagers. Unfortunately, they had the chattiest driver ever, and Drew was drawn into conversation with him despite himself. By the end of the ride, their new friend Miguel had given them the address of his favorite taco truck and his theories on gentrification.

Alexa giggled as they got on the elevator.

"What?" He pretended to scowl and pushed her against the back of the elevator. She didn't resist and kept laughing.

"You say I'm the politician, and yet tonight you bonded with our driver and had a long conversation with Nate, of all people. I think your whole sour-face thing the weekend of the wedding was all pretense."

He held on to her arm and trapped her against the wall.

"Keep talking like that, and I can't promise what will happen. Interesting things happen to us in elevators, you know."

She licked his neck, bit down, and licked again. Had he really planned to never see this girl again?

"I'm growing to like elevators quite a bit," she said as the doors opened for his floor.

He fumbled in his pocket for the door key and realized two things. One: he wanted to pick her up and throw her on his bed again. Two: he really had to pee. Shit. He'd better make it quick.

He pulled her inside the room.

"Don't move. Give me one second. I'll be right back." He flew into the bathroom and hoped that the look on her face hadn't been

irritation or—oh God—a change of heart. Maybe she'd remembered she was mad at him? That thought made him zip his pants
quickly, in case he had to convince her to stay.

When he opened the door, she wasn't standing in the entryway
where he'd left her. She hadn't left, had she? He looked around the
room and . . . holy shit.

She was propped up against the pillows on the bed, wearing
that leather jacket, those heels . . . and nothing else. He unbuckled
his belt.

"I thought I told you not to move?" he asked her as he approached the bed.

She nodded, her fingers zipping and unzipping the jacket like
he'd done earlier.

"It's true. You did tell me that. But you also told me you wanted
to see me in this jacket and nothing else. Do you want me to put
my clothes back on?"

He dropped his pants to the floor and stepped out of them,
kicking off his shoes in the process.

"Over my dead body." He crawled onto the bed and straddled
her. He grabbed her hands and pulled them away from that zipper.
She watched him play with it for a while, as her hands ran up and
down his body. Then, without any warning, she pulled off his tie
and threw it onto the floor.

"I've been wanting to do that all night."

He unzipped the jacket all the way, rolled over, and pulled her
on top of him. She sighed and leaned against his chest. He loved
the way she always relaxed into his arms whenever he touched her.
Even at the bar, when they hadn't seen each other for two weeks
and he knew she was mad at him, as soon as he'd pulled her against
him, her body had molded to his.

"I missed this," she said.

He turned them both over so he was on top of her again and kissed her in that hollow between her breasts that he loved so much.

"Did you miss this? Or did you miss . . . me?"

She opened her eyes and held his gaze for a long moment.

"Both."

He smiled.

"That's what I wanted you to tell me."

♥

"You have too many clothes on." Alexa unbuttoned his shirt all the way. He pulled it and his undershirt off and threw them across the room.

"I was in too much of a hurry to take them all off," he said.

She pushed him onto his back and enjoyed the sensation of the warm, firm skin of his chest under her fingers. It wasn't like she'd forgotten how much she liked having sex with him—that was impossible to forget. But somehow, she'd forgotten how free she felt with him. How she could relax enough to lie naked on his bed in only a leather jacket and high heels and wait for him. She'd never been this confident with anyone else.

"Drew?" She paused as her hand ventured lower on his body. "You do have condoms, don't you?"

He grinned without opening his eyes.

"The same box I bought the last time I was in a hotel room in San Francisco with you. I didn't take it out of my bag." He opened his eyes. "Why, is there something else you've been missing?"

She caressed his hips, and he closed his eyes again.

"Mmmmhmmmm," she said.

"Are you going to tell me what that is, or am I going to have to guess?"

"Hmmm, I think you should guess. But be quick about it. I've been missing . . . it so much. Everything feels so . . . ." She rubbed his chest again, up and down, and stopped just at the base of his stomach. "So sensitive. I feel like I'm going to explode for needing . . . it."

When he opened his eyes, the need on his face almost pushed her back against the bed. He jumped off the bed and dove for his luggage, coming up a few seconds later with a triumphant look on his face and a box of condoms.

"Oh, I have a guess." He dropped the box on the nightstand and tore open a condom packet as he stood next to the bed and looked at her. "I'm going to guess over and over again. All night long and most of the day tomorrow. We have to make up for lost time."

The next morning, Alexa sat back against the plush pillows of the hotel bed and watched him pour coffee from the room service carafe into her mug. He added one sugar and handed it to her before pouring his own.

She beamed down at her mug. She couldn't help it. He remembered how she took her coffee. She cupped her hands around the mug and let the warmth spread through her body.

He got in bed next to her and pulled the basket of pastries up to join them.

"One of the best things about hotels," he said, "is that you can get crumbs in the bed without worrying about it. I know it's no doughnut, but do you want the bear claw?"

He turned toward her halfway through his raspberry Danish.

"Hey, what's going on with your program for teenagers? The arts thing?"

She paused midway through pouring herself more coffee to smile at him. Wow, did it feel good for him to care enough to ask about that.

"I'm cautiously optimistic. The goal is to get it on the city council calendar for mid-July. Keep your fingers crossed."

He tore the top off the blueberry muffin and offered her half.

"Great, will do." He held up two crossed fingers and poured her more coffee.

"I saw Abby and Jack the other day, by the way. She told me about how much you're helping them. Thanks for that." He leaned over to kiss her. His lips were sprinkled with sugar. Perfect.

"When do we have to be out of here?" She looked around him to the clock radio on the bedside table. "It's almost ten. Wait, when's your flight?"

"Twelve thirty, but I can change it, like I . . ." His voice trailed away as he turned away from her to pick up his phone. "I can change to the flight at eight tonight?"

"Yeah, that works." She was glad he looked back down at his phone and couldn't see how wide her smile was.

He moved the pastry basket to the foot of the bed and put his arm around her.

"Last night . . . you didn't say whether *you* were sleeping with anyone else."

"Oh." She hadn't expected him to bring this up again. And her whole "don't overthink it" motto certainly wouldn't have let her do it. "No, I'm not."

"Good." He smiled and leaned down to kiss her, but she pulled away. Now that he *had* brought it up . . .

"I don't want this to be . . . but when you said you weren't sleeping with anyone else, did you mean . . . I know you meant the 'not at the moment' thing as a joke, but—"

He kissed her cheek and pulled her against him.

"What I mean by that is that you're the only person I've slept with since I met you in that elevator, and that as long as we're doing this thing, that will remain the case. Okay?"

"As long as we're doing this thing" rang in her ears. She knew it meant there was a time limit on their relationship, such as it was. But she didn't want to push this conversation too far; she didn't want to fight with him and spoil it all again, so she buried those misgivings.

She rested her head on his shoulder.

"Okay."

He lifted his hand to her cheek and rested it there for a moment before turning her toward him for a long, slow kiss.

"Now, let's make good use of our last hour of this hotel room, shall we?"

16

When Alexa got in Drew's car at LAX the following Saturday morning, he kissed her for so long that airport security banged on his window to move him along. Oops.

"How was the event last night?" he said when he finally drove away from the curb. The mayor had had a big charity event the night before, so Alexa couldn't fly down until Saturday morning. Drew was on call that night, so he couldn't fly up.

"It went well, I think. I haven't had a chance to check to see what the press said about it. I crashed when I got home, and the Wi-Fi was broken on the plane." She settled against the seat and grinned at him. "Is one of those coffee cups for me?"

He lifted the coffee he'd gotten her out of the cup holder and handed it to her.

"The drive from the coffee shop to the airport should have cooled it down enough for your delicate tongue."

She lifted the coffee halfway up, paused, and opened her mouth. He laughed.

"I love that you're going to make that joke, but I just meant you're always complaining about coffee being too hot."

She smirked and put her purse on the floor in front of her before she took a sip. Then she looked up at him.

"Hey, Drew?"

He fought back a smile. He knew what was coming.

"Hey, Alexa?"

"What's in this bag right here?" she asked, pointing to the waxy paper bag at her feet. They both knew what was inside.

He didn't fight his smile anymore.

"Why don't you open it up and see?"

"Doughnuts! And they're still warm? How did you manage that? You're my hero." She'd bitten into one almost before she finished that sentence. He looked over to see pure bliss on her face and grinned. The only other time her face looked like that was right after sex. Maybe he needed to work to keep that look on her face more often.

Thank God for that conference. He was so glad this woman was back in his life.

On the way back to his apartment, they drove by the Santa Monica Pier.

"I haven't been there since I was a kid," she said. "It was always so fun."

An SUV pulled out of a parking spot ahead of him, and he made a snap decision.

"No time like the present." He reversed into the spot and grabbed her hand. "Let's go."

When they got back to his apartment, they were both giddy, sunburned, and exhausted. They'd ridden the rides, played arcade games, eaten too much, and laughed even more. They'd even goaded each other into temporary tattoos—she'd gotten a flower on her cheek; he'd gotten an anchor on his bicep. Before they'd come back to his apartment, she'd made him run down into the water with her and shrieked when he splashed her.

They dropped down onto his couch as soon as they walked in the door. She leaned her head against his shoulder, and he pulled her tighter against him. She curled her legs up on the couch so that her body was tucked against his. He wanted to drag her into the bedroom for a long afternoon sex session, or even just have her here on the couch again. But right now they were so comfortable. He'd wait just a few minutes.

He woke up when the afternoon sun came through his kitchen windows and hit him in the eye. They'd somehow moved in their sleep to lying almost flat on the couch, but her head was still tucked in the nook of his shoulder, and his arm was still tight around her. He could stay like this for another few hours.

His stomach rumbled.

Oh, right. Except for that. The hot dogs and cotton candy from the pier couldn't hold him forever.

She squeezed her eyes together and stirred, turning into his chest, away from the light. She kissed his chest as she snuggled against him, and the warmth from her casual caress spread through his body.

"Mmmngry," she said into his collarbone.

"Hmmm?" He stroked her hair away from her face. Remnants of the flower were still on her cheek. He rubbed at it with his thumb.

She lifted her head a few centimeters.

"I can't believe you talked me into this flower. I'm sure I look ridiculous."

He smiled down at her, her cheek pink and creased from being against his chest.

"You look beautiful."

She pulled his head down to hers and kissed him, her hands in his hair.

"I'm hungry," she said against his lips. "You?"

He chuckled and ran his hands over her hair to her back, and then again. A woman after his own heart.

"Starving. What's your feeling on burgers and fries? We should probably eat here instead of going out, since I'm on call tonight . . ."

She kissed his collarbone again.

"I have very positive feelings about burgers and fries. Eating here is perfect, since I accidentally glued myself to this couch."

He kissed her ear to make her giggle and rolled out from underneath her and stood up.

"Good thing you have me. I'll go pick them up and bring them back here while you try desperately to unglue yourself."

So they ate their burgers on the couch while they watched terrible movies on Netflix and kept their fingers crossed that he wouldn't have to go into the hospital.

It was probably a real risk to pull her into the bedroom . . . but he was on call until six in the morning. Was he supposed to not have sex with her tonight?

Afterward, damp and panting, he reached blindly for his phone to make sure he hadn't missed a call. Just then it rang.

He kissed her hard and jumped out of bed after he got off the phone.

"I've got to go. Keep the bed warm for me, okay?"

She turned and looked up at him with that smile that always made his heart turn over.

"I'll be here when you get back," she said.

"I'm counting on it."

♥

It took Alexa a while to fall asleep after he left. It wasn't like she wasn't used to sleeping alone. But she missed him next to her.

She wouldn't admit this to anyone other than herself, and then only late at night, but ever since that first weekend with him, every night when she lay in bed she imagined him there with her. Even those nights right after their stupid fight. She would think of his strong arms around her, hear his slow, steady breathing, feel his chest rise and fall, and his warm body against hers, and it all lulled her to sleep. It felt silly to do it there in his bed alone, but she did it anyway.

She woke up in the middle of the night to feel him pull her against him. When his arms were around her, she felt like nothing else mattered. Like nothing bad could ever touch her.

"Everything okay?" she whispered.

He kissed her forehead.

"It is now. Go back to sleep."

After a lazy day on the beach the next day, they went out for Mexican food Sunday night. She took a sip of her margarita, and her lips puckered at the salty/sweet tang of the drink. She took a bite of a salsa-laden chip and smiled. Chips and salsa were tied up there with cheese and crackers for the perfect snack food. Maybe not as perfect for being stuck in an elevator, but . . . He interrupted her tequila-influenced musings.

"I'm not on call next weekend, so I can come up." He paused. "If that works for you."

She licked the salt from the corner of her mouth and noticed his eyes follow the movement of her tongue. She smiled and did it again.

"Yeah, that works for me."

She got to the office the next day, feeling much more wide awake than any woman who'd been on a seven a.m. flight from LAX had any reason to be. But when she had a wake-up call like Drew's . . . well, that was going to keep her awake all day.

Theo poked his head in her door on his way into the office.

"I don't need to ask how your weekend was; that look on your face says it all."

Her cheeks got hot, and she tried to tone down her smile, but when Theo plopped in her chair and handed her a doughnut, it blossomed again.

"I'll try to pull myself together by staff meeting."

Theo bit into his own doughnut and took a sip of her coffee. They'd long ago started taking coffee the same way to simplify their lives.

"You going to see him again? Or is that an 'of course'?"

She tried not to let her smile take over her whole face but probably failed.

"He's coming up this weekend."

She switched the conversation to work so she wouldn't get carried away.

"What do you think the press will say about my program? Who are we targeting to leak about it? Or do you think an interview?"

Theo stood up.

"That reminds me," he said. "We need to name this thing. It needs a good terrible acronym."

Just then, the mayor poked his head in Alexa's office.

"Thought I'd find you both here. Just wanted to let you know Richards is against the delinquent project. He fought me on it at dinner this weekend."

Shit. Richards was the city councilman from the Berkeley Hills, and a good friend of the mayor's. She opened her mouth to defend her project, point by point, when the mayor stopped her.

"Alexa. You don't need to argue with me on this. I'm on your side; this is our program now. I'm just telling you what we're up against and what work has to be done. Just huddle with Theo and figure out a plan, okay?"

She smiled at him.

"Yes, sir."

♥

Drew had driven straight to the hospital after dropping Alexa off at the airport. Even though that gave him plenty of time to get through his pile of stupid paperwork, he didn't get much done.

Usually when he got home in the middle of the night after a stressful surgery he felt exhausted and wrung dry. But Saturday night when he'd walked into his bedroom and seen her there in his bed, he'd felt a sense of homecoming that he hadn't felt in years. And when he'd wrapped his arms around her and she'd curled her body against his, his whole self had felt at peace.

He shook his head in an attempt to pull himself back to earth, or at least to his office. Why was he being such a teenager over this one girl? He was acting like this was the first girl he'd ever slept with.

He was going to have to break up with her soon. If he didn't, he'd invariably do something to fuck it all up again. How terrible would it be when she looked at him with loathing in her eyes instead of that smile?

He couldn't end things yet, though. They'd just started back up again. Maybe after this coming weekend.

He'd settled back in with the paperwork when his phone buzzed. He snatched at it, but it was just Carlos asking if he wanted anything from Starbucks.

Large with a shot of espresso.

He'd already had coffee with Alexa this morning, but after not a lot of sleep and getting up early to go to the airport, he'd need more caffeine than usual today.

As Carlos walked into his office, his phone buzzed again. This time, it *was* her.

Landed, but there were no doughnuts waiting for me at Oakland airport, terrible way to get off a plane.

He laughed down at his phone and looked up to see that smirk on Carlos's face.

"Good weekend, I take it?"

He picked up his coffee and took a sip.

"You can stop gloating anytime now. Yes, yes, you told me so." Carlos grinned.

"As long as you remember that. When're you seeing her again?"

He shrugged.

"This weekend I'm going up there." Carlos's grin got bigger. "Don't give me that look! Don't make a big deal out of this!"

Carlos rolled his eyes as he left the room.

17

Alexa and Theo and their deputies huddled and came up with an acronym (Teen Arts Rehabilitation Program, or TARP, a name she and Theo knew they'd be mocked about forever), a deadline (the city council meeting in July), and a schedule of community meetings to hopefully garner support. This all meant Alexa was at work until eight or nine the whole week, and spent a few more hours working at home on her couch every night.

She probably would have worked a few hours less that week if she hadn't been texting with Drew in between every meeting, but she couldn't help it. His texts always made her smile, made her relax after tense moments, and sometimes made her blush.

Him being so far away was starting to make her go crazy. Why couldn't she drive straight to his house from one of her long workdays to get rid of some of her frustration in the best possible way? Why couldn't she wake up with him in her bed in the mornings, so at least she'd have those five minutes before she pulled herself out of the warm circle of his arms to feel content and at peace?

Text messages were great and all, but . . . well, she was happy he was coming up this weekend.

♥

Drew loved feeling the buzz in his pocket and knowing it was her, that anticipation of reading what she'd said throughout the day, the smile she always put on his face. And he really loved the texts they sent each other late at night . . . and sometimes referred to throughout the day.

He told her about the baby who peed on him, causing both him and the baby's dad to double over with laughter; the five-year-old twins who both broke their arms when they jumped off the roof "just to see if they could"; the little girl who swallowed a penny during a temper tantrum and giggled uncontrollably when she saw it on her X-ray.

One day she had a meeting that he could tell stressed her out from just the length of her first text.

The good news is that my boss is firmly behind the project, and that is really good news . . . but the bad news is that some other important people aren't, and this is going to be a fight. I'm thrilled about the first thing but kind of freaking out about the second.

He tucked his files under his arm so he could respond.

That's awesome about your boss. You were worried, right?

Her response came a few seconds later.

Yeah, I was. Never realized he trusted me this much! But now I feel like I have to fight even harder.

He sat down on the exam room table to think about his response.

He didn't know anything about city politics in Berkeley other than what she'd told him. It wasn't like he could give her good or useful advice when she knew everything and he knew virtually nothing. All he could give her was his support, which felt like it didn't matter. He thought about texting, *You can do it!* but that felt stupid.

He's lucky to have you in his corner.

That was all he came up with. It didn't feel good enough.

Her response took enough time that he wondered if he'd gotten it totally wrong. He walked down the hall to his office. His phone buzzed just as he set his files down at his desk.

That means so much, thank you. I really appreciate it.

At first, he tried to keep himself from grinning at his phone. But Carlos wasn't around to gloat or make fun of him, so he stopped trying and smiled so hard his cheeks hurt.

♥

"I'm sorry I had to work all weekend," Alexa said as she drove him to the airport on Sunday night.

"Not *all* weekend," he said, his eyebrows dancing. She poked him and laughed.

"You know what I mean! Anyway, I know it was a boring weekend. I wish we could have gone out and done more, but these next few weeks are going to be so . . ." Just thinking about everything riding on her work made her anxious all over again.

He put his hand on her thigh. That got her attention in more than one way. His hand there, so big and strong and firm and gentle, made her think of all of the other places his hands had been that weekend. She blushed as she looked down at it.

"Monroe, stop apologizing. I had a great time with you. Hanging out on the couch together was fine. I know you have a lot going on. I'm glad you didn't want me to cancel my trip in the first place."

She put her hand on top of his and held it in place. No matter how much work she had, it had never occurred to her to ask him to cancel.

"I just wish I hadn't been on my laptop or on the phone with Theo half the time you were here." Was he mad about that? He hadn't seemed mad, but a few times when Theo had called and she'd picked up, he'd left the room.

He turned his hand over and interlaced his fingers with hers.

"It's okay. We'll have next time. It sucks that we can't do next weekend, though."

She had community meetings both Saturday and Sunday, and he was on call, so he couldn't fly up. It was for the best, anyway; her cousin Becca's engagement party was on Friday night, and it wasn't like she could bring him along with her to that. They had a sex-up-against-her-bedroom-wall kind of relationship, not a come-meet-my-family kind of relationship.

But she was really sad about not being able to see him for two weeks. She felt a little panicky about how sad she was.

And even though he seemed like he was sad about it, too, she still had "as long as we're doing this thing" echoing in her head.

She moved her hand back to the steering wheel.

"I don't know how you're going to survive without me for two whole weeks. Maybe Carlos will make fun of how much sugar you put in your coffee and how you can't handle spicy food, just to keep you on your toes."

He laughed and moved his hand off her knee. Hmmm. Just because she'd let go of his hand didn't mean she wanted him to move it.

"You and Carlos have only met each other twice. How is it that you're so in tune? He'll do that without any prompting. Don't worry about it."

He kissed her hard when she pulled up at the curb.

"See you in two weeks?" he asked, as his fingers stroked her cheek.

When he looked into her eyes like that, she would say yes to anything he asked her. *Do you want to rob a Vegas casino with me, I promise it's for a good cause? Let's go skydiving! Tell me all of your deepest and darkest secrets.* She'd have said yes to it all.

"Definitely."

♥

Drew took a picture of the cheese and cracker plate he'd bought at the airport and texted it to Alexa when he got on the plane.

Don't you wish you were sharing this with me?

He'd had such a good time with Alexa that weekend. This thing obviously couldn't last that much longer, but why mess with a good thing? Ever since they'd gotten back together, being with her had been so relaxed and fun. It felt so comfortable. Maybe a little too comfortable?

Perhaps it was good that he wasn't going to see her for two weeks. It made everything easier. More low-key. This was why she was the perfect person for him to date—she lived on the opposite end of the state, she had a super busy job, and they couldn't see each other that often. And when they did see each other, it was great. See, perfect.

He laughed when the flight landed and a text from her lit up his screen.

You ate me out of house and home this weekend, Nichols . . . and cheese and crackers.

Accompanying the text was a picture of three open and empty cracker boxes and a cheese rind.

He put his phone back in his pocket, still smiling.

He ignored the weight in his chest at the thought of not seeing her smile for fourteen days. It was probably just all of that cheese.

♥

Theo narrowed his eyes at her when she walked in on Monday morning.

"Coffee. Let's go." He had her outside before she could even put her purse down.

"What's wrong?" he asked, as soon as they were far enough away from the building so they wouldn't be overheard. "Were things bad this weekend? Was Drew an ass about you needing to work?"

She sighed. Had her poker face gotten that bad or did Theo know her that well?

"No, he was great. He was great about everything. It's just . . . we're both busy next weekend, so it's going to be a little while before we see each other again, that's all."

There were too many people they knew inside the coffee shop, so after they'd gotten their coffee, he steered her in the opposite direction of City Hall.

"You've been seeing each other every weekend, right?" Theo asked her.

She shrugged.

"Yeah. I mean, we hadn't planned on it that way. It just sort of happened." She avoided his eyes.

He tore off a piece of his pastry and handed it to her.

"This thing seems to be getting kind of serious. Have you guys talked about what's going on between you two?"

She shook her head. All she wanted was coffee. Why did she have to get the third degree? She was irritated with Theo for bringing this up, irritated with herself that tears had popped into her eyes. She blew into her coffee cup so Theo couldn't see them.

"Nah, it's just fun. It's not like it can go anywhere. He doesn't really do serious. Plus, I don't think either of us can keep up this kind of travel schedule for too long. My finances certainly aren't up to many more plane tickets. I'm just going to enjoy it while it lasts."

Theo was still looking at her. She took a sip of too-hot coffee to brace herself and winced. She looked back up at him with what she hoped looked like a genuine smile.

"Okay." He stopped on the corner, forcing her to stop, too. "If you say so. I'm just worried that—"

"Theo. Enough."

She hadn't meant to snap at him. She never snapped at Theo. But she couldn't handle this conversation anymore. She didn't want to think about this, let alone talk about it. She shook her head.

"Sorry, Teddy, I'm sorry. I just can't do this right now, okay?"

He threw an arm around her shoulder and pulled her into a side hug.

"It's okay. But you know, if you ever want to talk . . ."

She leaned into the hug.

"I know. Now, let's go get our TARP off the ground."

Theo groaned. She laughed.

"Oh, don't you worry, I'm going to make so many jokes like that in the next few weeks. It's going to be great."

♥

"You've sure been in a shitty mood this week," Carlos said as they walked to their cars after basketball on Wednesday night. "I can't wait for you to see Alexa this weekend so you stop knocking people down on the court."

Drew threw his gym bag in the trunk of his car.

"I didn't knock that guy down! I dove for the ball, and he happened to be in the way."

Carlos laughed at him and leaned against Drew's car, which prevented him from driving away in a huff. He could still do it; he'd just maybe back over his best friend. Which, given the way Carlos had been annoying him this week . . .

"You going up there this weekend or is she coming down? If she's coming here, you should bring her to Angie's party. It'll be a blast."

He should definitely back over him.

"Neither." He opened his door and waited for Carlos to take the hint and get in his own car.

He didn't.

"What do you mean, neither? Neither what?"

Drew sighed. Now Carlos was going to make a big deal about this.

"Neither going up nor coming down, is what I mean. We're not seeing each other this weekend. Other commitments."

There, that was easy, right? He got in the car, but before he could shut the door, Carlos grabbed it.

"*That's* why you're so crabby this week! You're not seeing your girl this weekend."

Drew shook his head.

"She's not—"

Carlos shut the door on him, but he could hear Carlos yelling anyway.

"And don't even try to say she's not your girl!"

♥

She missed Drew even more that week than she'd thought she would. It was weird to miss him so much on a Wednesday. They never saw each other on Wednesdays. But somehow just knowing that it would be another full week and a half before she saw him made it that much harder to be alone on her couch that night.

She looked over to the opposite end of the couch, picturing him there the way he'd been the weekend before. It had been so comfortable—her on her laptop, him half watching the basketball game and half reading through the pile of medical journal articles in his lap; not talking, just being together. Sometimes she would read part of her city council presentation out loud and he would help her wordsmith it, or ask her questions that made her realize she was using too much jargon and needed to simplify. She hadn't realized how helpful he could be.

Periodically, one of them would get up to fetch drinks or snacks for both of them. They'd share a quick kiss as they both settled back in to work . . . well, okay, sometimes the kisses hadn't been so quick, but only sometimes. She'd worried that he'd been bored, but then if he'd been bored, he wouldn't want her to go down there for 4th of July weekend, right?

She picked up her phone to text him but put it back down. It wasn't like she couldn't text him at all—they'd been texting each other plenty for the past few days—but in the maudlin mood she was in, she'd probably say, *Drew, I miss you, I wish I was seeing you this weekend, I'm counting the days until I see you next.* Which . . . that was all true, but some things she didn't need to share with him. Or anyone else.

♥

At Drew's sister Angela's party on Saturday night, Drew kept thinking about how much more fun it would be if Alexa was there with him. He tried to shake that thought off. He wasn't drinking, because he was on call; that was probably why he was so irritable.

But his irritation washed away when his phone buzzed in his pocket. He grinned at the text from her: a picture of a pile of doughnuts, arranged and stacked like a wedding cake.

Look at what they had at the community meeting!

He walked into the hallway to text her back.

They obviously don't know you that well. None of them have sprinkles.

After two more texts, he gave up on the party and disappeared out the back door to get to his car. He called her before his car was out of park.

"Hey!" she said, that warm sound of laughter in her voice. Was she laughing because of his texts, or was she out with other people?

"Hey! How was the meeting other than the doughnuts?"

He heard noise and chatter in the background. When she said a muffled, "Be right back," the noise receded. So she was with other people.

Not that she wasn't allowed to go out when he wasn't there, but he'd sort of pictured her sitting home on the couch missing him.

"It went really well, I think! I hope we have lots of parents and teachers on our side. Getting drinks with Theo and some others from work now."

"That's great. How many people were there?"

She gushed for a few more minutes about the meeting, before he heard a muffled voice saying, "Alexa! Another margarita?"

"Sounds like you should go," he didn't want to say but said anyway.

She laughed again, clearly in a great mood.

"Probably, otherwise they'll drink all of the tequila without me. Talk to you later?"

"Yeah, talk to you later."

Why wasn't he there with her and stupid Theo and her great mood right now? He should be there, to see that laughter on her face in person, to hug her after a good night, to throw his arm around her when she was relaxed and tipsy after a few margaritas and the high that comes from a job well done.

He was almost relieved to get a call from the hospital a few minutes later to get his mind off her.

18

Alexa woke up with a smile on her face on Sunday morning, after the meeting at the church on Saturday night and Drew's unexpected phone call. They almost never called each other—they mostly communicated via text or occasionally email. Maybe he'd missed her that weekend like she'd missed him?

But the smile got wiped off her face on Sunday afternoon. There was another community meeting in the Berkeley Hills about her program, and everyone there hated it. Well, they all pretended to like it, with all sorts of platitudes about how it would be a great thing if programs like this one worked, and how they cared so much about troubled children, and how great it was that the mayor had come up with such a creative plan.

The problem was that all of those sentences had a great big BUT in the middle of them: but how do we know this would work; but these kids would be out on the street and still in school; but they'd influence other kids in school and turn them to a life of crime; but shouldn't we put city resources into programs for *young* children so we could make sure they stayed on the right track in the first place; and on and on and on.

She'd prepared for this, of course. And the mayor had a list of talking points with answers to all of those questions. But she still felt deflated when she left.

She wished, not for the first time, that this program wasn't so important to her. That she didn't have so much of her own history and identity and absolution and vindication tied up in this one effort. She wished that this was just a regular run-of-the-mill project, like the playgrounds or the bike lanes or the farmers' market expansions, not one where, if this effort failed, she would feel like she'd failed her whole family.

She wanted to go home and call Drew and spill all of this out to him. She almost did, especially after his out-of-the-blue call from the night before.

But though they'd talked about a lot in the past month and a half, they hadn't gotten that personal. She didn't know if they had that kind of relationship yet. Or if they would ever. What if he checked out after she spilled her guts to him? Could she handle that?

Probably not. And that was the problem. She wanted him waiting for her when she got home; she wanted to talk to him about everything she was feeling; she wanted him to listen, to ask her questions, to reassure her, to tuck her into his chest and wrap his arms around her. But she knew none of those things were going to happen. She had to remember that.

She tried to push those wants down into the depths of her brain and stopped for ice cream on the way home instead.

♥

Tuesday afternoon, Drew had a follow-up appointment with Jack. Only Abby was with him this time, and after he exchanged fist bumps with Jack, she turned to him.

"So how's your . . . friend Alexa?"

He felt like he should shut down a question like this from a patient's mom, but he was too happy to talk about Alexa to someone who wouldn't make fun of him later that he couldn't.

"She's great. I'm sure she'll want me to say hi to you for her." He knew that her real question was whether "friend" was the right word to define Alexa, but he avoided answering that. "How did Jack do with the MRI yesterday? I know you were worried."

She patted Jack on the head. "He handled it with flying colors. Thanks for asking."

Drew smiled at Jack. "Good job, Jacky, staying in that machine like you did. Most kids your age couldn't manage that." He turned back to Abby. "I don't have his results yet, but they should have been here by now. Let me go check on that."

He found the report in his office. Read it once, then again. He ran across the hospital to find Dr. Montgomery and had him look at it, too. He sat down in his office with his eyes closed for a moment before he forced himself to walk back into the exam room.

Abby looked up from her book with a smile on her face when she saw him, but her smile dropped away. Thank God Jack had fallen asleep on the table.

"What is it?"

He sat down next to her and took a deep breath.

"Dr. Nichols, what is it?"

Shit, he just had to tell her. Why was doing this part of his job still so hard?

"Abby. I'm so sorry I kept you waiting, but I wanted to double-check a few things with another doctor here. We won't know for sure without additional testing, but there's a mass in one of Jack's lymph nodes. Initial indications are that it's cancer."

Abby went very still. She closed her book without marking the page and stared at him without a word.

He shouldn't have spit it out like that; he should have done a better job of leading up to the C word. Telling parents bad news was the worst part of his job.

"I've already called our best pediatric oncologist for a consult, so if you can bring him back in Thursday morning, we can start doing more testing and, if necessary, come up with a plan."

She stared back at him, still without saying anything. He wanted to touch her, or Jack, or say something to reassure her. But he couldn't do any of those things.

"Abby? Can I call someone? Should I call Fred?"

She stood up and swayed for a second. He jumped to his feet and reached out to steady her, but she pulled back.

"Okay. Can you . . . can you just have someone call me with details about the appointment on Thursday? I should take Jack home. I should call Fred. We need to . . ." Her voice trailed away as she picked Jack up and carried him out of the room.

Drew sat back down and put his head in his hands. There was probably no good way to have that conversation, but knowing that didn't make him feel any better.

When he stood up to go back to his office, he noticed Abby had left her book on the table. He tucked it in Jack's file, so it would be there for her on Thursday.

He stumbled through his next few appointments, the look on Abby's face in the forefront of his mind the whole time.

Thank God he was finished with appointments early that day. Hopefully, he could leave the office without running into anyone. He didn't want to see or talk to anyone. Well, there was one person he wanted to both see and talk to, but that was impossible. She was far away from this hospital right now.

Except . . . she wasn't that far, was she?

He made it to his car without talking to anyone and drove straight to LAX.

♥

Alexa was still depressed on Tuesday from the meeting on Sunday night. Even though she'd huddled with Theo and the mayor on Monday morning, she was convinced they had no chance of victory, at least not this time. The people in the hills had too much influence. They were rich and white; the teens she was trying to help were poor and brown. She knew who the city council was more likely to listen to.

She got home at seven that night and shed her dress, bra, and heels as soon as she walked in the front door, too tired and discouraged to bring them into her bedroom. She changed into yoga pants and a hoodie and stood in front of the open refrigerator, a glass of wine in her hand. She really should make herself a healthy dinner with all of those vegetables she'd bought at the farmers' market on Saturday morning.

Instead, she reached for the block of cheese in the drawer and brought it, a knife, and a box of crackers to the coffee table. Just as she sat down, her phone rang. She groaned. It was probably Theo, calling to tell her about a negative story that was going to be in the paper the next day, or someone from Councilman Watson's office giving her a heads-up that one of her few strong allies was going to defect. She took another swig of wine and reached for her phone anyway.

Drew. With her luck, he was calling to tell her not to come visit him this weekend. He'd probably realized during the weekend off from her how nice it was to hang out with other people, or he'd met some other girl after they'd hung up on Saturday night . . . or maybe even before he'd called.

Wait, was that why he'd called on Saturday night? To break up with her? But had he decided against it since she was with people?

She thought about letting him go to voice mail but decided to get this over with.

"Hey." She tucked herself back into her corner of the couch, wishing she'd brought the whole wine bottle to the living room. "How are you?"

"Are you at home?" He sounded breathless. Had he just been running or something? Probably another reason why he was going to break up with her. He went running after work; she put on her yoga pants to sit on the couch with wine and cheese and crackers.

"Yeah, why?" What she wanted to say was, *Why, do you need to know so you don't break up with me when I'm in public?* but she managed to not blurt that out.

"Great," he said. Her doorbell rang two seconds later. Wait, what?

She put her wineglass down and walked to the door, phone still in her hand. She saw him through the peephole with a bag over his shoulder and a tense look on his face. Damn it, she didn't even have a bra on.

She opened the door, and before she could say anything, he stepped inside and pulled her into his arms. He pushed the door closed with his elbow and leaned back against it, holding on tight, his head tucked into the curve of her neck.

She stroked his hair and kissed his ear, happier to see him than she could have thought possible. When he turned toward her, she felt dampness on his cheek.

"Drew, honey, what's wrong? What happened?" She wanted to kick herself for calling him "honey," but it had just slipped out.

He shook his head, so they stood there for a while without speaking, their arms around each other, her fingers moving back and forth through his hair and up and down his back, his rough breathing the only noise in the hallway.

Drew lifted his head and kissed her hard. He unzipped her hoodie and breathed in deeply when he found her topless underneath it.

"Do you always just walk around your house like this? I should show up with no warning more often."

He leaned down and kissed that hollow between her breasts, and felt her fingernails scrape his scalp.

"I didn't fly up here just to catch you shirtless in your house, but what a bonus," he said.

She kissed the top of his head, his cheek, his lips. He sighed and she pulled back.

"Why did you come? What's wrong? Tell me."

Drew stood up straight.

"Let's go sit down somewhere comfortable first."

Alexa looked into his eyes for a long time. When he felt the tears start to well up again, he turned away. He was already embarrassed enough that he'd cried in front of her; he couldn't do it again. She took his hand. They walked into the living room and she pointed at the couch.

"Sit. I'll get you wine. Have you eaten? Are you hungry?"

He sat, suddenly exhausted.

"No. I haven't eaten since . . . lunch? I should be hungry, but I'm not really."

She tossed him her phone.

"Pizza place is in my favorites. Call and order whatever while I get the wine. You know what I like."

She came back with a full glass of wine in one hand and the bottle in the other just as he got off the phone. She sank down on the couch next to him and handed him the glass. He put an arm around her and felt that feeling of homecoming as she tucked her feet up on the couch and laid her head against his shoulder. *This* was why he'd come.

He took a sip of wine and set the glass on the coffee table next to hers.

"I think . . . I'm pretty sure, actually, that Jack has leukemia."

She gasped and tried to sit up, but he tightened his grip around her shoulders, keeping her close to him.

"Oh, Drew, how terrible. When did you find out? Have you told them yet?"

He kissed her hair and released her enough so she could reach her wineglass. She took a sip and grasped his hand.

"This afternoon. Yeah, I told Abby right after I found out. I think I did a terrible job of it. She looked so . . . broken."

Alexa pushed his head down onto her shoulder. He went willingly. Her fingers combed back and forth through his hair. He felt better than he had all day. Better than he'd felt in over a week.

"Sweetheart, I don't think there's a good way of telling someone that their child has leukemia. I'm sure you did as good of a job as you could."

He shook his head but didn't bother to protest any more than that. He just wanted her to keep holding on to him like that, touching him like that. He spilled out the whole story, still resting his head on her shoulder.

"It was so awful. I've had patients with cancer before, but those times, I always knew in advance. It wasn't a kid I *knew*. Why am I not better at this? Why can't I feel distant and academic about it, like other doctors I know?"

She didn't answer him but raised his head and kissed his cheek, then his mouth. They kissed like they were just getting to know each other, like they'd known each other forever. They spent the next thirty minutes like that, taking periodic breaks for sips of the red wine that went straight to his head, then coming back together, whispering soft words in between kisses. They only separated when her doorbell rang.

"Pizza," she said, her hand still on his cheek.

He stood up, surprised to find himself unsteady on his feet. Maybe he really did need to eat. He stumbled to the front door and found his wallet in the gym bag that he'd grabbed out of his trunk in the airport parking lot. He handed the delivery guy a handful of bills and brought the pizza into the living room, just as Alexa was coming back from the kitchen with plates.

She poured herself more wine while he put pizza on their plates, and he quirked his eyebrows at her.

"My glass is empty, too, you know."

She shook her head and took a sip.

"None for you until you eat something. I'm not going to have you collapsing on me here from stress and too much wine and no food."

He started to argue, but the look on her face made him realize it was futile. He dove into the pepperoni, sausage, and extra cheese pizza and had finished two slices before he reached for his wineglass again. This time, she filled it up.

"I'm sorry I descended on you without any warning," he said. "I just . . . I just needed to see you. I should've called, but . . ." But he hadn't wanted to call; he hadn't wanted her to say that she had plans or was too busy and he shouldn't come.

"It's okay." She put her plate down and poured herself more wine. "I would have just finished this bottle on my own if you hadn't come. Glad you could join my pity party." She lifted her glass to his and he toasted her.

"Why were you having a pity party? What's wrong in Alexa world? I thought things were going well after the meeting on Saturday?"

♥

Alexa took another sip of her wine and fought the urge to lay her head on his shoulder. Then she wondered why she was fighting it. She curled up against him, and he put his arm around her.

"Yeah, so did I, but Sunday there was another meeting and it was . . . different."

He rubbed his hand up and down her arm.

"That doesn't sound good. What happened?"

She attempted to not sound as defeatist as she felt as she told him everything.

"Monroe, this is just one group of people. You don't know that they represent everyone in the hills," he said when she was done. "Plus, now you know exactly what you're up against, and this will make you all the more prepared for battle."

She smiled, buoyed by his confidence in her. Maybe she *should* have called him on Sunday night.

"I know, it's just . . ." She took another sip of her wine and put her glass down on the table. She twisted her fingers together and didn't look at him.

"What is it? Tell me." She finally looked up. He smiled at her, with such a tender, open expression on his face that she reached out and touched his cheek. He turned his head and kissed her palm. "Tell me what's wrong."

♥

Drew had always known there was something about this program that she wasn't telling him. He hadn't pushed her, hadn't wanted to push her. But now he needed her to trust him like he trusted her.

She took a deep breath and grasped his hand.

"This program, the whole idea of this program . . . it's a pretty personal one to me." She looked up at him. "You've probably fig-ured that out." He nodded. "I . . . We . . ." She sighed. "I don't know where to start this story."

He lifted their joined hands and kissed the back of hers.

"Wherever you want to start. We have all night."

She laughed, but it came out half like a sob.

"Okay." She turned so that she was facing away from him, but he didn't let go of her hand. "My sister, Olivia, and I. We're only two years apart. Growing up, she was my . . . my idol, my everything. I read books because she read them, I took ballet because she did, I played soccer because she did, though that one I was terrible at." He laughed. She looked up at him and laughed, too.

"It's true. I was. I would pick flowers in the outfield during the game and make little flower crowns for myself." They smiled at each other, and then her smile dropped away. "When I started high school, I was so excited to be back at the same school with Olivia. And, unlike my friends, I wasn't worried about starting high school, because I knew I had my sister there to watch out for me."

She got quiet. He waited for a moment, before he asked, "What happened?"

"One weekend night after a few months of school had gone by, Olivia and her friends got in trouble. They all got high and then drunk, or drunk and then high, and broke into the high school and stole some stuff. Someone heard them and called the cops. They got caught as they were on their way out."

She splashed more wine into both of their glasses and took a long sip of her own before she continued.

"And you have to understand, I was a good kid, a very never-get-in-trouble, obey-all-the-rules kind of kid. And I was so shocked that my sister, who I looked up to so much, who I thought was perfect, would do something like that. And then everyone found out, and I was so humiliated. I thought everyone would think badly about her now, and badly about our whole family. That my teachers would think less of me, that everyone would make fun of me." She glanced in his direction but didn't meet his eyes.

"Why was it such a big deal?" He set his wineglass down. "That sounds like typical teenage stuff. I did stuff like that when I was a teenager and never really got in big trouble, other than with my parents."

She raised her eyebrows and let go of his hand. He felt colder without her touching him.

"I know, but Drew, you're a white guy. Life is different for you. You were born with a benefit of the doubt that black kids never get."

He put his hand on his knee.

"That's true, but . . ." He didn't really know how to finish that sentence.

She took another sip of wine and didn't look at him.

"Come on, Drew. What would have happened if you'd gotten drunk and broken into your high school? What did happen when you did stuff like this? Someone yelled at you and told your parents, you maybe got grounded and got your car taken away, but the school didn't do anything big. Possibly a suspension, but probably not, because you were a golden boy; you were one of the smart, charming ones who everyone loved and everyone could see would eventually make it to medical school. Because you were a white kid. So they got mad at you but always with that smile behind their eyes, to let you know they didn't really mean it and they actually thought it was a little funny, and boys will be boys. Even if someone called the cops on you, which they probably didn't, the cops wouldn't arrest you; they would just give you a lecture, and then maybe tell a story about the time they did something bad when they were a teen like you. Right?"

That was frighteningly accurate. He flashed back to the time that Mrs. Mann had caught him and his buddy Toby stealing the principal's car for a prank, and had just winked at them and pretended she didn't see anything. They'd gotten the car up to the roof of one of the outbuildings of the school, and the principal went ballistic, but no one ever told him who did it. Would Mrs. Mann have done the same thing if it had been Malik, who was in his AP

Chemistry class, she'd seen in the driver's seat instead? He wanted to think so, but too much in the world had told him otherwise. What would have happened to *him*?

He felt like he was tiptoeing through this conversation right now. He wanted to ask questions, he wanted her to keep talking, but he didn't want to say or do the wrong thing, and he had no idea what the right thing was. While he thought, he slid another slice of the now lukewarm pizza on her plate. She smiled her thanks but didn't pick it up. And she still didn't look at him.

"Yeah," he finally said. "You're right. That's exactly how it happened with me. I should have . . . I should have thought of that. What happened to your sister?"

To his relief, she answered.

"She was arrested, along with all of her friends. It was . . . it was a pretty terrible night. I . . . ." She started to say something else and trailed off.

"Did she have to go to jail?"

She shook her head. "In Oakland then, there was a pilot program sort of like TARP." Her voice went back to her chief of staff cadence. "It only lasted for a year, but it was just at the right time for Olivia, so instead of having to serve a sentence or have it on her record, she did the program. And since I know what a difference it made for her, I feel like it could . . . it *would* make a difference for teens in Berkeley today. Olivia got to achieve everything she wanted to, because people gave her a chance."

She still wasn't looking at him. He picked up his wineglass, put it down.

"What are you not telling me?"

She shifted on the couch, pulled her knees up, and put her arms around them so her body was one tight ball.

"Oh, Drew, I was so mean to her." Her voice caught. She stopped, closed her eyes, and swallowed before continuing. "I was mean and snotty and insulting. I made her feel so bad for what happened. I did it on purpose! I became a tattletale to our parents for everything I thought she was doing wrong. We barely spoke for the better part of a year, and even after that, our relationship was fractious and difficult for years. We didn't really start becoming friends again until I was in college, and even then, it took years for us to be close." She paused, clearly lost in thought, and shook her head. "I feel like . . . if I manage to make this happen, it would be my way of making up for everything."

He moved across the couch and put his arm around her. She was so tense he wasn't sure how she'd react to his touch. But she relaxed against him and released her knees.

"And if you don't manage to make this happen? What then?"

She shook her head as it rested against his shoulder. He turned toward her and kissed her hair. He felt her sigh.

"Then it's me failing her again. If I can't do this one thing for my sister, for my family, for all of those other kids who need something like this like she did . . ."

He pulled her closer to him, so happy to be with her. It felt wrong to be happy when she was on the point of tears, but he was honored that she was sharing this with him. This conversation felt like a gift.

"You know that's not true, right? That if it doesn't pass this time it's not your fault? That all you can do is give everything you have to this, and you know you have been? You do know all that?"

She shrugged and turned away from him. Okay. Did that mean she didn't want to talk about this anymore? He wasn't sure if he should keep talking, but he had one more question for her.

"Have you talked to Olivia about this? Have you told her what you're trying to do, and why?"

She hesitated and shook her head.

"We haven't . . . We don't really talk about that at all. At first, I was too ashamed to say anything, and now it seems like it's been too long."

He didn't respond at first, not quite sure what to say. She reached for the slice of pizza he'd put on her plate and had eaten half of it before he spoke again.

"So, if TARP did pass, how were you going to tell her? You *were* going to tell her, right?"

She swallowed, took a sip of her wine, and swallowed again.

"Yeah. I've thought about that. I was going to email her a link to a news article about it. With something like, 'Look what your little sister has been up to?' or, 'Terrible name, great program, right?'" She sighed. "Okay, maybe both of those ideas are stupid, but you know what I mean."

He laughed and squeezed her hand. The tense look on her face relaxed and she squeezed back.

"Maybe you should talk to her. Before the hearing, I mean. About TARP, yeah—this is a great thing you're trying to do, and I know she'd be proud. But also about the other stuff you told me. I'm sure she would want to know."

She shook her head again but didn't let go of his hand.

"It was so hard for me to tell you, Drew. I don't even know how I would tell her how I felt, or what I would say."

He turned her so that her legs were draped over his and took her face in both his hands.

"Say to her what you said to me. Just think about it, okay? I think it would make you feel better."

She leaned her forehead against his and closed her eyes. He wrapped his arms around her, and they sat there for a while, breathing each other in.

"I'll think about it," she said. He moved an inch closer to her, and their lips clung together slowly, gently. He wanted to deepen the kiss but pulled away.

"Now, finish that slice of pizza so you don't have a hangover in the morning. Your doctor insists on it."

She laughed, as he'd been hoping she would.

"How many children do you have to advise about hangovers, Dr. Nichols?"

He stood up to take the pizza box and the empty wine bottle to the kitchen.

"You'd be surprised. Though most of my patients have hang-overs of the Halloween-candy variety."

Her laughter echoed through the house as he walked to the kitchen. He was so glad he'd come.

♥

When he came back from the kitchen, Alexa had dutifully eaten all of her pizza but the crust. He made fun of her for that, as he'd done when she was in L.A.

"Yet another similarity you have with my patients." He grabbed her hands and pulled her to her feet. "You eat your pizza like a toddler."

She kept her hands in his and looked up at him. She felt wrung out emotionally, but she couldn't stop smiling at him. It was so nice to have him here, in her living room, just being here with her, on a Tuesday night. She could get used to this.

She shook that thought away.

"Did you have any plans in mind for the rest of the night?" she asked him.

He pulled her close to him.

"Mmm, I don't know. What were you thinking?"

"Hmmm." His lips trailed down her neck as she considered. "We could check out a show on Netflix? Or, ooh, I'm listening to this great audiobook about segregation in American cities. We could listen together." He unzipped her hoodie and bit her shoulder. She gasped and giggled all at the same time. "Unless you had another plan?"

He straightened up, his eyes focused on her face as he ran his hands down her body. She closed her eyes against the sensation and moaned.

She opened her eyes to see him looking down at her. His shirt was half unbuttoned, his hair was on end, his eyes focused on her and only her. He looked like he'd been sculpted from her wildest fantasies.

"You drive me crazy, Alexa. Did you know that?"

She shook her head and licked her suddenly dry lips.

Holy shit, how did this man still do this to her? Shouldn't this hunger for him and his body and his touch have worn off already? But no, it only seemed stronger now. He squeezed her nipple and she moaned again.

"My plan, you tease, was to spend the next few hours hearing you make that noise over and over again. What do you think about *that* plan, hmmm?" He pulled her closer to him and kissed that spot on her neck that she loved. She sighed.

"It's no Netflix or audiobook, but it'll do."

He laughed, and before she could blink, he'd picked her up and thrown her over his shoulder. She pounded her hands on his back as he strode down the hall to her bedroom.

"What do you think you're doing?"

He turned on the light in her bedroom and kicked a pair of shoes out of his way.

"Less talk, Monroe." He dropped her on the bed. "More action."

♥

How did the sex just keep getting better with her? Drew turned over onto his back, rolling her on top of him.

"Was there an earthquake, or a bomb, or a building collapse or something?" he asked.

"Mmm, I don't think so. Why?" She turned her head to look out the window.

"Because my ears are ringing."

He felt rather than heard her laugh. She laid her head on his chest and ran her hands up and down his still-tingling body. His hands went to her hair, and he held them there, just enjoying the sensation of being with her again.

"When do you have to go back?" she said against his chest.

Oh right. He had to go back.

"My flight's at seven in the morning." He pushed her hair over to the side so he could see her face. "I'm so glad I came."

She looked back at him and smiled, that wide smile that shone from every part of her face. He loved that smile.

"Me, too."

19

Alexa got to work the next morning groggy but blissful. In the middle of the night she'd woken up to him kissing the back of her neck and turned to give him access to the rest of her body. This time it was slower, gentler, quieter, but the fireworks had gone off just the same.

He'd refused to let her drive him to the airport that morning. He'd insisted it was too early and she should get some of the sleep that he'd robbed her of. She hadn't gotten any of that sleep—she'd jumped in the shower as soon as they'd kissed good-bye at her front door—but she'd loved him for saying so.

She sank into her desk chair and barely managed to avoid spilling her coffee as that thought sank in.

Loved him? Wait, no, that's not what she'd meant. She couldn't feel that way about him. That way was surely headed for heartbreak with a guy like Drew.

But he clearly cared about her, right? He jumped on a plane to come see her for less than twelve hours; he had to feel something for her. Or was she just trying to believe he felt something for her because, despite what she was trying to tell herself, she felt something for him?

Damn it, this wasn't what was supposed to happen. This thing was supposed to be easy and fun and light. Maybe she could ignore these feelings and hope they went away?

Should she try to talk to Drew about how she felt? She shook her head. The only time she'd tried to talk about their relationship to Drew it had been an unmitigated disaster. She didn't want to go through that again. Plus, she'd almost certainly scared him away after all of that race talk the night before. White men hated it when you reminded them of their privilege, she knew that all too well.

But what was she supposed to do with all of these feelings now?

Bury them in a corner, drink her damn coffee, and stop having major life crises at eight a.m., that's what.

She managed to distract herself with work for most of the day, but by five thirty she gave up and called Maddie. She knew Maddie would tell her what to do.

♥

Drew walked into the hospital straight from the airport, thankful he'd had an extra shirt in his gym bag so he didn't have to stop at home. Now that he was away from Alexa, he felt stupid about dropping everything to go see her, even though it had felt great in the moment. Good God, he was an adult, he'd been a doctor for four years, and yet he got bad news about one of his patients and flew five hundred miles just to hug one woman?

He was getting in too deep. It was going to hurt way too much when it ended. It was going to hurt even more when she hated him. Like Molly had.

He never should have flown up there. The whole thing . . . it had been too much. Too intimate.

Part of him wanted to flee, never answer her text messages again, never see her again, forget he'd ever known her.

But the thought of never seeing Alexa again made his stomach clench. He'd only left her this morning, and he still couldn't wait to see her this weekend.

Of course the first person he saw when he stepped off the elevator was Carlos.

"Hey, man, you look like shit," was Carlos's friendly greeting. He paused and his smile fell. "Oh wait. I heard about Jack. That sucks. I'm sorry."

Drew shrugged. What was he supposed to say? *That's okay?* It wasn't, really, and Carlos knew that. So he said nothing.

"Where were you last night?" Carlos followed him into his office. "I called you, but your phone was off."

He thought about lying, but he knew Carlos would find out eventually. He was like that.

"I went up to Berkeley."

Carlos stopped halfway into the chair. Damn it, he should have lied; he knew Carlos would make this into a bigger deal than it was.

"Oh? Hard day, you needed a hug from your girl?" He settled into the chair and looked up at Drew with a smug expression. Drew was too tired and irritable for this.

"Whatever, that wasn't it." He shrugged and smirked. "I just needed some stress relief that I couldn't get from basketball. You know how it is."

Carlos laughed, and for a minute, Drew thought Carlos would let it go.

"That's how you're going to play it? It was just a booty call, right? Give me a break, you *like* this girl. You flew to the other end of the state to see her! Don't get me wrong—she's great, and I approve completely, but . . ."

Drew cut him off before he went too far.

"Okay, I knew you'd do this. Calm down. It was just an hour flight. I've driven to the Valley to get laid before, same difference."

Carlos rolled his eyes. Why was he friends with this guy again?

"First of all, no, you haven't."

Okay, fine, he was right. Not that Drew was going to let him know that.

"Second, there's nothing wrong with going to hang out with your girl when you're upset. I'm glad she was there for you, man." Carlos took a sip of his coffee.

Drew shook his head.

"That's not how it was." That was exactly how it was. "I don't know why you keep acting like this thing with Alexa is some big deal, anyway. It's probably not going to last all that much longer."

Carlos stared at him.

"Why wouldn't it? What did you do?"

Drew resisted the urge to flip him off, but only because a nurse walked by his open door.

"I didn't do anything! It's just . . . it's been going on for a while; we've had a good run. Better to end things while they're still good."

Carlos's phone buzzed and he glanced at it, then back up at Drew.

"No offense, man, but don't be such a fucking idiot. I've *seen* the way you look at this girl. I've never seen you look at anyone or anything like you look at her. And you're just going to throw all of that away for some bullshit reason? Because you're too scared for something real?"

Carlos checked his phone again and stood up.

"I gotta go. But dude, stop being the idiot you always have been."

♥

Maddie was borrowing her car for the weekend, so she drove Alexa to the airport on Friday night.

"How're you feeling?" Maddie asked.

Could she even describe how she felt about seeing Drew this weekend? Excited to see him, on edge about what the weekend could bring, relaxed at just the thought of being around him . . .

"Nervous."

She had to talk to him. She had to know what was going on and how he felt before it was too late. Though she was afraid that ship had sailed.

"It was a lot easier when I wasn't overthinking this."

Maddie turned to her at the stoplight.

"Didn't we both know that that could only last a weekend with you? Maybe a long weekend, *maximum*."

They both laughed.

"Do you want a pep talk, or do you want to talk about something else?" Maddie asked her.

She thought for a second. A pep talk would just hype her up too much.

"Something else, please. Tell me about what's-her-name, your crazy new client."

Maddie laughed.

"Oh my God, Alexa. Did I tell you what she wanted the other day? She needed cute exercise clothes, because she always runs into people she knows at the gym, right? But instead of Lululemon, she wanted exercise clothes that no one else has, so I had to dive into the world of $500 yoga pants and $200 sports bras, and let me tell you, that is a crazy world."

They gossiped the rest of the way to the airport, and Maddie hugged her when she got out of the car.

"Good luck this weekend, Lex. Thanks for letting me use your car, and have a great trip."

She hugged Maddie back.

"Anytime, Mads, you know that. And thanks."

♥

Drew left straight from the hospital to pick Alexa up at the airport. Carlos high-fived him as he walked down the hall toward the elevator.

"You'll be at Heather's 4th of July party on Sunday, right?"

Drew nodded as he got in the elevator.

"See you there."

Alexa walked out of the terminal just as he drove up, and he jumped out of the car to kiss her. Okay, maybe he was being hasty about ending things. Maybe Carlos was right. He'd just been overtired and still upset about Jack on Wednesday morning. They could keep this going a little longer.

He squeezed her hand as he got on the freeway toward his house. Did she look tense? She looked tense. Should he ask why?

"Hungry?" That was an easier question.

She shrugged off her cardigan. She was still in business mode, wearing one of those conservative dresses that he secretly loved. "Starving. I barely had time for lunch, and I've depleted all of my office snacks this week."

"You want to go straight to dinner, then? That burger place again, maybe?"

She turned toward him and grabbed his knee. Man, he loved it every time she touched him. Yeah, they could definitely keep this thing going for a while longer.

"Yes, and can we get that Tater Tot casserole this time? I can't promise to eat it all, but it looked amazing."

Apparently, many people had had the same idea for dinner that night. They stood together at the bar while they waited for a table, drinking beer and talking about everything and nothing.

He didn't talk about Jack. He'd already texted her that the test results had come back positive, and he didn't want to bring both of them down. She didn't bring up her program, and he didn't ask, although he was dying to know whether she was going to talk to her sister about it.

Instead, he told her about the kid who kept throwing things across the exam room and giggling, and how he had to step out in the hallway to laugh. She told him about the naked protestors who kept following the mayor around. As they laughed, the tense look on her face relaxed. Maybe it was the beer, but he hoped it was being with him.

Just as he was about to ask her if she wanted another beer, he heard his name. He turned and saw his friends Robin and Lucy walking toward him.

"Hey!" He hugged them both, then turned to introduce Alexa to them.

"Hey guys, this is my . . . this is Alexa. Alexa, meet Lucy and

Robin." He'd almost slipped and called her his girlfriend. How the hell had that happened?

No one had seemed to notice his flub, and Alexa was chatting away with Lucy, so he turned to Robin.

"You going to Heather's party on Sunday?"

"Yeah, you?"

Just as he nodded, the hostess called his name, so they said their good-byes and followed her to the table.

♥

This is my . . . What was he going to say? What was going to be the end of that sentence? Alexa guessed it didn't matter, because he hadn't finished it, so whatever he'd been about to say, he hadn't really meant. Still, she spent the entire time they were at dinner with that sentence fragment running through her head.

Okay, maybe not the entire time. The rest of the time, she compared herself and the dowdy navy blue sheath dress she'd worn to work that day to Lucy and Robin in their cute little sundresses. And her didn't-look-good-in-a-cute-little-sundress-anyway figure to their nonexistent hips and thighs. And the salads on their table to her Tater Tot casserole.

Good God, she was a disaster. Why would she even think that he would finish that sentence the way she wanted him to?

"Monroe, is everything okay? You look worried about something." Drew leaned over and smoothed out the furrow between her eyebrows with his thumb. She couldn't help but smile when he did that.

She almost asked him all of the questions in her head but decided against it. It wasn't the right time. She'd been stressed all week; she needed to relax tonight.

Plus, what would happen if all of his answers were the wrong ones? She'd spend the rest of the weekend miserable and pretending to smile?

"It's fine. I mean, I'm fine. I was just trying to decide between another beer or a glass of wine."

They woke up the next morning wrapped around each other, the cool ocean breeze blowing in on them from his open window. She must have stirred, because his hand moved from her hip to her breast.

"Good morning," he said against her ear. He caressed her body and she sighed in response.

"Mmm, she likes that. Weird, I thought I heard someone say she couldn't take it anymore just a few hours ago."

She held his hand in place when he tried to move it.

"If you heard that, and I'm not confirming that you did, whoever said that probably said 'until morning' at the end there but it was muffled somehow. In a pillow, maybe."

He laughed and kissed her ear, her cheek, her neck, as his fingers kept moving. Okay, he definitely enjoyed some things about her body, whether it was built for little sundresses or not.

"Coffee?" she said into the pillow a while later.

He turned her over and smiled down at her, his eyes roaming over her from her waist to the top of her head. She pulled his head down to hers and kissed him along his jawline.

"How about"—he turned his head and returned the kiss—"while I make coffee, you get ready so we can go to breakfast?"

His hand was on her hip, his thumb drawing figure eights on her hip bone, and his eyes were locked on hers. Between all of that, she was powerless to say no to anything he asked.

♥

After breakfast at Drew's favorite diner, they stumbled back into his apartment and collapsed on the couch.

"Good Lord, why have you never taken me to that place before?" Alexa asked him. "I've never had pancakes that good."

He laughed.

"I knew you'd like the pancakes, even though the biscuits are my favorite."

He pulled out her ponytail so he could run his fingers through her hair, and she sighed and rested her head against his shoulder.

"Monroe?"

She turned and smiled at him, but she looked anxious again, like she had the night before.

Maybe she needed to get work done? Yeah, that was probably it. She always needed to get work done.

"I was maybe going to go for a run. Did you . . . is that cool? You'll be okay here for a while, right?"

She turned away from him and sat up.

"Yeah, that's fine. I can get some work done while you're gone."

Yeah, he'd figured. He kissed her again as he stood up to go change into his running clothes. When he came back into the living room, her laptop was on her lap and she had that worried look on her face again. Still.

"Everything okay?"

She jumped at the sound of his face and looked up.

"Oh . . . yeah, fine. Just checking my email."

He didn't quite believe that. He wanted to sit down next to her and ask more questions, find out what was really upsetting her. Or was it that she would rather email with her buddy Theo than talk to him? But her eyes were back on her screen, not him. He'd been dismissed.

"Okay. I'll be back in an hour or so."

"Okay." She didn't look up as he shut the door.

♥

Had he wanted her to go running with him? And had he changed his mind once he looked at her? Did he want to say that they should both go running after eating all that food but decided that would hurt her feelings? Why had she been so filled with hope when he said *"Monroe?"* like that? What did she think he was going to say?

Was she going to drive herself insane asking herself questions like this all weekend? *Signs point to yes.*

She took a shower to clear her head, pulled on a tank top and yoga pants, and got back on the couch to check her email for real.

Forty-five minutes later, he burst through the front door, his face pink, his shirt sticking to his chest, and holy shit, she wanted to pull his clothes off immediately.

"How was your run?" she asked him.

He tugged his shirt off and wiped his face with it. Now she really couldn't stop staring at him.

"You changed." His chest was glistening, and his dark brown chest hairs stuck to his body. And those shorts . . . Did he have anything on under those shorts? She put her laptop on the coffee table.

"Mmmhmm, I took a shower."

He kicked his shoes into the corner of the room and took a step toward her.

"If you keep looking at me that way, I'm going to pull you into the shower with me in about thirty seconds flat."

With him closer to her now, her head was just about even with his waist.

"Ten seconds."

She hooked her thumbs around his waistband and pulled his shorts down.

It took closer to fifteen seconds, but only because she stopped to throw off her clothes before he turned on the water. Thank goodness she'd packed her blow-dryer.

20

"So who all is going to be at this party?" Alexa asked him on Sunday as they ate a late breakfast on the couch. She'd convinced him to make her pancakes this time. And not to toot his own horn, but they turned out pretty great.

"A bunch of people you've probably heard me talk about—the guys from my basketball league; Carlos; Robin and Lucy, those girls you met last night; lots of other people I don't know." He paused. "Some of the dudes from my basketball league who'll be there are black. FYI."

She smiled and squeezed his hand.

"Thanks for letting me know." She took another sip of coffee. "Whose party is it again?"

"Heather's. She's an old friend of mine. She's got a great house, right on the beach."

He should probably mention that he'd dated her, just so she wouldn't find out from someone else.

"Uh, Heather and I used to sort of date, but that was a long time ago."

"Oh." She twisted a finger around a lock of her hair. "Okay." She looked down at her half-eaten pancakes, so he couldn't see her face. "What time should we go?"

Did she not care that he'd dated Heather? It's not like he wanted her to be all jealous about it. Okay, maybe just a little jealous would be nice.

"I kind of wanted to go on the early side, since I'm on call tonight. So, like, four or five?"

She opened her mouth, closed it, and drew her knees up against her chest.

"Maybe"—he wrapped his arms around her, knees included—"I can go for another run, and it can end like it did yesterday?"

"Mmmm." She turned her head back toward him, and he claimed her mouth. "You taste like syrup," she said, when they ended the kiss.

"If you like that, I have plenty more syrup, you know. There are many things we can do with it that don't involve pancakes."

She turned more fully around.

"Hmmm, that sounds interesting. Waffles, you mean? Do you have a waffle iron?"

He shook his head.

"Biscuits? My mom always puts syrup on biscuits."

He ran his hand down that deep V of his flannel robe that she loved to wear. And that he loved for her to wear.

"Nope," he said, his hand lingering at her left breast.

"Hmmm." She wiggled her shoulder, and the robe fell. "Then I don't know. Tell me."

He leaned forward to whisper in her ear as his hands roamed over her body.

He didn't have time for a run before the party.

♥

Alexa realized after thirty seconds at Heather's party that she was out of her element. Maybe every woman at the party wasn't blond, but wow, did it sure look like it. And not just blond, but that perfect honey blond with golden highlights, all either up in swinging pony-tails or down in flowing waves, in utter defiance of the humid air from the coast.

And it wasn't just the hair. They were all wearing those barely there dresses—the kind that you couldn't wear a bra with, the kind that Alexa always walked right by in the store—and their bodies looked perfect in them. She looked down at herself in the forgiving red and white polka-dot A-line dress she'd felt cute in before leaving Drew's apartment and sighed.

She saw at a glance she was the only black person there, but at least she knew more would show up eventually. She squeezed Drew's hand, grateful again to him for thinking to tell her that. He smiled down at her.

"Oh great, there's Heather," Drew said.

Oh great. His ex.

She had originally been glad he'd told her that tidbit of infor-mation before they'd arrived at the party. Way better than if she found out from another guest, or even worse, from Heather herself. But right now, as tall, thin, blond Heather turned to greet her, she wished she didn't know.

"Heather, this is Alexa," Drew was saying. Alexa noticed that he didn't hesitate this time. She wasn't even "my . . ." today, huh? "Alexa, Heather. We brought beer."

"Drew, good to see you!" Heather hugged first him, then Alexa. Given no choice in the matter, Alexa returned the hug. "Nice to meet you! Beer goes in the kitchen. Go outside and join the party. I've got lots of beer and sangria, and the grills are all going."

They joined a group of people outside, Drew with a beer and Alexa with a glass of sangria. She almost coughed when she took a sip; there was a lot more alcohol in that sangria than she'd been expecting. Drew introduced her to more people, and she tried to deal with this party the way she would at work: smile, make small talk, ask questions, get people talking about themselves. Like the way she'd done at the wedding.

The thing was, right now she was too anxious to be professional Alexa. When she was at work events, she was confident. There, she knew who she was and what she was doing. The wedding had been a lark, with a guy she barely knew, where she was just playing a role. Here, none of those things were true. She felt uncertain. Off-kilter. She took another sip of sangria and plastered a smile on her face.

She fell back on the time-honored way to befriend strange women: compliments.

"I love your sandals!" she said to a woman named Emma. At least she was strawberry blond.

"Thanks!" Emma said. Like lobbing a tennis ball back to Alexa, she returned the compliment. "Great lipstick! I always wish I could wear red lipstick, but with this hair, I feel like it always clashes."

"Oh no, I think there's a perfect red lipstick for everyone; it just takes trial and error. You need plenty of time at Sephora and a friend you trust."

They talked about makeup for a while longer. Either the conversation or the glass of sangria relaxed Alexa enough so that she stopped scanning the party for someone with brown skin or an errant eyebrow hair or even a tiny roll of fat.

She walked over to refill her glass of sangria. A guy Drew had just introduced her to followed her.

"Alexa, right? Having fun so far?" He put an arm around her. Lots of huggers at this party.

"Yeah, it's great." She stepped to the side so she could pour her drink. "Mike, right?"

"Yeah, so smart of you to remember." Mike liked to stand close, didn't he? "So Alexa, where are you from?"

She took a sip of her sangria and a half step backward.

"Berkeley. I'm just down here for the weekend."

Oh look, he'd moved closer.

"You live in Berkeley? That's cool. But I meant, like, where are you really from?"

Now she knew where this was going. Like she couldn't "really" be from California? Why did people always try to ask her about her ethnicity in the clumsiest of all possible ways? Getting this question, especially in this way, always made her feel like such an object of curiosity. Today it made her feel like even more of an Other in this party full of golden-haired beauty queens.

Now she was doubly annoyed with Mr. Stands Too Close. So she was going to fuck with him.

"Oh, not that far from there. I grew up in Oakland. Northern California girl!" She gave him her biggest, fakest grin.

He chuckled and took another swig of his beer.

"No, no, like where are you *from* from? Where are your *parents* from?"

This conversation was so predictable. Yet this dance people did was irritating every time.

"My parents are from California, too. My dad grew up here in L.A., actually, and my mom up in the Bay Area. What about yours?"

She felt a hand land on the small of her back and relaxed. She turned and saw Drew there next to her, as she knew he would be.

"Is Mike monopolizing you?" He grinned at Mike and did that hand slap thing guys did instead of hugging. "How's it going, man?"

Mike's eyes flashed to Drew's arm disappearing around her back, and he took a step backward.

"Good, good, just stopped to chat here with your friend Alisha."

She gritted her teeth, not even caring anymore if it looked like a smile.

"Alexa."

Mike laughed and lifted his glass of sangria to hers.

"Right, right, Alexa, of course. Nice to talk to you."

She walked with Drew toward the grills. As soon as they were out of earshot, she said, "I don't like that guy."

He stopped walking and turned to her.

"Why, what did he do?"

She made a face.

"Remember that Bill guy from the wedding? Creepy and border-line offensive?"

Now he stopped walking.

"It wasn't borderline. Mike's like that guy? Damn it, I'm sorry. I should have come to find you earlier."

He believed her. Just like that. So often, guys would jump in to defend other men when women said they'd crossed a line. It had happened to her over and over again.

But Drew had immediately believed her. Why did a little thing like that touch her so much? She reached for his hand.

"No, it was okay, I handled it. Just . . . come over if you see him cornering me again?"

He squeezed her hand and smiled.

"Absolutely. Here, let's go talk to some better people."

He introduced her to his friend Luke, another doctor at his hospital, and Luke's husband, Brendan, one of the aforementioned dudes from his basketball league.

"Ahh, you're the reason for Drew's mysterious trips up to the Bay Area as of late," Luke said. "So nice to meet you."

Did . . . Was Drew blushing? It could just be sunburn, but she hadn't noticed his cheeks that color pink five minutes ago.

"Nice to meet you, too, Luke, Brendan."

Brendan gestured at her drink.

"Is that the sangria? How is it?"

She took another sip and realized she was almost halfway through this glass.

"It's great, but be forewarned, it has more of a kick to it than I expected. If Drew has to carry me out of here in a few hours, it's because I had more than two glasses of this stuff."

"Uh-oh," Drew said. "Should I go get us some food to soak up all of that alcohol? There are burgers, hot dogs, sausages . . ."

"Definitely a hot dog," Alexa said. "It's the 4th of July. It's un-American not to have a hot dog!"

Luke's eyebrows went up and he opened his mouth. Brendan kicked him and he closed it.

"I saw that," Alexa said, and all four of them laughed.

"I don't know you quite well enough for a sausage joke yet, so pretend you didn't see that." Luke paused. "I can tell it after you've had that third sangria."

Drew groaned.

"Oh no, I'm scared to leave you with these two now. God only knows what they're going to do or say."

Alexa waved Drew away.

"Go on, get me my hot dog, I can't wait to see the looks on their faces as I eat it and they have to hold their jokes in. Maybe for dessert there will be popsicles?"

After all four of them ate hot dogs—with most of the jokes at Drew's expense—Alexa excused herself to both refresh her sangria and go to the bathroom. Coming out of the bathroom, she ran into Heather and Emma, along with Lucy and Robin from the night before.

"Hey, Alexa!" Heather said. "Having fun? I was just taking this crew to the kitchen for some of the white sangria, I haven't put it out yet. Do you want to try it?"

Never one to say no to an offer like that, Alexa followed the other women into the kitchen.

"So Alexa," Heather said as she poured the sangria, "do you live here in Santa Monica?"

Alexa glanced around the room to see if the others were all looking at her. Not yet, at least. How long ago had Heather and Drew dated? She wondered if the ranks were going to close against her like with Molly's bridesmaids at the wedding.

"No, just here for the weekend. I live up in Berkeley, actually."

Lucy's eyes shot to her face. What had she said?

"Are you from there? What do you do up there?" Lucy took a sip of her own sangria without her eyes leaving Alexa's face.

"Yeah. I mean, yeah, I'm from the Bay Area. I work for the mayor of Berkeley."

The other three women burst out laughing. She looked around at the four of them with raised eyebrows.

"What did I say?" Was this going to be like junior high, where people would corner you and laugh in your face?

Robin took a sip of her sangria and grinned.

"Oh, we're just laughing because we know Lucy isn't going to leave your side for the rest of the night."

Lucy rolled her eyes.

"Don't worry, they're making fun of me, not you. See, I keep talking about quitting my job as a teacher and going to law school, and the law school at Berkeley is supposed to be great for the kind of law I want to do. But just because you work for the mayor and live there doesn't mean you're an expert on the law school . . . does it?"

Alexa held her glass out to Heather for a refill.

"Maybe not an expert, but I did graduate from Berkeley Law School, so . . ."

Lucy crossed the room so fast she almost knocked into Heather.

"Tell me everything."

♥

After Alexa went inside, Drew got his share of teasing from Luke and Brendan.

"Good God, you should see the way you look at her," Luke said. "It's like me when I'm looking at . . ."

"A really fat sausage?" Brendan suggested.

"Oh, shut up, both of you," Drew said, after Luke and Brendan recovered from their peals of laughter.

"No, no, but it's cute," Brendan said. "Look at you—you keep glancing toward the house to see if she's coming back and trying to pretend that you're just looking at your drink."

Drew shifted his eyes back in their direction. Okay, fine, they caught him looking for her. He was just trying to make sure she made it back outside okay. No, that excuse didn't even work in his own head.

Eventually, Kat, another doctor at the hospital, came over to them.

"Hey, Drew," she said. "Did I see you running on the beach yesterday? I shouted to you, but if it was you, you didn't answer." Kat lived not far from him, and they went running together sometimes.

"Around noon? Yeah, that was me. I guess I was preoccupied. Sorry I didn't say hi." He glanced toward the house again.

"Huh, what could you have been preoccupied with this weekend?" Brendan said, between bites of hot dog. "Or should I say, who?"

"You two are such assholes," Drew said. He didn't know if they heard him through their laughter.

♥

"Enough law school talk," Heather ordered. By this time, they were all sitting around the kitchen table. "Let's talk about something more interesting. Alexa, how did you meet Drew?"

Hmm, which story was she supposed to tell? They hadn't really discussed that.

"We met at a wedding." She took another sip. Oh well, if Drew didn't want her to tell the truth, he should have told her their cover story before she'd had all of this sangria. "Sort of. In the elevator a few days before his ex-girlfriend's wedding, actually. He needed a date, and I was free that night, so . . ."

The whole table cracked up, Alexa included.

"Oh, that's such a Drew story," Robin said. "Meets a girl in an elevator, convinces her to go with him to a wedding that night."

"It wasn't that night. It was . . ."

Emma broke in.

"Was this that wedding in May? Oh man, I was supposed to go with him to that wedding, but my dad had surgery so I couldn't go."

Wait, this was *that* Emma? Had everyone at this table dated Drew?

"Has everyone at this table dated Drew?" Shit, she probably shouldn't have said that out loud. But at least now she'd get an answer.

"Not me!" Lucy said. But Heather, Emma, and Robin all rose their hands. Huh.

"He's a sweetheart," Robin said. "We had a great time while it lasted."

Everyone else at the table nodded.

"How long did . . . Why did it end?" Alexa asked them. What was she supposed to do, *not* ask these women who had all dated Drew that, when she was both tipsy and had been thinking about that very topic for days? She did not have that much willpower.

Heather was the one who answered her.

"At least for me, it was when it was going really well. I was starting to think . . . well, whatever, I've been over it for a while. But after about two months, he came over one night and gave me a little speech about how it was best to end things when we—"

"Were still friends?" Emma jumped in. "Yeah, I got that same speech. He was really sweet about it, though. Even sent me flowers afterward, to make sure there were no hard feelings."

Robin laughed.

"I got the same speech, also after about two months, but no flowers. The flowers must be new."

Heather jumped in.

"It's a testament to what a great guy Drew is that we all still like him. And one another. He obviously only dates great women." She stood up and refilled everyone's sangria cups.

"So what did you put in that sangria anyway?" she asked. The subject changed to cocktail recipes. Alexa did her best to chime in with her favorites as her mind was swirling.

Maybe she didn't want to get those answers from Drew after all.

♥

Drew almost went into the house to find Alexa at least three times and stopped himself each time. Finally, he saw her walking across the lawn with Lucy and Robin.

He and Kat wandered over to them. When he put his hand on the small of her back, she jumped.

"Hey, it's just me." She'd probably been on edge from Mike irritating her earlier. "You having fun?"

"Yeah." She took a step away from him and looked at the group around them. "It's great."

She reached her hand out to Kat, that smile from the wedding on her face again.

"Hi, I'm Alexa."

"Oh, I'm sorry." Drew jumped in. "Kat, this is Alexa. She's

here visiting this weekend. Alexa, this is Kat. She's also a doctor, and a sometime running buddy of mine."

"Great. So nice to meet you, Kat!" Alexa took another sip of her drink and turned back to Lucy and Robin.

Was something wrong? It felt like something was wrong.

"What were you ladies up to inside for so long?" Brendan asked as he came up to the group.

Robin, Lucy, and Alexa all laughed. Alexa was looking at them, not at him. Why wasn't she sharing this laughter with him?

"Oh, just chatting," Lucy said. "Well, drinking and chatting, anyway." She turned to Alexa. "Oh God, Alexa, I forgot to tell you that story about how two of my students got arrested—it tested every instinct I had when they told me about it, because I wanted to laugh so hard but I knew I shouldn't."

As Lucy went on to tell a long story about her students and a cemetery and getting chased by security guards into blackberry bushes, Drew watched Alexa. She was totally relaxed with the other women, smiling and laughing without that fake smile that he hated on her face. That smile had been his sign to come over when she was talking to Mike.

But she still had that tense look around her eyes. When he touched her arm, she turned toward him, but her body was stiff.

"Everything okay?" he said in a low voice.

She flashed a smile, but it didn't reassure him. It didn't have that glitter of joy hovering behind her eyes like her real smiles usually did.

"Fine," she said. "Want to get me more sangria?"

When he came back with the sangria, he brought a plate of chips and guacamole for them to share. This time when he joined the group he slid an arm around her waist, but she stepped away from him.

"Oh look, Heather's bringing out the cupcakes. Let me go see if she needs help."

So she walked off to help Heather with the cupcakes, leaving him with one arm empty, and one hand weighed down with a full plate of chips.

"Those for me?" Carlos asked from behind him.

"Hey, man, when'd you get here?"

Carlos reached for a handful of his chips.

"Just now. Why are you looking so forlorn? Where's Alexa?"

He gestured with his empty hand.

"She's over there, asshole. Helping Heather do something with cupcakes . . ." He paused as he saw Alexa and Heather talking to three men he didn't know. "I guess Heather introduced her to some more people."

Carlos looked at him for a long moment but just nodded.

"Cool, I'll go say hi. Where are the drinks?"

Drew pointed and went back to munching on chips and listening to Lucy and Brendan talk about surfing. Forlorn? He wasn't forlorn. It was *possible* he would prefer Alexa to be standing next to him than over on the other side of the party talking to three strange men, but he wasn't *forlorn*.

He watched Carlos approach her group and tap her on the shoulder. Alexa threw her arms around Carlos and beamed her hundred-watt smile at him and absorbed him in her cozy little group. Drew waited for her to look around for him. She was probably just waiting to catch his eye to signal to him to come join them. But she didn't turn her head.

21

Alexa was glad she hadn't tried to have the Talk with Drew before coming to the party. She would have made some humiliating speech about how she felt about him and how she wanted a relationship with him, and he would have looked at her with pity in his eyes.

She'd always known what the deal was. That was the worst part. She'd known from the beginning who and what he was—he'd told her so. What did she think, someone like her was going to change him?

She kept trying to snap out of it, to give herself a mental pep talk. But every time she caught a glimpse of Drew standing next to Kat, his hot blond "running buddy," she needed more sangria to wash down the bitter taste of shame.

Thank God at least no one knew. She hadn't told Drew how she felt, and she was almost certain she'd managed to keep her face relaxed and jokey in the kitchen with the other women. She wouldn't be able to handle their sympathy on top of the sadness that she knew was hovering in the back of her eyes.

It would be so much easier if she could be mad at Drew. But Drew had done nothing wrong. He'd been perfectly honest with her the whole time. It was her own fault for making up stories in her head about what it meant that he looked at her this way or touched her that way or had that tone in his voice when he talked to her.

Twenty-four hours until her plane left LAX. She could keep pushing that sadness in its little box for twenty-four hours until she'd be able to let it out.

She kept unconsciously looking around the party for a friendly face. Someone familiar, who she could relax around, not be so *on* with, just be herself. Someone who she didn't have to smile and fake it with. But the only person like that was Drew, and looking at him hurt now.

After another glass of sangria, she felt a hand on her shoulder and turned.

"Carlos!" Finally, someone she'd known more than an hour. "I was hoping you were going to be here. How've you been?" She hugged him, not sure if the tears that shot to her eyes during the hug were because she was glad to see him, or because of the sangria. Probably a little of both. At least she'd get to say good-bye to Carlos. He'd been so nice to her.

"Great." He toasted her plastic cup with his bottle of beer, his arm slung around her shoulder. "I knew *you'd* be here, Drew's found ways to mention you all week."

She looked down at her cup. Sure he had.

Drew came over to join their group, but this time she saw him coming, so she could dodge his touch without being obvious about it. She couldn't handle that warm, firm touch on her back or around her waist right now. She'd taken such comfort in it, thought it meant so much.

But it had turned out to mean nothing at all. Instead of soothing her, now it made her angry. Mostly at herself.

She left Drew and Carlos behind and walked with Lucy to get more of the white sangria. Intellectually, she knew that she should probably stop drinking so much, but following Lucy was a good way to escape. As was the sangria itself.

♥

Was it his imagination that Alexa was avoiding him? Probably. It was probably his imagination. But the thing was, for the past hour, she'd walked around with Heather and Emma, and Robin and Lucy, and chatted with a whole group of guys he'd never met. Every time he walked up to her, she'd moved when he'd touched her and had some reason to walk away after a minute or so.

He left her alone for a while and talked to other people, but he was always aware of where she was and who she was talking to. He told himself it was just so he could rescue her from Mike if necessary. Even in his head he knew that wasn't true.

Finally, he saw her standing alone over by the drinks table and walked toward her, determined to figure out what was wrong. Before he could get there, Carlos came up to her, threw an arm around her, and said something in her ear that made her laugh so hard he could hear it from across the backyard. When he reached the two of them, they were both still giggling.

"Hey guys, having fun over here?" He reached for Alexa's hand, but she switched her drink from her left to right. She'd looked in his direction but turned back to Carlos, the smile still on her face but no longer in her eyes.

Carlos grinned at him, but was that guilt in his face? What was Carlos whispering to his girlfriend about, anyway?

"Yeah, we were just talking . . . about the party," Carlos said, flashing his eyes back toward Alexa. They shared a grin that made Drew feel like a third wheel.

"You two are looking kind of cozy. What are you, planning your escape so you can be alone together?" Drew joked. Except somehow it didn't really come out like a joke.

Alexa looked straight at him for what felt like the first time that afternoon.

"Was that some kind of accusation? Because it felt like it."

Carlos's arm dropped from around Alexa's shoulders. Drew felt a flash of anger that it had been there in the first place, especially when she hadn't wanted *him* to touch her all day.

"Looks like I struck a nerve." Why did he even say that? He didn't really believe something was going on with Carlos and Alexa . . . did he?

"I don't know, Drew," Alexa shot back. "You planning your escape from me so you can figure out which of the women here will be your new 'friend'? I can go home now so you don't have an inconvenient sandwich at this buffet."

Okay, something was definitely wrong.

"What the fuck is that supposed to mean?" Drew said.

Alexa's lips curved into what some people might think was a smile.

"Pretty much exactly what I said." She took the last sip of her drink and put it down. "Wait, you probably don't remember—in this instance, the sandwich and the buffet are a metaphor for—"

"I know what it's a fucking metaphor for, Alexa. I remember. What's your problem today?"

"Good luck with this," Carlos muttered from behind him as he backed away.

"What's my problem today?" Alexa wasn't even pretending to smile anymore. "My *problem* is that I'm tired of meeting all of your perfectly nice friends who are checking my forehead for my Drew Nichols expiration date. It was cute at the wedding, but it's not fun or funny for me anymore, especially since I have a strong feeling that my expiration date is July 5th."

He grabbed her hand hard enough that she couldn't pull away and marched her into Heather's house and up the stairs. He closed the door once they got inside Heather's bedroom.

"Okay, now can we please talk about this without an audience?" The walk up the stairs had calmed him down. "What's going on here? I was just kidding about the Carlos thing. I shouldn't have said that."

She laughed. Her laugh didn't sound like Alexa's laugh.

"What would it matter to you anyway if I was fucking Carlos? Like you would care."

Whoa, where had that come from?

"What the fuck, Alexa? You know that's not true. Come on, what happened? What changed between now and this morning?" He took a step toward her and she backed away.

"Nothing you need to worry about, Drew. Go back outside, hang out with your friend Kat. I can occupy myself."

His shoulders relaxed. She was jealous! He could fix this; it was going to be okay.

"Is that what this is about? Monroe, nothing is going on between me and Kat—we're just friends." Something suddenly occurred to him. "I should have told you—I used to date Robin . . .

and Emma. Did they tell you that? Were they weird to you? Is that why you're mad?"

Alexa threw up her hands.

"No, Drew, everyone here is great. The women are nice and collegial, all welcoming me to the club of people who have had their month or so of sleeping with the great Drew Nichols, with that slight pity in their eyes when they look at me because they know what's coming. The men all look me up and down like they're ready to jump me as soon as you're done with me, because they assume there must be something good in there if I'm worthy of you. Same as it's ever been since the wedding, honestly."

He still didn't understand what was wrong. Maybe he was never going to understand women.

"Why do you keep bringing up the wedding? I thought everything was fine at the wedding. Better than fine."

She took a step toward him. Finally, she wasn't backing away anymore.

"Everything was fine at the wedding because the wedding wasn't real! I'd met you two days before, I didn't know you, I didn't know anything about you, and I didn't care about you then."

He smiled and reached for her.

"Does that mean you care about me now?"

She dodged his hand and stepped around him toward the bedroom door.

"Fuck you, Drew."

Apparently, that had been the wrong thing to say.

"No, wait, Alexa. I didn't . . . I don't understand. Please don't leave." He needed to fix this. He didn't want her to be mad. He didn't want this to be over.

Her hand dropped from the doorknob, but her back was still to him. He had to say something to get her to turn around. Maybe honesty would work.

"What do you mean the wedding wasn't real? It felt real to me." It had. From the moment he'd first touched her, it had felt like she'd belonged there by his side, smiling at him, joking with him, confiding in him, listening to him, being silent with him. Everything about this had felt real from the beginning, even when he barely knew her.

Now that he really knew her, and she knew him, it felt more than real. It felt like his life finally made sense.

He'd tried to pretend to himself all week that he would end things with her after this weekend, but he'd known as soon as he saw her at the airport that that wasn't true. Not only that he wouldn't, but he couldn't.

She turned around, and for a minute he felt like he'd said the right thing. That was, until he saw the look on her face.

"Here's how I know the wedding wasn't real, Drew. Because at the wedding, you called me your girlfriend. In real life, I'm nothing to you."

He shook his head. She was so far from nothing.

"That's not—"

"It *is* true! Since the wedding, I've been just Alexa, or sometimes 'my *friend* Alexa,' or occasionally *dramatic pause* Alexa. But never your girlfriend, because in real life, Drew Nichols doesn't do girlfriends. Which is fine—that's fine, at least you're honest—but don't try to pretend that I'm making this up right now."

♥

Oh, thank God, she could finally legitimately be mad at Drew. She'd felt guilty being mad at him earlier; it hadn't been his fault that she had feelings for him, or that she'd wanted him to return those feelings so much she'd almost convinced herself that he did.

But it was his fault that he was now trying to act like he'd wanted her with him at the wedding for anything more than a shield. And it sure as hell was his fault he sounded so smug she'd admitted she cared about him.

He rubbed his eyes and ran his fingers through his hair. Even after all of this, she had to fight to not reach up and touch it.

"Alexa, can we talk about this, please?"

She shook her head. The patented Drew breakup talk was the last thing she wanted right now.

"No need for a conversation. I know the drill."

He stepped closer to her. She was annoyed that even in the midst of this fight they were never going to come back from, she just wanted to step into his arms and have him tell her everything was going to be okay.

"Come on, can you calm down for a minute and let me say something?"

That solved that problem. Nothing pissed her off more than a man telling her to calm down.

"I get it, my feelings aren't worth anything to you, but I can be as un-calm as I want about this."

"No, no, that's not what I meant. I just want to . . ." He paused and put his hand on her arm. "I just want to explain."

At his touch, tears shot to her eyes. She shook his arm off and turned away from him.

"Don't worry about it, Drew. You don't need to explain. Your feelings come through loud and clear." She opened the door and ran back downstairs before he could reach for her again.

Thank God no one was in the bathroom. She ducked in there

for a few minutes to take a deep breath and swallow the tears that had threatened. She washed her hands, dabbed cold water under her eyes, and faked a smile at herself in the mirror like she hadn't just had a sangria-fueled relationship-ending fight in the middle of a party.

When she walked out of the bathroom, she ran into Heather, coming out of the kitchen with more cupcakes.

"Awesome, you can help me carry these." Heather handed her a tray of cupcakes. Thankful for something to do, Alexa carried them outside. She took a deep breath before she walked through the door, but a quick scan of the crowd showed her no evidence of either Drew or Carlos in the yard. She did see Lucy, though, and put two red velvet cupcakes on a plate for the two of them.

"You said this was your favorite, right?" Alexa held out the plate to Lucy, and soon they both had red tongues and lips smeared in cream cheese frosting. Robin joined them with a cupcake of her own and a pile of napkins. Alexa had just relaxed a little and wiped her mouth when the circle opened and she heard Drew's voice.

"Alexa." His voice was steady, like their fight had made no impact on him. "I got a call. I've got to be at the hospital in thirty minutes." He touched his hand to her shoulder and dropped it almost as quickly. "Sorry to do this to you guys, but I have to take Alexa away from you: duty calls."

She thought about telling him that she'd stay, that she could get a ride home later, and also that he could go fuck himself.

But her political training hadn't completely deserted her; not even this much sangria would allow her to let all of these people know her business. So instead, she gave everyone in the group hugs good-bye amid false promises of getting drinks "the next time she was in town" and followed Drew to his car.

♥

Drew had stayed in Heather's bedroom for a while after Alexa had fled. He'd wanted to run after her, to tell her no, she'd gotten it all wrong, that wasn't how he felt. But he'd already made a mess of this conversation, so he figured he should maybe wait and try again when they got home after the party and could really talk.

But then he got the call from the hospital and had to run outside and grab her in a hurry. He'd thought about asking Carlos to drive her home, but after basically accusing Carlos of hitting on her, he wasn't in the best position to ask Carlos for a favor. Plus, he didn't want Alexa to think he was pissed at her and had ditched her at the party.

However, from the look on her face and the way she refused to meet his eyes when he found her outside, he thought for a second that she'd tell him to go on without her. That would have pissed him off. That he could tell she'd considered it even pissed him off.

They drove without talking for a few minutes, the only noise in the car the pop music she'd been singing along to on the way there. She broke the silence before he could.

"Did you really get a call from the hospital, or was that just your excuse to leave?"

That's when he lost his temper.

"What the fuck, Alexa? Really? You really think I would make up a call from the hospital just to get you out of there? Do you think I'm that much of a child?"

She didn't respond, and when he glanced her way, she just shrugged. That made his temper flare even higher.

"Really? You have that low of an opinion of me, just because I didn't introduce you to people as my girlfriend? Just because I don't use the exact word that you want me to use to describe you, you decide I'm the kind of asshole who would lie to you and all of my friends like that? When you decided to push back our dinner reservations by an hour last night because you were on the phone with your buddy *Teddy* writing one fucking sentence together for forty-five minutes, did I call you a controlling bitch workaholic who doesn't pay attention to anyone else's feelings? No, I didn't, but I sure as hell could have."

He thought he saw her flinch out of the corner of his eye, but when he turned to look at her, her face was impassive.

"At least I finally know what you really think of me."

He turned into his parking spot, his sudden anger gone as quickly as it had come.

"No, Alexa, I didn't . . ." She was out of the car before he could say anything else. He followed her up to his apartment, unlocked the door, and pushed it open for her before following her inside.

"I shouldn't have said that. I didn't mean it—that's not how I feel," he said as soon as he'd shut the door. Her back was still to him as she walked around the living room picking up her stuff.

"Alexa! Come on, talk to me." She finally turned to him. He looked at the pile of her stuff in her hands. "Wait a minute, what are you doing?"

She neatly piled it all into the big purse she always used on the airplane.

"What does it look like I'm doing? Why are you still here? Don't you have to go to the hospital?"

He shook his head in reaction to what she'd said. In reaction to everything.

"No! I mean, yes, I have to go to the hospital, but no, please don't pack. Don't leave now! You can't leave now. I have to talk to you."

She stood there, silently, staring somewhere around the base of his neck but not meeting his eyes. He closed the distance between them and held on to her shoulders. She finally looked up at him but still didn't say anything.

"Promise me. Promise you won't leave. If this . . . if this has meant anything to you at all, promise me you won't leave while I'm at the hospital."

She closed her eyes and dropped her head, but he didn't let go of her. Finally, she whispered, "Okay. I promise."

He pulled her into his arms. She leaned her head against his shoulder for a quick second before she stepped backward.

"Go. You're going to be late."

She was right. He looked back over his shoulder at her on his way out the door, but she had already turned to look out the window.

♥

Alexa dropped into a chair and put her head in her hands as soon as he walked out the door. What a fucking nightmare the past few hours had been. She'd planned the whole way home in the car to pack and take a cab to the airport as soon as he left for the hospital, but now she couldn't even do that.

She was usually the last person who would leave in the middle of a fight. She liked to finish any discussion, she liked closure, and she always wanted to know exactly where she stood.

But this time she couldn't wait to get out of there. She already knew where she stood; she didn't need him to say it out loud. She didn't want to finish this fight, didn't want him to tell her what she knew was coming, didn't want to have to deal with the pain of listening to the gentle breakup speech he'd perfected on the dozen women who came before her.

What would be even worse was if he didn't give her the breakup speech today. If instead he found some way to convince her to stay with him. That would just postpone the inevitable and make it hurt all the more when he finally decided to move on. And make her feel even more stupid when he did.

That's why she had to get out of there. Fly back to Berkeley so she could hide inside of her apartment and eat ice cream and cry for an entire day before she had to face anyone.

But now she'd promised him she wouldn't leave, and as much as she wanted to break that promise, she wouldn't. And now she had to sit here and wait, with only her own thoughts for company.

She thought about calling Maddie, but she knew if she did she would break down on the phone, and the last thing she wanted was to have Drew walk in on her while she was sobbing her heart out over him.

Instead, she changed, finished packing, and tried and failed to concentrate on work. Finally, she got into Drew's bed and pulled up *Anne of Green Gables* on her iPad. Anne was right to smash her slate over Gilbert's head—fuck him for calling her Carrots.

♥

Drew got home much later that night, after an easy but long surgery. Thank God it had been an easy one; his mind was half on Alexa the entire time. Part of him was pissed at her that she'd started a fight over what seemed like nothing, but the rest of him was terrified that she'd left and he'd never see her again.

One thing she'd said at the party had kept ringing in his ears: *"In real life, I'm nothing to you."* Was that how she really felt? Was that how he'd made her feel? Because now he realized how far from the truth that was. She meant more to him than he could say. Than he knew how to say.

The whole way up the stairs to his apartment, he prayed that she'd kept her promise and was still there. He tiptoed into his bedroom, hoping she was there, not sure what to do if she was. He'd been rehearsing what to say the whole drive home, but now everything that he'd thought of seemed stupid and inadequate.

He stopped in the doorway of his bedroom and sighed in relief. All of his lights were on, and Alexa was asleep in that way that was so familiar to him now, curled up on her side in his bed, the covers pulled up to her chin, her iPad resting on her face.

He turned the lights off and undressed in the dark. He moved the iPad to the bedside table and crawled in next to her.

He'd always loved getting in bed with her. It was one of his favorite things about her, the way she would melt into his arms every time he put his arms around her. But this time, she stiffened at his touch. It broke his heart.

He tightened his arms around her and kissed her neck, her hair, the side of her face. After a few seconds, he felt her relax. He reached up and stroked her hair.

"Alexa, please. Please, can we talk?"

She turned in his arms and rested her head against his chest but didn't say anything.

"I'm sorry about what I said earlier. I got frustrated, and I didn't mean it. Please, forgive me, sweetheart?"

Her face was hidden in his chest, so at first, he only heard her irregular breathing and didn't realize the cause. But when he reached down to stroke her face and tilt it up toward his, he felt the tears on her face.

"Oh no, Alexa. Oh, please no, don't cry." He kissed her forehead and pulled her closer to his chest, but she only cried harder.

"I can't do this, Drew." He could barely understand her through her sobs. "This is too . . . It hurts too much. We can't do this anymore."

"No!" He hoped that he'd heard her wrong, but he knew that wasn't the case. "No, that's not . . . Please don't do this. Don't do this to me. To us. Alexa, please. I want this more than anything. You make me so happy. *We* make me so happy."

She shook her head and sobbed harder.

"Oh, Drew, you're so . . . Please don't make this even . . ."

He bent down to kiss her wet face, cutting her off before she could finish talking. She kissed him back hard, still hiccupping as her hands roamed his body. He caressed her breasts as he kissed her. He cut off the kiss just long enough to pull her tank top over her head and moved down her body. She dug her fingernails into his shoulders, and he hissed, but she didn't stop. He didn't want her to stop.

He moved farther down her body, knowing by her slightest twist and moan and gasp where he should linger. Her hands were tight in his hair, and he felt the tug on his scalp just before he heard her gasp and felt her contract around him. He lifted his head and looked down at her. Her eyes were closed, but the tears were once again running down her cheeks. He kissed them away.

♥

She opened her eyes when she heard the crinkle of the condom wrapper opening. He was kneeling between her thighs, looking at her in that way he'd looked at her since the beginning, like he couldn't wait to touch her, like he couldn't wait for her to touch him. She couldn't wait, either.

She ran her hands up and down his warm chest. He picked up her hands and kissed them. He pinned them above her head, holding on to her wrists with one hand.

He bent closer to her until his mouth was almost on hers, his body inches away, but he didn't close the short distance. She moved to meet him, but he moved away, a faint smile dancing around his lips.

"You know what I want," he said. "Tell me. Tell me what you want."

She looked at him, all warm and golden and strong above her. She said what was in her heart.

"You. I want you."

He pushed her legs wide open and slid inside of her. Their twin moans echoed around the room. Too quickly, her whole body tensed and she exploded, tears once again streaming from her eyes, words she knew she would be embarrassed about later coming from her mouth.

He quickened his pace and came, collapsing on top of her when the tremors throughout his body finally stopped.

"You have me," he said in her ear, so low she wasn't sure if she'd heard him right.

22

When Drew woke up the next morning, she was gone. He turned over in bed and reached for her, but her side of the bed was empty and cold. He sat up and looked around the room. The floor was bare in that corner where he'd been tripping over her suitcase all weekend.

"Goddamn it!" He got out of bed and looked around the apartment, but all evidence of her was gone. He looked for his phone and found it sitting in the middle of the coffee table. Waiting for him.

I'm sorry about how I acted at the party. You and I both know this is over. I had a great time with you, Drew.

That was it? That was motherfucking it? "I had a great time with you"??? He'd told her how he felt last night, and then she fucking disappeared in the morning like he was some one-night stand she couldn't wait to get away from?

He lay flat on his back on the sofa, still naked.

How fucking perfect that the first time he'd really cared about

a woman in years she'd fled the scene without even saying good-
bye. He should tell Molly about this; she'd get a good laugh out
of it.

He sat up and grabbed his phone. He was going to text Alexa
back, tell her to get back here, that he wanted to talk to her, this
was more than just a great time, why the fuck had she left before
they had a chance to talk? He typed out the text to her in a flurry.

Right before he was about to hit send, he dropped the phone.
He tucked it under the couch cushions and sat on it for good
measure.

He flopped onto his back again and covered his head with a
couch cushion. Why was he being so fucking emotional? He'd
ended things with girls lots of times. Was this how they all felt
when he did it?

He hoped not, otherwise he would feel like an asshole.

He felt his ass vibrate, sat bolt upright, and fished the phone
from underneath it. Maybe she was at the airport and had second
thoughts and was texting him to say that she was on her way back.
Maybe she was right outside and was texting him to say she was
about to knock on the door.

It was Carlos. Not Alexa.

Hey man, everything cool with you and Alexa? You disappeared
from Heather's last night.

Oh, fuck. On top of everything else, he had to apologize to
Carlos.

Hey. Sorry I was an asshole last night.

He stood up to go flick the switch on the coffeepot, glad that
he'd set it up yesterday afternoon.

We're cool. I don't think I'm the one you have to worry about,
though.

He stared at his coffeepot, now brewing twice as much coffee as he would need.

Tell me about it.

He shook his head. Fuck Alexa. She wasn't worth all of this. Fuck this emotional bullshit. He was going for a run. Maybe he'd run into Kat.

♥

Alexa sat on the airplane at LAX and buckled her seat belt. She hoped this damn plane would take off soon so she wouldn't grab her bag and run back to Drew's. She'd been sitting at the airport for the past two hours, unshowered, her hair in a messy topknot, no makeup on. And the whole time she'd resisted the temptation to turn around and jump back under his covers and next to his warm, sleeping body before he even realized she was gone.

Last night before she'd gone to sleep, she'd planned on having an adult conversation with Drew. She wasn't going to tell him how strong her feelings were for him, because he didn't need to know that. The last thing she wanted was his pity.

She'd planned to tell him it was nothing against him, but she knew how he felt about relationships, and she couldn't do this anymore. She would have just blamed the distance making it tough, and how she couldn't keep flying up and down the state anymore, how this had been fun for a couple of months, but they both knew it couldn't last much longer.

All of that had the benefit of being the truth. It just wasn't the whole truth.

But then he'd crawled into bed with her in the middle of the night and put his arms around her and she'd broken down. All she'd wanted in that moment was to stay right there in his arms forever, to ignore everything in her head telling her this was never going to work and they were too different and wanted different things, and just give in to the warmth and security of his arms.

The impossibility of that had made her burst into tears. Her, Alexa Monroe, who never cried.

And when he said sweet things about making it work, she'd lost it completely and sobbed so hard she'd hiccupped. She knew what his version of "making things work" was—they'd just keep going the same way they'd been going for a while longer, a few more weeks, a month even, before she'd get his breakup speech and he'd disappear.

But she wanted so much for it to be true, that he did want to make it work for real. She wanted him to love her and for them to push through all of their problems together because they loved each other enough to be able to do it.

So she cried to mourn what could have been, how good his arms felt around her and his chest felt against her face, and how she would never get to feel that again. Her tears had revealed her feelings for him even more than words could have.

How humiliating. She'd cultivated her poker face for years, and in the most important moment she'd had in years, it had betrayed her in the worst possible way.

She'd woken up this morning with his arms still around her. She'd been too scared and ashamed to face him and have to see the look of pity on his face, or listen to his platitudes about how it wasn't her, it was him, and how he hoped they could stay friends. So instead, she'd tiptoed out of his apartment early this morning and dragged her suitcase blocks away so she could get a cab to the airport.

Was that cowardly of her? Probably, but she'd rather be a coward than break down in front of him again, and in broad daylight this time, so he could see how bad she looked when she cried.

And then once she actually got to the airport, she had to pay way too much money to get her flight changed from her original one. Maddie, God bless her, had asked no questions when she'd texted her to pick her up from the airport.

Maddie was waiting at the curb when Alexa walked out of the airport. Maddie took a long look at her face when she got in the passenger seat.

"First: are we going to your house or my house?"

Alexa considered as Maddie drove out of the airport.

"Do you still need my car until you can pick yours up tomorrow? If so, my house."

"Okay." There was silence as Maddie got on the freeway toward Berkeley. "Do you want to talk about it?"

Alexa dropped her head back against the headrest and closed her eyes.

"I don't know. I just want to be somewhere and not not cry." She sighed. "I've spent the past five hours doing everything in my power to not cry. At his house, at the airport, on the plane." She checked her phone again to see if he'd called. He hadn't. "Now I can at least stop fighting it."

Maddie reached for her hand and squeezed it.

"You want me to drive through In-N-Out on the way?"

Alexa shrugged.

"I'm not really hungry."

Maddie shook her head.

"Now I know you're in a bad place. I'm getting you In-N-Out whether you like it or not."

When they walked through Alexa's front door, everything in

her house reminded her of Drew. The couch where he'd cried on her shoulder. The towel he'd stolen from the hotel for them to lie on in Dolores Park, now hanging up in her bathroom. The coffee table where he'd set her coffee while she was working. The hoodie that he'd left here on his impromptu trip and that she'd "forgotten" to bring back to him this weekend.

She lowered herself down on the couch and put her head in her hands.

"Lex." She felt Maddie's hand on her shoulder and leaned into it. Maddie wrapped her arms around her. They sat there like that on the couch for a while, not talking. Eventually, Alexa sighed.

"You were right—I want some French fries. You got us ketchup, right?"

"Of course." Maddie ripped the bags open and unpacked the food on top of the makeshift place mats. "Now. Talk to me."

Alexa dropped her head into her hands.

"Oh, Mad. I fucked it all up."

Maddie pulled her head onto her shoulder.

"What happened?"

"It was all going okay. I mean, we hadn't talked about anything, but the weekend was fine. Great. And then we went to the 4th of July party." She thought about the party, and the humiliation hit her all over again. "And all of these other women . . . They were so nice . . . but they said . . . and he didn't . . . I'd had too much sangria but . . . ." Oh, look, she was sobbing again. Maddie folded her into her arms and let her cry on her shoulder until she was too tired to cry anymore.

She sat up and took a sip of her drink and ate a handful of cold fries.

"I guess I should start over again." She told Maddie the whole story, except for the part about the sex they'd had when she was weeping. That seemed too intimate, too personal, even to tell Maddie. She managed to get through the whole thing without crying, but she'd probably cried out all of her tears.

"Honey." Maddie stroked her hair. "Alexa, I love you. I would do anything for you. You know that, right?"

She sighed and nodded. She'd heard this before from Maddie. Enough to know to worry about what was coming next.

"Okay. Why didn't you just tell him how you felt about him? And tell him what you wanted? Why did you just disappear this morning?"

She pushed herself to the other side of the couch.

"I knew what he was going to say, okay? I didn't need to hear it."

Maddie looked at her. She didn't smile, or raise her eyebrows, or tilt her head. She just looked at her and wouldn't let her look away.

"I was scared! Is that what you want to hear? Okay, fine: I was scared to talk to him! I was scared I would pour out my heart and he would tell me he hoped we could stay friends, I was scared I would see in his face when I started talking that he felt sorry for me, I was scared I'd lay myself bare for nothing, and I was scared I would reveal my whole self to him and he would avert his eyes." She sighed. "I was scared."

Maddie wrapped her back up in a hug.

"Oh, honey."

Alexa rested her head on Maddie's shoulder. Oh, look, she did have more tears in there.

Maddie sat up.

"Does cookie dough ice cream go better with red or white wine?"

Alexa half laughed, half sobbed.

"I guess we're about to find out."

♥

Drew saw Kat on his run, but he dodged behind a truck at the last minute to avoid her. He got home in as shitty a mood as when he'd left. He ordered an enormous Hawaiian pizza and opened a bottle of rum, mostly because Alexa hated both. By seven p.m. he never wanted to see another pineapple, but he finished the pizza just to spite her.

Not that she would ever know, but maybe somewhere she had a terrible taste in her mouth and it was thanks to him.

He dragged himself into the hospital on Tuesday morning and managed to avoid having a conversation with anyone but his patients and their parents until almost one o'clock. Of course that's when Carlos burst into his office.

Fuck. He was grumpy and hungover. He didn't need to deal with Carlos.

"Never learned to knock, huh?" He kept his head buried in his stack of files.

"How was the rest of your weekend? Everything cool with you and—"

Drew didn't even want to hear her name.

"Leave it alone, Carlos."

Carlos moved the stack of books Drew had put on the guest office chair to the floor and plopped down in the chair. Drew scowled. He'd left those books on the chair to keep anyone from sitting there. He should have known that that wouldn't stop Carlos for a second.

"No, really, what happened? She looked pissed at the party even before you said—"

Drew looked up from the stupid files.

"I said leave it alone, Carlos."

Did that stop him? No, of course not.

"Come on, man. You have a fight? It was bound to happen eventually. Tell Dr. Carlos about it. I'll get you all fixed up."

Drew couldn't take it anymore. He'd slept like shit, because of the rum and the pizza and the absence of Alexa's soft, welcoming body next to him, his stomach was full of nothing but strong coffee, he had the worst possible taste in his mouth, and Carlos apparently wasn't getting the message that he didn't fucking want to talk about it. He pushed himself up from his desk, and his chair slammed back against the wall behind him.

"I SAID, leave it alone."

He threw open his office door, ignored the stunned look on Carlos's face, and walked out of the hospital to his car. He had thirty minutes before his next patient; that was enough time to eat something disgusting and terrible for him.

♥

Alexa walked into City Hall bright and early Tuesday morning. She'd been up since four, so at five thirty she'd given up on more sleep and had gotten ready for work.

At least she hadn't dreamed about Drew, though her anxiety dreams all had very loud Drew subtext. Awake, he was never far from her thoughts. She kept thinking of what he would say about her presentation, if he'd thought about her at all, the look on his face when they'd made love that last time, the way he always held her as they slept. It was a lot easier to think about work.

She brought a carafe of coffee and a box of doughnuts into the office, along with a bag of doughnut holes. She ate the doughnut holes all morning while catching up on email and expense reports, and got so absorbed in the mindlessness of it that she jumped when Sloane exclaimed from her office doorway. "You brought doughnuts, thank GOD." Sloane walked in and popped open the box. "Wait, all dozen are still here? You haven't had one yet?"

If she hadn't bought herself the bag of doughnut holes, she would have demolished the entire box of doughnuts before anyone else had gotten there.

Theo walked in right behind Sloane and dove into the doughnut box. He came up with the maple bar that she'd gotten for him.

"You're a queen among women, Lex."

"She is, isn't she?" Sloane picked up the box. "Want me to bring this out to my desk? Need more coffee?" Alexa nodded to both questions. Theo dropped into her office chair as soon as Sloane left.

"Got your email last night. Did you see mine?"

She nodded. She'd seen it at four this morning when she'd woken up and checked her phone. They talked city council strategy as they drank coffee and ate their doughnuts, and argued about whether they could count on Councilman Goode to be on their side or not. The conversation soothed her. This she knew how to do. This she was good at.

Theo reached for her bag of doughnut holes.

"Hey, how was your weekend in L.A.?"

She shook her head. If she said anything to Theo, she might break down again, and work was the last place she wanted to do that.

Well, the last place was probably Drew's bed at one in the morning with him there to witness it, but work was second to that.

"Oh no, what happened?" Theo asked.

She shook her head again before he could finish his sentence. He reached for her hand and squeezed it. She squeezed back and let go.

"I can't, Teddy. Maybe later."

He nodded.

"Okay. But you know that if you ever want to talk . . ."

She nodded down into her coffee. Yes, she did know.

Theo took a deep breath. "Okay, onto another topic that may also be sensitive: have you talked to Olivia about any of the TARP stuff yet?"

Alexa looked up from her coffee. Theo was one of the only other people who knew about the history with Olivia. She'd told him all about it on a drunken night last year, right after they'd both had a terrible day at work and when she was already anxious about Olivia coming to visit that weekend.

"What? No, why?"

He sat back in the chair, crossed his legs and uncrossed them, and sat up again.

"You don't have to, of course. But I know we talked a while ago about how she might have some ideas that we hadn't thought of."

She started to interrupt, but he kept going.

"And also . . . we have all of those personal stories from people who went through programs like this and turned their lives around, and I thought maybe Olivia might be willing to write something up for us, or . . ."

Alexa looked down into her coffee again, gazing into the dark brown liquid like it was Dumbledore's Pensieve. She knew Theo too well to be fooled by this. He was just making up reasons for her to talk to Olivia about TARP. But maybe he was right?

"I never thought of that," she said, not looking up at Theo.

He stood up and walked toward her office door.

"You don't have to, of course. But . . . maybe you want to? I think she'd be pleased to hear you're doing this. I bet she'd be pretty touched."

Alexa looked up at him, the tears threatening again.

"Somebody . . . somebody else said that, too. Maybe I will."

Theo's eyebrows went up.

"You told . . ." She looked down at her desk, and his voice trailed away. After a minute, he said, "Think about it. It might be good for you to talk to her about it."

She'd think about it. Maybe Drew had been right about this. Damn him.

Theo was halfway through her office door before she stopped him.

"Teddy."

He turned around.

"Yeah?"

"Thanks. For . . . everything."

"Anytime."

23

Friday after work Drew went home and changed into his running clothes. He ran on the beach for ten miles, trying to exhaust himself so much he didn't think about Alexa, and how he should be on a plane to go see her at that very moment. It didn't work.

The shameful thing was that he'd already bought a ticket to fly up there that weekend. He'd bought it the day before she flew in for the 4th of July weekend, and he hadn't canceled it yet. He kept thinking he'd hear from her; he'd feel his phone vibrate in his pocket and it would be a text from her. She'd say she was wrong to leave, she'd missed the hell out of him all week just like he'd missed her. And then he would fly up there this weekend, and . . . but that hadn't happened.

So he'd canceled his flight right before leaving the office, and now he was even grumpier than he'd been all week. Now it truly felt over.

He climbed up the stairs to his apartment after his run, hot and sweaty and irritable, but no longer in the kind of mood where he would knock over small children in his path. That mood had been kind of inconvenient for a pediatrician.

He pulled his house key out of the pocket in his running shorts, confused by the sound of the TV. It must be his neighbors, though they usually . . . oh no.

"Who the fuck told you to come over?" he said as he opened the door, knowing what he would find. Yep, Carlos sitting on his couch with a beer in his hand.

"Hey, man." Carlos gestured to the spread on the coffee table. "I brought burgers. And beer."

Drew looked at the food. His disloyal stomach growled. Okay, fine. He dried his face with a paper towel and opened the fridge for one of Carlos's beers. This was bribery, but it's not like he was going to reject beer. Carlos would just have to deal with his sweat; he's the one who'd barged in uninvited in the first place.

He finished a burger and a beer without them saying much to each other except for grunts at the Dodgers game on the TV. Carlos went back to the kitchen and opened two more bottles. Maybe he'd just come over because he wanted company. Maybe Drew had been ignoring his friends because of Alexa, and Carlos had missed him, and was taking advantage of this Friday night that Drew was in town to hang out, watch baseball, eat burgers, drink beer. Maybe . . .

"All right." Carlos turned off the TV and set a beer in front of Drew. "How drunk do I have to get you before you tell me why you've been scaring the nurses and making your patients cry all week?"

Maybe not.

"I don't know what you're talking about." Drew downed half the beer. "And that kid always cries—it wasn't my fault."

Carlos shook his head and took a handful of fries.

"His *mom* was crying this time, too."

Drew banged the beer down on the table, making it almost overflow.

"Just because I told her if she had been paying attention to her child, he wouldn't have gotten injured like that, now I'm the bad guy?" He turned to Carlos, whose mouth was wide open.

Drew finished his beer and sighed.

"Fine, I am the bad guy. Get me another beer."

Carlos passed him his own untouched beer and stood up to get more.

"Just tell me what happened," he said when he got back to the couch. "It might make you feel better. I assume this is about Alexa, since you're all sweaty from a run on the beach on Friday night and not from . . ."

Drew kicked Carlos and he laughed.

"What, you told me yourself that when the two of you get together, it's all—"

Drew threw a French fry at him.

"Do you want to hear this fucking story, or are you going to keep sitting there making jokes about my girlfriend?" He sighed. "Forget I said that; she's not my girlfriend. She was never my girlfriend."

Carlos grabbed a handful of French fries.

"Did you . . . want her to be your girlfriend?"

Drew gulped the third beer.

"I don't know. Maybe. It doesn't matter, though. She hates me now."

Carlos raised his eyebrows.

"Do you not have eyes? Because that's some bullshit right there.

You forget, I've seen the two of you together. I've seen the way she looks at you. Unless you did something terrible that I don't know about . . ."

Drew shook his head. Yeah, maybe she had looked at him like that, but that was before.

"I'll tell you the whole story, then you'll see." Apparently the answer to Carlos's earlier question was: "Three beers."

It took him another beer to get all the way to the text message from Monday morning. Why did it hurt so much to tell Carlos what happened?

"See? I should have ended this a long time ago, before she could hate me."

Carlos looked at the phone for a few seconds, and then up at Drew.

"No, you shouldn't have ended it a long time ago. What the fuck is wrong with you? You know, I always thought you were kind of an idiot, but I never knew you were this fucking stupid."

Drew stood up and kicked the table. Ketchup flew across the floor.

"I bare my fucking soul to you, tell you how a girl left me asleep and naked in my bed, and this is what I get? Fuck you. Why don't you spend time dealing with your own fucked-up life, instead of worrying about mine?"

Carlos looked up at him from the couch with a blank expression on his face. He didn't budge.

Drew put his head in his hands and shook his head. What was wrong with him? Carlos didn't deserve that.

"Sorry. That was a shitty thing to say."

Carlos nodded.

"It was. Sit down."

Drew looked at him, looked at the mess on the floor, then at Carlos again. He sat back down on the couch.

Carlos sighed and leaned back against the couch cushions.

"Okay, look. I wasn't sure whether to tell you this, but after what happened, I think I have to."

Drew lunged for him.

"Did you actually hit on her? You fucking asshole, I never really thought—"

Carlos pushed him back down on the couch.

"Relax, dude, of course not. Come on, you know me better than that."

Drew leaned back against the couch cushions and sighed.

"I do. I'm sorry. I'm a jackass. What terrible thing are you going to tell me now?"

Carlos stood up and dragged the coffee table back in place.

"It's something Emma told me after you guys left the party. She said she was feeling kind of bad, because when she and Heather and Robin and Lucy were all in the kitchen with Alexa, they started talking about you."

Drew slumped down and reached for a bottle, but they were all empty. Carlos went to the kitchen for more beer for both of them.

"This must be bad if you're bringing me more beer. What did they say?"

Carlos opened both bottles and sighed.

"Well, I guess Alexa asked a few questions about you . . . and then they all ended up telling their, um, strikingly similar, I guess, stories of how you broke up with them."

Shit. Drew dropped his head in his hands. That was why Alexa had been so upset all of a sudden. Carlos kept talking.

"She didn't tell me exactly what they said, and she said Alexa didn't seem upset about it, but . . ."

Drew lifted his head.

"She does a great fake smile. It fools most people."

"But not you?" Carlos asked, sliding him his beer. Drew pushed it away.

"But not me." He sighed. "She didn't tell you what they said?"

Carlos took a handful of fries.

"No, but I can guess." He raised his eyebrows, and Drew waved at him to continue. Better to get this over with. "I mean, I've seen your pattern. After a month or two, when things are going well, you give them the 'Let's be friends' speech. Maybe she thought that was about to happen to her?"

He closed his eyes. Of course she'd thought that.

Carlos patted him on the shoulder.

"It's okay, man. I think you can fix this." He paused. "If you want to fix it?"

He couldn't remember ever wanting something more.

"Of course I want to fix it, just like I want my med school loans to be magically wiped out, and every sick kid in our hospital to be well, and my knee to stop hurting when I run more than ten miles, but I know all of that is impossible, too." He sat back against the couch cushions, taking his beer with him.

Carlos put down his food and stood up.

"So you're just going to give up? You're not even going to try to get her back?"

"What good would it do?" He sighed. "Plus, it's not like I know how to have a real relationship. Even if it did work, I'd just fuck it up again."

Carlos sat back down in the corner of the couch. The asshole was in Alexa's spot.

"Did you tell her how you felt about her? How you really feel?"

He'd tried, but . . . He shrugged.

"Forget whether she hates you—she doesn't—or if you'd fuck things up again—you would, but you'd figure it out." Carlos pushed a burger in his direction. He ignored it. "The real question is: how *do* you feel about Alexa? Because if you can't answer that question—honestly, and in a way that satisfies her—there's no real point in even trying to fix this."

Drew closed his eyes. He pictured Alexa laughing up at him in the elevator, Alexa dancing with him at the wedding, Alexa smiling at him from their pilfered towel in Dolores Park, Alexa eating tacos on his couch, Alexa frowning at her computer screen, oblivious to him, Alexa whispering "coffee" in his ear early in the morning, Alexa pulling his head down onto her shoulder when he'd flown to her side, Alexa tucked inside the curve of his arms in his bed.

He opened his mouth. But the words stuck in his throat.

Carlos shook his head.

"It's okay, man. You don't have to tell me. But you've got to tell her."

Drew put his head in his hands.

"I don't know if I can do this."

Carlos leaned back against the couch cushions and propped his feet up on an empty spot on the coffee table.

"There's only one way to find out."

24

Alexa woke up on Saturday morning, determined that this would be the day that she called Olivia.

Wednesday, she'd decided for sure to talk to her sister. But she hadn't wanted to do it when either one of them was at work, because that wasn't a conversation she wanted to have inside her office when she might be overheard.

Thursday, she decided to call her when she got home after work, since it would only be around nine or ten New York time and Olivia would still be awake. But by the time she got home that night, it was seven thirty and she decided that was too late.

Friday, she'd admitted to herself she was procrastinating. But she decided Saturday was a better day for a conversation like this anyway. Which meant she had to actually make that call today.

Or Sunday? Maybe Sunday was an even *better* day for a call like this?

She threw back the covers and forced herself out of bed to make

coffee. No, she had to do it today. She'd barely been able to concentrate on anything this week, between this hanging over her
head and the thoughts of Drew, which were constantly *in* her head.

Maddie was right. She should have told him how she'd felt. At
least then she wouldn't have this constant, overwhelming feeling
of regret.

And at least she wouldn't feel like such a coward.

She downed a cup of coffee and shook off the thoughts of Drew.
She just needed to get through this week. If she got through the city
council meeting on Thursday, win or lose, she could spend the entire next weekend in bed wallowing with French fries and ice cream.

And Theo—and Drew—were both right that she had to talk
to Olivia before the meeting.

The coffee swirled around in her empty stomach as she picked
up the phone. Someday she really should switch to tea. She re-
treated to bed and got under the covers before she scrolled to Olivia's name in her phone.

"Hey, kiddo!" Alexa heard street noise in the background.
"How are you this Saturday afternoon?" Olivia laughed. "Morning still for you, I guess."

"Good!" Alexa could tell her voice was too high and tried to
moderate it. "Um, where are you? Are you busy?"

Maybe she'd be too busy to talk right now and they wouldn't
have to have this conversation?

"No, no, just walking home from brunch. What are you up to?"

Shit, okay, she had to do it, then.

"Just drinking coffee at home, trying to take a deep breath after
a long week." Well, that was an understatement.

"Yeah? What's going on? How's work going?"

She just needed to get it out. It was the only way to start this.

"Actually, that's why I called. I've been . . . The mayor has a new initiative for an arts program for at-risk youth, and that's what I—"

"Yeah, I've been reading about that! I had a feeling it was your idea. Great job, kiddo."

Alexa took the phone away from her ear and looked at it. Olivia already knew?

"I, um—you've been reading about it?"

Alexa could hear an elevator ding through Olivia's laughter.

"Of course I've been reading about it. You think I don't pay attention to what my little sister is doing? I'm so proud of you for this. City council meeting is this week, right?"

Alexa sat up in bed. This conversation was not going the way she'd anticipated.

"Yeah, Thursday. I didn't know . . ." She stopped and started again. She'd missed out on the opportunity to be honest with Drew; the least she could do was be honest with her own sister. "I was scared to tell you. I didn't realize you already knew."

Alexa could hear Olivia open and close her front door.

"Lexie, why were you scared to tell me? This is a great thing you're doing."

She teared up at the nickname.

"I wanted to tell you, but we still don't know if it's going to get through the council. I didn't want to tell you anything was in the works until it passed. I didn't want to fail you again."

Alexa picked up her coffee cup, realized her hand was shaking, and put it back down on her bedside table.

"Again? What do you mean, again?"

Alexa twisted her sheets around her fingers to stop the trembling.

"I was so . . . I was terrible to you. When we were in high school and everything blew up, I mean. I was such a bad sister, and I wanted . . . I wanted to make up for that."

Oh God, this was even harder than she'd thought it would be. Tears were running down her face now. She hadn't cried this much in one week since that week she'd gotten her period right before the bar exam.

"You've been worried about that all this time? You don't have anything to make up for. I know there's still friction between us sometimes, but that's not because I'm still mad at you, or hold anything against you for what happened back then. Yes, things were pretty bad that year, but we were kids."

Alexa let out a sob. She wiped her face with the bottom of her tank top.

"I know, but that doesn't make it okay. I wish I hadn't been like that to you."

"Lexie, you've done so much for me!" Olivia said. "You've supported me during times when I needed you the most. You flew to New York at the last minute to move me out of that terrible apartment when I'd gotten dumped, remember? And you—"

Alexa broke in, still sniffling.

"But I've never told you how sorry I am! I'm sorry, Livie. I'm so sorry for what I said and how I acted. I've regretted it for years, but I've been too ashamed and too scared to apologize. I guess this program was going to be my apology, but whether or not the council passes it, I need to say it out loud, too."

She could hear sniffling on the other side of the phone now.

"Oh, honey, apology accepted. I'm glad you said it, but I didn't need to hear it. I always knew you were sorry. I'm so glad my experience inspired you. The teens of Berkeley are lucky to have you championing them."

Alexa's tears kept falling, but they were happy ones now. She got up to pour herself more coffee, and maybe make some toast to settle her stomach.

"Thank you. That means so much for you to say."

She could hear the gurgle of Olivia's coffee maker in the background and almost laughed. Like sister, like sister.

"Okay, so tell me everything about this TARP program of yours that hasn't been in the paper—terrible acronym, by the way. Who came up with that? And what ever happened with the dude from the elevator?"

Alexa reached for the expensive jam from Paris she'd been saving. She deserved it today.

"Oh, Liv, I have so much to tell you."

♥

Drew walked through the hospital on Sunday morning, relieved that he'd finally recovered from his hangover from Friday night. Copious amounts of junk food the day before and a long run where alcohol came out of his pores were the only things that stopped his curses at Carlos and all of that damn beer he'd bought.

If only the solution to what he would do about Alexa was so easy to find. Could he tell her how he felt about her? What if she didn't feel the same way? Wouldn't it be easier to pretend he'd never met her?

These were the questions that had been spinning through his mind for a day and a half, with no answers. He'd been all ready to text her on Friday night, but Carlos confiscated his phone. Probably for the best; the half-written text he saw when he woke up Saturday morning said something nonsensical about how much he missed her naked body against his—while that was *true*, it was probably the wrong way to approach this problem. He didn't know the right way yet.

He got up to the fifth floor and waved at the nurse at the desk. He ducked his head into the third room on the left and found who he was looking for.

"Hey, buddy, how are you doing?"

"Dr. Nick!" Jack grinned at him from his chair and waved. "Did you come to visit me?"

He walked over and sat down next to him, exchanging smiles with Abby.

"Sure did. Haven't seen you in a little while. Wanted to check and see how one of my favorite dudes is doing."

He sat back and let Jack's animated chatter wash over him until it slowed and finally stopped.

"He's asleep," he said to Abby. She'd been pretending to read her book the whole time they talked, but he'd noticed that she hadn't turned a page.

"Yeah, the chemo takes a lot out of him." She closed her book and smiled at him. "Thanks for coming by, though. I know he loved seeing you."

He looked over at Jack, who looked even younger than usual, sound asleep and hooked up to multiple IVs.

"I loved seeing him, too, even though it's tough to see him like this." Tears jumped to Abby's eyes, and he felt like an ass. If it was hard for him to see Jack like this, how did he think his mother felt? "I talked to Dr. Sullivan, though; she said his prognosis is good. She seemed very hopeful."

Abby wiped the tears out of her eyes and smiled at him.

"She said that to us, too, but it's good that wasn't just what she says to parents. Thanks for telling me that. I know doctors tell one another the real story."

He touched Jack's head, careful not to wake him up.

"No problem. I was . . . I was pretty worried about him. I was very relieved when I talked to Dr. Sullivan, though—"

Abby closed her book and tucked it in her purse.

"I know, there are no guarantees. Thanks, regardless." She looked at his hand, still on Jack's head. "How's your friend Alexa?"

He sighed. He should have anticipated that Abby would bring up Alexa.

"That bad, huh?" Abby said, as he looked for a way to answer. "Can I assume that she is . . . or was . . . more than a friend?"

He made a face at her, and she laughed.

"Like you didn't already know that." He sighed. "This is not a normal doctor-patient conversation, but . . . we hit a roadblock. Time will tell if it's a bump in the road or more of a brick wall."

She sat back in her chair and folded her hands.

"I'm guessing from the look on your face that you want it to be the former?"

He moved his hand from Jack's head and looked her in the eye.

"More than anything. I just don't quite know how to make that happen."

She smiled at him.

"Oh, that's easy. What does *she* want more than anything, even if she hasn't told you? Do that for her."

He let out a bark of laughter, checked to make sure he hadn't woken Jack up, and kept laughing more quietly.

"That's easy? Good Lord, what's hard to you?" He glanced back at Jack. "Oh."

Now Abby laughed.

"I wasn't even going to play the kid-with-cancer card, but you did it for me. Look, if you want to be with her, which from the look on your face you do, find a way to be with her. It's really as simple as that, once you clear away everything else."

He laughed again.

"Well, when you put it that way . . ." Actually, when she put it that way, it really was that simple.

He closed his eyes and nodded. Now he knew what he had to do. What he wanted to do. He just hoped this was what Alexa wanted, too. Or else he'd look like a real idiot.

"When you put it that way, you might be right." He stood up. "Thanks, Abby. I hope you've solved my problem for me."

She smiled at him and ran her hand over Jack's head.

"I hope so, too. Keep me posted, will you?"

He saluted her on his way out of the room.

"Absolutely."

He went straight to his office. He had a phone call to make.

25

Alexa was at work by seven in the morning on the day of the city council meeting, even though it didn't start until six that night. At this point, being at work was easier than being at home. At work there was something for her to do, she felt needed, she felt important. At home she was alone with her thoughts and with reminders of Drew. They'd known each other for two months, and he'd only been to her house a handful of times, so why did she see him everywhere there?

At some point, she hoped that would fade. Maybe after the council meeting and she had her ritual fire of everything Drew related.

She was only kidding about that ritual fire. Sort of.

She was in her office on her third run through of her city council presentation when Sloane carried in two big pink bakery boxes.

"Delivery for you, Alexa, but if this is what I think it is, you'd better share."

Alexa perched on the corner of her desk and opened both

boxes. They were overflowing with doughnuts of every variety. Four pink frosted doughnuts with sprinkles were in the center of each box.

"Where did this come from? I was going to bring doughnuts this morning but had too much to carry on my way in to pick these up. Who got these, Theo?"

Sloane flipped one of the boxes closed and pointed to the note on top that Alexa had overlooked.

"Look and see."

She pulled the folded white envelope from the top of the box and opened it.

Alexa—Good luck today! Drew

She hadn't heard from him since she left his bed at dawn almost two weeks ago, and he'd sent her doughnuts? And he'd remembered when the city council meeting was? Was this the Alexa version of Emma's breakup flowers?

She tucked the card back in its envelope and slid it into her purse anyway.

"Can you put these in the kitchen, Sloane? And send out an email to everyone to let them know there are doughnuts? Wait, hold on a second." She plucked two of the pink frosted ones out of one of the boxes. "Okay, now you can take them away."

Sloane picked up both boxes and turned to leave.

"You're going to kill it today, boss."

Alexa put her doughnuts on a napkin.

"Thanks, Sloane. I hope so. I told you to order pizza for everyone's lunch, right?"

"Already done," Sloane called out from the doorway.

The day dragged, as days with something important at the end
of them always did, but finally the clock hit five, her signal to close
her office door and change into her lucky suit and heels. She opened
her door when she was done to find Theo standing behind it.

"Armor on?" he asked. "Are we ready to go?"

She grinned at him, suddenly full of adrenaline.

"You know it. Let's go kick some city council ass."

♥

Drew slipped through the doorway of the city council chambers
right at six. He'd wanted to get there early, but he didn't want
Alexa to see him before the meeting started. She hadn't acknowl-
edged the doughnuts, but he knew she'd gotten them; he'd followed
the delivery guy to her office to make sure.

He found one of the only empty seats in the back of the council
chamber, next to a black woman with lots of curly hair who looked
vaguely familiar. She looked up and smiled at him for a second before
looking back down her phone, her thumbs flying across the screen.

He saw Alexa up at the front of the room, sitting next to Theo
and behind a white-haired man he assumed was the mayor. Damn,
it felt so good to see her again, even from across the room. She was
sitting there, intent on the proceedings, in one of those suits he
loved, looking like she was in her element. She *was* in her element.

Maybe she was relieved to not have him taking up her time
anymore. Maybe Theo had already pounced—see, right there,
he'd put his hand on her shoulder—and they were as happy as
could be together. Had he flown up here for nothing?

He took a deep breath. He couldn't back out now—both Abby
and Carlos would kill him, among other things. Hell with it, he
didn't want to back out now; he had to know for sure.

He saw on the agenda that there was some business to get through first, so he pulled his phone out to pass the time.

"What are you here for?" the woman next to him whispered.

"Oh, the teen arts thing." He smiled and gestured to the front of the room. "My . . . A friend of mine works for the mayor, so I wanted to be here for her."

Her eyes narrowed.

"Oh? Who's your friend?"

He hesitated before he answered, but she was looking at him so intently that he had to.

"Alexa Monroe, she's the mayor's chief of staff." He couldn't keep the smile off his face as he said her name.

The woman dropped her phone into her purse and turned to him with a wide smile. Why was he reminded of a wolf?

"You must be Drew," she said.

At that, everything clicked. Boy, did he feel like an idiot for not figuring this out sooner. He sat up straight.

"And you must be Olivia?" That's why she looked familiar; he'd seen pictures of her around Alexa's house.

She nodded and reached out her hand. He hadn't been so nervous about a handshake since his med school interviews.

"I was under the impression that you and my sister were no longer . . . friends?" She still had that smile on her face.

He nodded, then shook his head. Words, Drew, it was time for words.

"I hope . . . There have been some problems, but my hope is that we're still friends." He laughed under his breath. "No, that's not what I want. I don't want to be friends with your sister—I want a lot more."

Olivia's smile lost some of the animosity.

"Good. Because if you answered that question a different way, I was going to tell you to walk out of this room right now and get your ass back to Los Angeles."

He laughed again, louder this time, causing the people in front of him to turn around and frown. He muttered an apology.

He turned back to Alexa's sister.

"She doesn't know I'm here. So if you could . . ."

She patted him on the shoulder.

"Don't worry, I won't spoil your surprise. I wouldn't anyway, but she doesn't know I'm here, either, so I'd spoil my own surprise, too."

He suddenly realized something: if Olivia was here, Alexa must have taken his advice and told her about the program. He couldn't believe she'd listened to him.

He turned to Olivia to say something else, but she shushed him and pointed to the front of the room.

"They're talking about it now."

♥

Alexa had expected to be jittery, but she'd felt a weird sense of calm descend upon her as soon as she'd walked into the chambers. She'd done all that she could do, and whether she won or lost, she knew she'd won in the eyes of her sister, no matter what.

But she still wanted to *win*.

She spent the first half of the meeting scribbling notes to both the mayor and Theo, and getting scribbled notes from them in return. They'd learned the hard way to always write their notes to one another during council meetings on paper instead of via email or text, since that time a local newspaper had tweeted a picture of the mayor looking at his phone during a council meeting and he'd gotten roundly mocked.

When it was time for her presentation, she stood in front of the podium, all of her anxiety for the week gone. The city council had already gotten her report, so this part was pure theater.

"Mayor, Councilwomen, Councilmen, you've all seen the proposal about the Teen Arts Rehabilitation Program, or TARP. At this point, I'll just go into a few details about the program before alumni of similar programs report to you about the benefits they received from it, and then we'll open it up to questions and public comment."

She went through her presentation, pleased that almost everyone on the council nodded and smiled at her, and the only ones who didn't were the two who'd been opposed to the program from the beginning.

Then came the alumni of various programs, handpicked by Theo: one was a student at UC Berkeley who had done a program like this in East L.A.; another was a recently published author who credited her youth arts and writing program for putting her on the path to where she was. Theo had spent days coaching them on what to emphasize, and Alexa saw him tense up and lean in their direction as they started talking. But after a few initial stumbles, both of them had the council in the palm of their hands.

The council chair opened up the discussion for public comment, and now it was Alexa's turn to tense up. After that meeting in the hills, she was afraid of who was going to be at this meeting, and what they would say. Sure, they'd reached out to all of the communities who they knew supported the program to encourage them to come, and Alexa could see a good number of them in the audience, but there were also lots of faces there that she didn't recognize. Who knew what they would say?

The first two speakers were people she knew were on their side.

But the next two were people who had been visibly skeptical at the meeting in the hills. And yet, they both spoke in support of the program.

She looked over at Theo, who stared straight back at her, his eyes dancing, and down at Maddie, in one of the front rows. She couldn't smile, not yet.

But it kept going on like that. Sure, there were a few people who opposed it, who said that kids needed discipline, needed to be punished for their transgressions, that this was soft on crime, and all of those reasons she'd heard before. But the vast majority of the crowd was on their side. She couldn't believe it.

She looked down at her notebook to doodle something so she wouldn't grin like a loon. When she looked up, she almost jumped out of her seat. Standing there at the microphone was Olivia.

"Mayor, Councilwomen, Councilmen, thank you for this opportunity. As some of you may know, I grew up right here in the Bay Area, though I live far away now. I spent my time in high school getting in and out of trouble, and finally I went too far. Thank God I got sent to a program very much like the one being debated today. That program opened my eyes to all of the things that I could do, all of the things that I could accomplish, if I moved beyond my teenage rebellion and concentrated on what mattered. Since then, I've graduated from two top schools and have recently become a partner at a law firm in New York City. There are many teenagers out there like I was, teens who need someone to help put them on the right track, but who could so easily get pushed onto the wrong path altogether, and never find a way off it. I'm so glad that my arts rehabilitation program showed me my path to success, and I hope you'll open up those pathways for the youth of Berkeley who need it the most."

Alexa had tears in her eyes by the middle of Olivia's speech, and had to look up at the ceiling by the end of it so the tears wouldn't fall. When she managed to look down, Olivia was looking right at her, and they smiled at each other during the loud applause.

No one was surprised when the council voted to approve the pilot program, not after that speech. Alexa was grateful Theo grabbed her in a big bear hug, so she could hide her huge grin against his shoulder. She was so amped up that she could barely concentrate on the thirty minutes of public debate about the new bike lane on Oxford Street.

Finally, the meeting ended and Alexa jumped to her feet, intent on finding Olivia. She couldn't get to her right away, because almost everyone on the council walked up to thank her. And then when the council was done, it was the mayor's turn to wrap her up in a hug.

"You made me proud tonight, Alexa."

She wiped her eyes as she pulled back. This time, she wasn't even ashamed.

"Don't make me cry, sir. Just doing my job."

He laughed and patted her on the shoulder.

"You'd better not be in the office until noon tomorrow, and that's an order, you hear me?"

She didn't even attempt to argue.

"Aye aye, sir."

He grabbed Theo's shoulder, hugged him, too, and handed him a few twenties.

"I know your whole crew likely has plans for drinks. You all have fun. I'm going home." He winked. "Don't do anything I wouldn't do."

They waved good-bye to the mayor, and Alexa picked up her overstuffed purse. Okay, NOW she could go find her sister.

She walked down into the audience seats of the council chamber, her eyes intent on Olivia's hair; it made her easy to find.

"Olivia!" She shouted her sister's name, no longer worried about keeping to her inside voice. When Olivia turned around, the man beside her turned along with her. Alexa took a step back.

"Drew?"

He was in front of her in a flash, Olivia behind him.

"Hi. Great job up there," he said.

She couldn't believe he was here.

"Drew?" She needed to come up with something more to say than just his name. She wanted to reach for him, throw her arms around him, bury her face in his warm chest and let him hold her for days, pull him into her house and never let him out. "Have you been . . . What are you doing here?"

He crossed his arms, then uncrossed them.

"I came to see your night of triumph. Are you, um, glad that I'm here?"

She smiled. After the night that she'd had, any sort of prevarication was impossible.

"I couldn't be gladder that you're here. Although"—she looked around him to meet Olivia's eyes—"I'm pretty happy to see my sister, too."

Drew and Olivia looked at each other and laughed.

"We didn't plan this! We promise!" Olivia said, and pulled her into a hard hug. "I'm going to follow Theo and the rest of your little band. I assume you're all off for a drink or five?"

Alexa nodded. This might be one of the weirdest nights of her life.

"Yeah, at the Blue Lounge, but wait—"

Olivia shook her head and gestured to Drew.

"You have other things to deal with right now. Don't worry, we'll catch up later."

Had Olivia and Drew talked about her? Where had they even met? What was he doing here? Alexa reached out and grabbed Olivia's hand before she walked away.

"Wait, Livie . . . Thank you."

Olivia squeezed her hand.

"You're welcome, kiddo. It was my pleasure."

By the time Olivia walked out the door with Theo and Maddie, the council chambers were deserted. Just Alexa and Drew were left.

"Thank you for the doughnuts," she said. "That was so sweet."

"You're very welcome." He reached out to her and touched her upper arm. She had to fight to not sway toward him. "I hoped they would start the day out on a good note."

She smiled, thinking back to her first bite into the still-warm doughnut.

"They did." She gave up the fight and leaned into his hand for a moment. "Drew, what are you doing here?"

He dropped his hand. It was probably for the best, but she still missed his touch.

"I'm here . . . Shit, I had a whole beginning to this, and now I've forgotten it all." He took a deep breath. "Everything went wrong that weekend."

Now she reached out and grabbed his hand. She couldn't help herself.

"Drew, that's all my fault. I shouldn't have started that fight at the party. And I shouldn't have left without saying good-bye. I'm sorry. I should have just talked to you like a grown-up."

He tightened his grip on her hand when she went to pull away.

"I'm sorry, too. I should have been honest about how I felt."

She didn't want to hear the rest. Not tonight. Probably not ever.

"No, don't worry about it. You didn't have to come all the way up here about that. I know how you feel; it's okay." Shit, was she going to start crying again? At this point, she couldn't even be embarrassed about it.

"No, Alexa. You don't know." He released her hand and took a step back. "I never told you this, but I changed my flight back to L.A. that day, so I could spend more time with you."

She looked up at him and narrowed her eyes. Why was he telling her something she already knew?

"I knew that. I was right there when you changed it."

He shook his head.

"No. Not after the conference. After the wedding."

She let her purse slide off her shoulder and onto the floor. Her mind was a jumble. She felt drunk. Was it all of the doughnuts and pizza? Or maybe the many cups of coffee?

"What do you mean, after the wedding? Your flight was that night, right?"

He shook his head.

"My flight was at noon. When you were in the bathroom that morning, I changed my flight so I could spend the day with you. I should have realized then that I could never get enough of you."

What was he saying? Why was he saying this now?

"Drew, I . . ."

He reached for her hand again.

"No, let me finish, let me get this out. You . . . I . . . Alexa, I can't imagine my life without you. I haven't been able to since I first met you in that elevator. When I woke up that morning and you weren't there . . . it broke me. I tried to live without you, but I couldn't. I can't." He took a deep breath. "Alexa, I love you. I love you so much."

She tried to release his hand, but he held on tight. Her eyes filled with tears.

"Drew, I . . . Are you sure?"

He smiled and took another step toward her.

"I've never been more sure about anything."

♥

Telling Alexa that he'd loved her hadn't been as hard as he'd thought it would be. As a matter of fact, he wanted to keep saying it, over and over. But did she feel the same way? He couldn't tell. All he knew was her hand was in his and she was here with him.

He might as well tell her everything.

"Look." He held out his phone to her. She looked at him with a question in her eyes but took it anyway. "This is how sure I am. Read this email."

She cleared her throat and looked at his phone. He was still gripping her hand.

"Drew Nichols, Children's Hospital of Oakland is pleased to offer you the position of . . ." Her voice trailed away. "Is this for real?"

He took the phone out of her hand.

"Very much for real. I called my mentor on Sunday. He told me when I saw him before the wedding that there was going to be a job opening up here and tried to get me to apply for it. I said no then, but . . . I changed my mind. It was a little more complicated than he'd implied, and I can't start until—"

She threw her arms around him and buried her head in his chest. She was crying again, but he hoped that these were good tears. He pulled her tight against him.

"I'm only going to take it if you want me to," he said against her ear. "Please tell me you do?"

She turned her head and pulled his head down to hers for a long kiss. Eventually, he pulled back and wiped the tears from her face with his thumb. My God, he'd missed her so much.

"Tell me."

She smiled up at him, her eyes sparkling through her tears.

"Yes, I want you to take it."

He kissed her eyelids, her cheeks, her hair.

"Don't you have something else to tell me?" he said, his lips a breath away from hers.

"I love you." The tears streamed from her eyes as she said it. "Oh, Drew, I love you so much. I've been trying to deny to myself all week how much I love you."

He brushed her tears away.

"I've been trying to admit to myself how much I love you."

He held her face in his hands and kissed her, their tears mingling with each other's, their bodies fitting together like they were made to be just like that.

"Mizz Monroe?" The voice came from the doorway. Alexa put her head on his shoulder, laughing into his mascara-stained shirt before she turned toward the security guy. "I was going to lock up. Should I, um . . ."

Alexa cleared her throat.

"Sorry about this, Stu. You can lock up. Let me just get my stuff."

She picked her purse back up from where she'd dropped it on the ground and took Drew's hand.

"Let's go home."

He squeezed her hand and walked with her out the door.

"Aren't you forgetting that we have to meet up with everyone from your office?"

She stopped and laughed as she wiped her face with the sleeve of her suit jacket.

"I can't believe it, but I had forgotten that. I'll text Theo; he'll understand. Olivia can come over . . . a little bit later."

Drew shook his head. He wanted nothing more than to take her straight home and make up for all of their lost time, but he knew she'd regret missing out on this night with her crew.

"No, no, you can't not go. This is your night of triumph!" He took her heavy bag from her and tossed it over his own shoulder.

She smiled up at him.

"See, this is why I love you."

He laughed.

"This is it? Of all the things it could be, me sending you out to have drinks with your coworkers instead of locking you in the bedroom with me is why you love me?"

She reached for his hand and squeezed it.

"Yeah. It is."

He lifted their joined hands and kissed hers.

"Now, let's get you into the bathroom to wash your face before your whole office sees you with raccoon eyes. Plus, if you walk in there looking like that, your sister is going to draw and quarter me."

She laughed.

"Come with me upstairs to my office so I can repair myself." She pulled his face down so she could whisper in his ear. "And you know, my office door locks, so no one will interrupt us there."

He liked the sound of that. He gestured to the hallway with his free hand.

"Lead the way, Monroe."

Epilogue

"Why can't Carlos meet us at the restaurant?"

They walked into the Fairmont, almost a year after they'd met there. Carlos was in town and was staying there for some reason, instead of one of the more convenient hotels downtown. Drew had insisted on meeting him in his room, instead of at the restaurant where they were having dinner. Alexa was trying not to complain about it, but it was a Thursday night at seven, she'd had a long day, and she was ready for a cocktail and an enormous plate of French fries.

"He needs your opinion on his outfit. I don't know." Drew had been distracted their whole drive there and kept checking his phone. She knew he had a few patients he was worried about, but this was unusual for him.

She pressed the button for the elevator and looked up at him and smiled, ready to reminisce about *their* elevator, but he wasn't looking at her; he was looking off in the distance. Okay. She tried not to take it personally.

In the past year, they'd had their ups and downs. They'd learned how to deal with two busy careers and a relationship, too; what the other person was like on an early Monday morning and a stressful Thursday night instead of just their idyllic weekends; that she never made the bed; that Drew always left the lights on.

They'd also learned how to talk to each other about their feelings, even when they were scary. And throughout everything, they'd loved each other. Those two things helped them get over all of the bumps, big and little.

The corner elevator—their elevator—opened, and he grabbed her hand and led her inside. She looked up at him to ask another question, saw something out of the corner of her eye, and turned.

There were bouquets of flowers lining the elevator. Deep red roses, fat pink peonies, bright orange gerbera daisies, golden yellow daffodils, purple lilacs, all in vases along the floor. In one corner was a picnic basket, in another was an ice bucket with a bottle of champagne inside, and a pink bakery box was in the middle.

"Drew? What's . . . Is this . . . Are we . . ." She didn't even know what to ask him. At first, she'd thought it must be some mistake, but then she saw the way he was smiling at her, looking relaxed for the first time that day. He took both of her hands in his, and her whole body warmed at his touch.

"Alexa. I love you. I love you so much. You know that, right?"

She nodded, tears springing into her eyes. Damn this man for always making her cry. Except now, almost always, it was from joy.

"Me, too. I love you so much, too."

The elevator shuddered to a stop, and she looked around and laughed.

He kissed one of her hands.

"I know you do. We met right here, three hundred sixty-four days ago, and it was the best thing that's ever happened to me." He pulled her down to the floor, where they sat cross-legged, like they had the last time they'd been stuck in an elevator together. "Alexa Monroe, will you marry me?"

A tear slid down her cheek. At least she'd switched to water-proof mascara ever since Drew had moved to Berkeley.

"Yes, I'll marry you. I would LOVE to marry you." She pulled his face toward hers, and they kissed until they were lying on the floor, the flowers surrounding them.

He pulled back and smiled at her, then sat bolt upright.

"Wait! I forgot something!" He reached in his pocket and pulled out a jewelry box. "Do you like it? I had Maddie give me some ideas, but if you . . ."

She held out her left hand for him to slide the ring on her finger. She glanced down and saw the sparkle but couldn't keep her eyes off the look on his face. She couldn't remember ever having been this happy in her life.

"The ring is perfect, and I can't believe Maddie was able to keep this secret from me." She looked around at the elevator. "How did you manage to do this? How long do we get the elevator for? Wait. Carlos isn't really upstairs, is he?"

He intertwined their hands and laughed.

"Nope, safe and sound in L.A. We only get the elevator for thirty minutes, and that took a lot of sweet-talking to the hotel manager and implied promises of having a wedding here. I wanted to do this tomorrow, on our actual elevator anniversary, but I had to compromise. I hope you don't mind."

"I don't mind a single thing right now."

He grinned at her.

"I'm going to open that bottle of champagne as soon as I manage to let go of you. We don't have much time to drink it."

He seemed in no hurry to let go of her, though, and she was in no hurry for him to let her go. He wrapped his arms around her again, and they sat there on the floor together, her head against his chest. After a minute or so, he gestured to the picnic basket and said the magic words.

"I brought the fancy cheese and crackers this time."

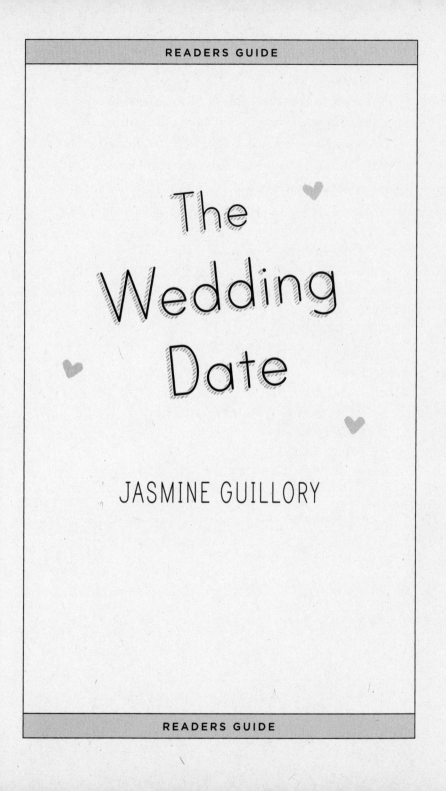

The Wedding Date

JASMINE GUILLORY

Reading Group Discussion Questions

1. Would you be able to choose your career over a possible long-term relationship, much like Alexa did?

2. Was there a time when you were incredibly passionate about a project, whether at work or at home, and felt stymied about getting it through? What were you able to do to finish it?

3. Theo is Alexa's work husband—he's there for her, encourages her, and is all-around her closest confidante at work. How important is it to have a work bestie? Do you have one?

4. When was there a time you knew a relationship wasn't going to work out, much like Drew's situation? You weren't in love with the other person, and you knew it was best to end the relationship. How difficult was it? Talk about your experience.

5. There are several instances of racism throughout the novel, both subtle and obvious. Have you observed racist behavior in your life, and if so, how were you affected by it? Did it cause you to act? Why or why not?

6. Drew doesn't see himself as a "player," even though many of his ex-girlfriends do. Do you think he is one, or does he just have a different understanding of what defines a "player"?

7. Communication is important in relationships. With all the different ways of communicating that technology now offers, have you ever had a text or email exchange that was misinterpreted and that led to conflict?

8. Alexa has a lot of guilt about her past with her sister. Do you think she's right or wrong to feel guilty about her past behavior? Have you done something that you still feel guilty about, even if the other people affected have forgiven you and moved on?

9. Alexa and Drew bond over a mutual love of food. How important a role does food play in your own relationships?

A Conversation with Jasmine Guillory

1. *The Wedding Date* is your first novel. What made you decide you wanted to write?

I've been a voracious reader my entire life, but for some reason, it never occurred to me to write. But there was a point about six or seven years ago when I realized that while my job was great for me in many ways, I had no creative outlet in my life. I thought about writing, but I'd spent so many years thinking about writing as something other people did that at first I shied away from the idea. But a good friend of mine is a writer, so when I tentatively broached the idea to her, she was so enthusiastic and encouraging that I thought, "Okay, maybe this *could* be something I could try." And when I finally started writing, I had so much fun with it that I realized it was the piece missing from my life.

2. How did you come up with the idea for *The Wedding Date*?

Right around the time I started thinking through a story about two people who meet in a broken elevator, my friend Nicole came to San Francisco for a wedding and stayed at the Fairmont. I met her there for a drink at the bar, and as we sat in that romantic, old-school atmosphere, I wondered what would happen if my as-yet-unnamed doctor from Los Angeles and mayor's chief of staff from Berkeley were at a wedding in that hotel together, just days after they met. I've always loved weddings, and I think they're full of so much fodder for writers. They can be wonderful and full of joy, but they can also be incredibly stressful, both for the couple getting married and for the guests. When you're a guest at a wedding full of people you have a long history with, you never know what stories they're going to bring up, or what age you might revert to around them. I wanted that wedding to be the worst possible kind of wedding to go dateless to, so I realized it had to be his ex-girlfriend's wedding. I pulled out my phone and jotted down a quick outline (which still lives in the Notes app of my phone), and *The Wedding Date* was born.

3. Have you had work friendships that became lasting friendships, like the relationship Alexa has with Theo and the one Drew has with Carlos? How have you managed to deepen those friendships?

Some of my closest friendships started as work friendships. I met two friends because we were on a huge work project together. It was one of those projects where you're working with each other constantly—we saw each other far more than anyone on the case saw their spouses—and when you're working twelve hours a day, seven days a week with people, you either come out of it hating them, or friends forever. We were lucky that we were the latter. I think the thing that made the difference for us is that we got to know and care about each other as people, not just as coworkers. When you get to the point with people where you learn not just what makes them laugh, but what makes them cry, those are people you have to hold on to. And a few years later, when two of us were bridesmaids in the third's wedding, we knew exactly how to deal with her wedding-related stress! (Brownies and wine.)

4. Knowing that you have a full-time career outside of writing, how do you balance your life?

When I'm working on a book, I have to keep myself to a pretty strict schedule and steal time whenever I can find it. No matter what, I write every day, usually from about 9–11 P.M. I've tried to get up early to write, but mornings have never been my strong point (to put it mildly). I took the good advice of a writer friend to just keep doing what works for me, and writing at night is what's always worked for me, so I'm not going to fix what's not broken. But it helps that I enjoy writing so much that I'm happy to make time for it. When I was writing the first draft of *The Wedding Date*, my job was really hectic, but I would steal away to Starbucks with my laptop for half an hour most afternoons and write as much as I could. It really taught me how to find those hidden pockets of time in my day and make use of them.

That said, making time for my family and friends is also very important to me, and I would never sacrifice those relationships. Sometimes I meet friends for brunch instead of dinner, or I make them come to meet me at a restaurant five minutes from my house so I can get back to work faster. But my family and friends are very supportive of my writing, so we all make it work. Last summer, on girls' weekend away, I had a great dinner with my friends. Afterward, they went to bed, and I stayed up for two more hours with my laptop. I was a little groggy the next morning, but then, this is where the secret of many writers comes in: coffee!

5. Do you have any advice to share for aspiring writers?

Keep going. We all struggle with self-doubt, rejection, and anxiety, and we all think maybe we should quit. Keep writing, keep reading, and keep improving your craft. *The Wedding Date* may be my debut novel, but it's the third book I wrote, and the lessons I learned from writing the first two taught me so much. Ask other writers for advice and guidance, and see if any of their tricks or tips are right for you; you'll get a ton of conflicting advice, because all writers do this stuff differently. There's no right or wrong here! Some of my most helpful writing experiments have been failed experiments, because learning what doesn't work for me is almost as helpful as learning what does. Read widely—fiction and non-fiction, children's and adult, literary and commercial. Take note of what you like and why, and just as important, what you *don't* like and why. And keep writing.

6. Alexa and Drew initially got together because Drew needed a date for his ex-girlfriend's wedding. Have you ever asked a complete or near stranger to be your plus-one at a wedding? Or do you think it's better to go dateless, or with just a friend?

Unless I'm seriously dating someone, I always go single to weddings. So often, weddings are a time when I get to see friends I haven't seen in years, or family I only see for major occasions, so

I'd rather spend my time at the wedding catching up and having fun with them instead of shepherding around a near stranger my friends will likely never meet again anyway. Plus, my friend Colleen was very correct about that "Don't bring a sandwich to a buffet" line—I've had more than one romantic connection begin at a wedding.

However, I will say that there have been a few weddings where I wished I'd brought a date. At weddings where the couple getting married were the only two people I knew there, it would have been far more fun to have someone I knew and liked at my side. Plus, when seated at the "we don't know where to put these people" table, a date would have saved me from having to make small talk with strangers for hours. And then there's family weddings. I have a really big family, and sometimes at weddings of distant family members, I think it would be far easier to have a date at my side to avoid all the questions about my love life. The problem with that is I'd be answering "What ever happened to that date you brought to . . ." questions until the end of time. I probably chose correctly.

Nik Paterson looked around at the perfect Los Angeles day: clear blue sky, bright green baseball field, warm sun shining down on the thousands of people with her at Dodger Stadium. There was only one thought on her mind: *when can I get out of here?*

Fisher was next to her, his blond man bun golden in the sun, laughing as he drank warm beer to celebrate his birthday. He and his buddies were talking about lifting, or their latest auditions, or their upcoming car purchases. All of the things his friends always talked about—all of the things Nik couldn't care less about. If she'd known that this birthday outing was going to include a bunch of Fisher's friends, she would have at least gotten one of her girlfriends to come along so she would have someone to talk to.

To be fair, it was possible Fisher had told her his friends were coming and she hadn't been paying attention. She tended not to pay that much attention when Fisher talked. But then, she hadn't been dating him for the past five months for his conversational skills.

Nik looked back up at the scoreboard and sighed. It was still only the fifth inning. She probably had at least an hour, maybe an hour and a half, more of this.

She didn't have anything against baseball, exactly. It was just that she'd rather be spending this beautiful spring day at home with her laptop and a glass of bourbon on the rocks than outside at a baseball stadium with a warm beer. But when the hot dude you were sleeping with wanted to go to a Dodger game for his birthday, you sucked it up and went along with him and his bros.

She sighed again and reached for her phone. Maybe she could get some work done as she sat there.

Just as she was starting to make some actual progress on a draft of an article, Fisher nudged her hard.

"Nik! Put your phone down, you can't miss this!" He threw his arm around her and kissed her on the cheek. She pressed save and tucked her phone back in her pocket. His favorite baseball player must be coming up to bat or something.

She looked down at the field, but nothing was going on there. She followed Fisher's pointed finger and instead looked up at the scoreboard, just in time to see on the screen:

NICOLE: I LOVE YOU. WILL YOU MARRY ME? FISHER.

She turned to Fisher, her mouth wide open.

"What the hell is going on?"

To her horror, he dropped down onto one knee, on top of the peanut shells that carpeted the concrete, dangerously close to the puddle of spilled beer.

Oh God. He had a ring box in his hand.

"Nikole." He tucked a strand of hair behind his ear and opened the ring box. She averted her eyes. "Will you make me the happiest man in the world?"

Was she asleep? This definitely felt like a nightmare.

Good God, they'd only been dating for five months! That he loved her was news to her—he'd certainly never said *that* before—but a proposal? He didn't even know how to spell her name!

She tried to put on a smile, but she'd never had the best poker face—except, strangely, when she was actually playing poker. Not even his best friends would call Fisher perceptive, but even he could tell something was off with his happy moment.

"Nik, did you hear me? You're just standing there. You haven't even put the ring on!"

"I don't . . ." She cleared her throat and tried to talk in a low voice, so that the whole damn stadium couldn't tell what was going on. "It's just that we've never discussed this. We aren't really in a place to . . . I didn't . . . I just wish you'd brought this up before . . . before now."

"Are you saying no?"

He was still on one knee. God.

"I'm saying this isn't really the place to have this conversation."

He snapped the ring box closed.

"Are you saying no?" he repeated.

She took a deep breath.

"I'm trying not to say that out loud so everyone can hear me."

She was still hoping this was some sort of a joke. That any minute, he would reveal that this was for a commercial or something, and they would all laugh and go back to not paying attention to the game.

"I can't believe you're doing this to me." He stood up and tossed his head. The head toss didn't work as well when his hair was in the bun. "Rejecting me in public! On my birthday! What kind of a person are you?"

He stormed off and ran up the stadium stairs. So it wasn't a joke, then.

She looked at his bros, and his bros looked at her. They shook their heads like they were disappointed in her, turned, and filed out of the row after him.

Which left Nik alone to face the 45,000 pairs of eyes on her.

♥

Carlos nudged his sister Angela as the blond dude and his bros stalked up the stairs and out of the stadium.

"Now I know what to tell your boyfriend not to do."

Angela rolled her eyes.

"Nice try, but I don't have a boyfriend."

Damn. She consistently refused to let him meet guys she was dating, so he was reduced to trying to trick her into admitting she had a boyfriend. Either he never managed to catch her off guard enough to admit it, or she'd never had a boyfriend since he started trying this. He was betting on the former.

"You have one good point," Angela said. "Anyone dating me should definitely not do that." Her hand gestures got bigger as she talked. "She said they hadn't discussed it. Who proposes to someone if they haven't even discussed it? Especially in public?"

He looked back down at the woman—Nikole—now alone in her row. She'd sat back down and was typing something on her phone. The sun picked out the golden highlights in her dark curly hair. She was doing a very good job of pretending that the whole stadium wasn't talking about her.

"I feel so bad for her." He couldn't believe she hadn't jumped up to flee the building. The game had started back up again, but no one was watching. Everyone was looking at her. Including Carlos.

"So do I," Angela said.

Nikole twirled one of her curls around her finger and pretended to watch the game. Carlos realized he was staring at her and forced himself to look away.

"I get trying to make a big romantic gesture and all, and wanting a surprise, but . . ."

"Deciding to spend your life together shouldn't be a surprise," Angela said. "It should be something the two of you talk about first!"

"Oh hey, speaking of," he said, "did I tell you that Drew proposed to his girlfriend a few days ago?"

She laughed.

"Really? That's fantastic. I never would have thought a year ago that Drew would be engaged." She looked up at the Jumbotron, and then at Carlos. "She did say yes, right?"

He laughed.

"She did. But then, they'd talked about it first."

Carlos looked back down at the woman two rows down, who had *not* said yes. She was aggressively not looking at anyone around her. Her hair moved in the breezes that blew through the stadium, and her dark brown skin glowed in the sun. He'd only seen her face briefly up on the Jumbotron, until he'd realized that this real-life drama was going on just ten feet below him, but he'd seen a striking face, with big dark eyes and bright red lips. He wondered how long she was going to stay at her seat. She probably hadn't wanted to leave right away for fear of running into the man bun guy, which made sense. But if he knew anything about the way things happened in L.A., if she sat here too long, she was in danger of . . .

Yep, there it was. The camera crew.

He poked his sister. She looked down and saw the problem immediately.

"Oh my God, what a nightmare," she said.

"We've got to save her," he said.

"How do you propose we do that? Pun not intended."

"Follow my lead." He stood up and made his way out of their row, Angie right behind him.

He walked down the wide stadium stairs, eyes on the field. When he got two rows down, he paused and glanced to the side. *I hope this works*, he thought, before he went in.

"Nikole? Nikole, it is you!" he said, loud enough that she, the entire camera crew, and the other rows around them all turned to look. "Angela, look, it's Nikole! We haven't seen you for . . . my God, how many years has it been?"

Angela took up his prompt as Carlos pushed the camera crew aside to get to Nikole.

"At least five years, it's got to be? Nikole, how are you?" Angela threw her arms around the grinning woman, and whispered something in her ear before the embrace ended.

"It's so great to see you after all this time!" Angela said. She looked around with a huge smile on her face, and appeared to notice the camera crew for the first time. "Oh my goodness, are we interrupting something? I am so sorry, guys! We haven't seen each other for so long!"

"Oh wow, how do you know each—"

Carlos stepped in front of the guy with the camera. If the dude got aggressive, well, Carlos was pretty sure he had at least four inches and thirty pounds on him.

"We were just heading to get more beer and Dodger dogs. Want to come with?"

"Great idea, I'm starving." Nikole wiggled past the cameraman. "Chat with you guys later!" she called back to them, as she, Carlos, and Angie raced up the stairs.

They kept up the pretense on their way up the stairs. When

they got inside the stadium, the three of them all leaned against the nearest wall and erupted with laughter.

"Thank you guys SO MUCH for saving me," Nikole said when she finally stopped laughing.

"You're not safe yet," Carlos said. He put his hand on her back and grabbed his sister by the arm. "We've got to get you out of this stadium. They'll find you again if you stick around. Did you drive here? Or was your . . . or did you get a ride?"

She shrugged.

"My ride seems to be long gone, but I'm sure there's another way to get back to the Eastside from here. Isn't there a shuttle or something? Or I can get a ride, I have all of those apps."

"You live on the Eastside?" Angie asked.

"Yeah, Silver Lake."

"Silver Lake is in our direction, more or less," Carlos said. "We can give you a ride back."

She raised her eyebrows at him and shook her head.

"No, seriously, that's okay. You two probably have other things you'd rather be doing than driving a stranger around Los Angeles."

Angela looked confused and then laughed.

"Oh wait, did you think we were on a date? Ugh no, he's my brother. Trust me, I'd rather be driving you around L.A. than watching baseball with him."

Nikole looked at Carlos.

"Are you sure? You really don't have to."

He grinned and threw his arms around both women.

"Call it my good deed for the week," he said.

Jasmine Guillory is a graduate of Wellesley College and Stanford Law School. She is a Bay Area native who lives in Oakland, California. She has towering stacks of books in her living room, a cake recipe for every occasion, and upwards of fifty lipsticks. Visit her online at jasmineguillory.com and twitter.com/thebestjasmine.